NIGHTFIRE

TOR PUBLISHING GROUP

NEW YORK

MAEVE FLY

CJ LEEDE

MAEVE FLY

A Nightfire Book
Published by Tom Doherty Associates / Tor Publishing Group
120 Broadway
New York, NY 10271

www.torpublishinggroup.com

Nightfire™ is a trademark of Macmillan Publishing Group, LLC.

The Library of Congress has cataloged the hardcover edition as follows:

Names: Leede, CJ, author.
Title: Maeve fly / CJ Leede.
Description: First edition. | New York : Tor Publishing Group, 2023. |
   "A Nightfire Book"—Title page verso.
Identifiers: LCCN 2023007669 (print) | LCCN 2023007670 (ebook) |
   ISBN 9781250857859 (hardback) | ISBN 9781250857873 (ebook)
Subjects: LCGFT: Horror fiction. | Novels.
Classification: LCC PS3612.E34895 M34 2023 (print) | LCC PS3612.E34895
   (ebook) | DDC 813/.6—dc23/eng/20230308
LC record available at https://lccn.loc.gov/2023007669
LC ebook record available at https://lccn.loc.gov/2023007670

ISBN 978-1-250-85786-6 (trade paperback)

Our books may be purchased in bulk for promotional, educational, or business use. Please contact your local bookseller or the Macmillan Corporate and Premium Sales Department at 1-800-221-7945, extension 5442, or by email at MacmillanSpecialMarkets@macmillan.com.

First Nightfire Trade Paperback Edition: 2024

Printed in the United States of America

0 9 8 7 6 5 4 3 2 1

TO KYLE,

for staring joyfully into the void with me,

every day

I am a sick man, I am a spiteful man.

—Fyodor Dostoyevsky,
Notes from Underground

My kind of debauchery soils not only my body and my thoughts, but also . . . the vast starry universe, which merely serves as a backdrop.

—Georges Bataille,
Story of the Eye

This is not an exit.

—Bret Easton Ellis,
American Psycho

MAEVE FLY

I

Every man shares the same fantasy, and it is this:

He will marry a universally beloved sweetheart. Live a noble life and succeed in all the ways his father taught were best. And when he stands at the pinnacle of filial and paternal achievement, when he has finally reached that great height of goodness, honor, and inarguable virility, then and only then, his wife, child, and pet should be ripped from him. Violently, unforgivably.

Restoring, ultimately, freedom.

Because he has done the good thing, the right thing, and only then become the victim of its vanishing, this virtuous man may now turn with the full support of any onlooker to violence, rage, nihilism, and debauchery. Which were his ultimate true aims all along. To lose himself in the glorious, sanctioned rapture of retribution. How many husbands of wives have lined up at the box office to live out this exact fantasy that they deeply, fundamentally, and brutally desire?

Men are insipid, stupid creatures.

Here is the truth, the one that so few of us know:

You do not need a moral and noble story to do what you want. You do not first need to be a victim to become a monster. Your loved ones need not be taken from you so that you might drink and brutalize and chase the sublime. Life is fleeting and mean-ingless and crying to be seized from behind and fucked into obscurity.

This is my story, and you cannot control it. No more than you can the ever-lower dangle of your sex or the warming of this fat, lazy prison rock floating in the semen-splotched dark.

My name is Maeve Fly.

I work at the happiest place in the world.

II

Kate and I kneel opposite each other in the ice queen castle room, costumed in our uniform princess dresses, as we are every day. I watch as a single bead of blood plops, and then another, from Kate's nose down to the head of the child sitting in her lap.

Kate is beautiful and hungover, and she is a dulled but still precious gem in a dark and faux-Nordic cave of artifice. I mean that literally. They've painted the walls to look like an amalgam generic Scandinavian castle, which looks nothing like the few actual Scandinavian castles in existence. Kate is twenty-six, one year younger than I am. The kid in her lap is wearing some kind of cartoon sport-player shirt and has dried cotton candy stuck to the side of his face. Her blood can only improve upon an already bleak image. The mother does not seem to have noticed. Today is a Tuesday in September, and the parents shiver in their Southern California sweat, cooled and sickening in the artificial air.

"Wow, what a lovely dress you have on! It looks even better on you than it does me!" Kate says to the little girl who sits next to me. They are siblings, the children, and I cannot help but see them as competitors to each other. One will eat the other someday, one will steal the other's spouse. The little boy, the one with the sugar and the blood, he can't be older than four, but even so, there is a mind at work.

And all at once, he seems to understand, with great clarity, the
fleeting and fortuitous situation he has found himself in. Sitting with his face very near the firm young breasts of a woman
who is not a familial blood-tie. His mouth is open, and his eyes
fix on one of Kate's nipples. We're supposed to wear bras with
the costumes, but it's standard for Kate to forget. I'm not complaining. Neither is this kid.

The little girl beside me twirls in her princess dress. Kate's
character is the younger sister to mine. Kate smiles benevolently
down at her. No one has noticed that her nose is bleeding. The
little boy, slowly, as if it might not be real, reaches his hand up,
just a couple inches, toward the fruit of his adoration. He stops
himself. He looks at me: Is this okay? Will I be punished? What
all men want to know. I smile and give him a wink. We'll all be
punished eventually. Why not?

I love playing my princess. Of all the little girls who come,
most seem to resonate with Kate's, since she's the sister who is
unwaveringly virtuous, the protagonist who not only saves the
village but also falls in love with a large handsome Scandinavian to produce more beautiful large Scandinavians. It's only
the kind of fucked-up girls who like my princess, the sister with
the destructive powers, the one without a husband. The one
who occupies the space of both princess and villainess. We'll
discuss that further later, but my princess is significant, a rare
archetypal defiance in a world so blandly predictable. She is
beyond glorious. The only downside to our particular appointment is the song of the snowman, Kate's oafish bumbling trav-
eling companion, which plays at intervals throughout the day
and is a truly unbearable one minute and fifty-one seconds of
nasal-voiced torment. The children live for it.

This particular little boy though is really getting his parents'
money's worth and pays no mind to the song in the slightest.

His attention has returned to the breast, and there is a new determination in his eyes. Kate's nose drips another drop of red, mingling with his hair, and I am filled with a deep and unwavering love. For Kate. For this job. For all of it.

Kate and I place our arms around the little girl and lean in for their parents' photo. There's a line, and we can't keep the other kids waiting. We are very popular in the park. The most popular, in fact.

As we lean in, the boy looks to me, and I feel the moment just as he does. This will be the pinnacle of his early youth, this brave young knight on his first true quest. And I am bearing witness to such honor. I nod in stolid encouragement. He understands and prepares to move forward, on his course of destiny.

He reaches upward.

"Say CHEESE!" the mother shouts.

The boy gives Kate's breast a firm, whole-handed squeeze.

The flash shines bright. The mother cries out. Kate laughs. The father tries to look appalled, but it is plainly there in the barely concealed smirk, the adjustment in stance. He is so proud of his son. He wishes it were him with his hand there on this faux-princess's chest. He indulges, finally, the fantasy he has not until this point allowed himself, standing before us. The soft firmness of it compared to his now-maternal wife's, the illicit glory of a mammary yet untouched, unconquered by *him*. How the fathers envy their progeny. How they cling to that envy forever.

I raise my eyebrow at him, and he shrugs, unapologetic. He knows instinctively that I know. The ones who know always do.

We get a half-hour break in the afternoon. We head into the break room. Cinderella and Snow White are eating fat-free, sugar-free, dairy-free yogurt. They glare at us. There is a distinct hierarchy among the princesses, and Kate's and mine, as two of the newest of them, are the most popular. Children have really all but forgotten the old ones. Additionally, it's worth noting that we are all—Kate, Cinderella, Snow White, the others, and I—lower on the totem pole than the princesses working at the main park. We work at the newer park next door, which holds more adult rides, and the children's attractions—such as meeting princesses—are very much afterthoughts. Our park also always holds fewer guests than its next-door sister park, the original. It opens later, closes earlier. So to be Cinderella or Snow White at our park is to be the B Team of the B Team, and they are both extremely bitter about it. I would be too.

Kate and I ignore them and step into the locker room beyond the break room. We both immediately pull our wigs off. My hair is not far off from my character's white blonde, but they require that we wear the wigs anyway. Kate's hair, unlike that of her red-brown wig, is as bloodred as hair gets without dye. It is fascinating, sometimes I am caught staring at it for too long. Copper wire, pyroclast, menstrual blood. She lays out the lines for us on a paper plate from the break room, and we suck them up through tampon straws. I stick a little up in my gums. We slouch against the lockers on the floor, towels between our costumes and the ground, and chew the gummy bears I flirted the 7-Eleven guy out of this morning. The fluorescents gleam off Kate's hair. Her skin is so translucent I can see the veins beneath.

The break room door opens, and Liz comes in.

Liz is everything that is abysmal in a human being, and is, consequently, my nemesis. She is both loathsome and curiously fascinating. Liz adores rules, loves adhering to them, upholding them, sucking their little metaphorical dicks with the love and patience of a saint or a woman getting paid. She is also our supervisor. Sort of.

I watch as her face turns red at the sight of us. This is one of Liz's two modes. Both insufferable, though I find this one at least somewhat amusing. Kate sniffs once, and Liz crosses her hands beneath her fantastic breasts, the source well of all her despair. Fun bags. Sweater globes. She used to be a princess, like us, but one day, she woke up to find that her chest had inexplicably grown to such an extreme degree overnight that she suddenly no longer fit in her uniform costume. Well, she fit in it, but she looked enough like a porn star that Management sat her down and told her that her princess days were behind her. This is the greatest wound and disappointment of her life, and she will never emotionally recover. Liz is stupidly hot, and to outgrow her dress only to become the pinnacle of what every woman in this town wants to be, in fact pay ample money for, is to Liz the death of all that is good in the world.

It makes Kate insane. Kate who, beautiful herself, might kill for Liz's body. Enter a reactionary self-flagellating donut addiction on Liz's part that never makes her gain a pound anywhere and a general off-putting sense of prolonged adolescence, and any chance she stood with Kate was gone forever. I could give two fucks about any of it. For me, it is just *her*. At all times either policing or indulging in interminable longing for something that will never return, and the most un-self-aware person I have ever encountered in this town. The wistfulness, the laborious sighs and ravenous gazes clinging to us in our dresses, a yearning so deep that it makes me sick. Liz is, in every way and above all else, the worst and most basic thing anyone can choose to be. A victim.

Now Liz plays a fur character, sometimes a chipmunk, sometimes a lady mouse, and she put up such a fuss when she lost her princess role that Management, in an effort to appease her extreme desire to contribute and to save themselves the lawsuit they believed would come (though Liz would never do anything to besmirch their name), bestowed upon her the semiofficial title of Princess Supervisor. This is not a real appointment and resulted in no pay bump, which I know because Kate and I snuck into her locker and opened her paychecks to find out, or any discernible benefit beyond the fact that she felt it gave her some small semblance of power over us.

"Again? *Again?* I am going to have you fired, you two are so done!" Liz spits out in a fevered whisper.

"Lighten up, Liz. Have a bump," Kate says.

"If you think that you can get away with—"

"Sorry, what was that? What can I not get away with?" Kate says. "I seem to remember something that *you* might not get away with, Liz, if I were to, you know," she inspects her fingernails, "say something to upper management. Maybe . . . *show* them something?"

Liz's face pales.

Liz loves the park. Liz loves the park more than any place on earth. Her dream is to get engaged in matching mouse ears with a park-loving husband-to-be, to marry in Cinderella's castle, spend a magical night botching her purity, discarding it swiftly in the coveted castle suite in the East Coast park which she will never be able to reserve. The whole of her room in her shared, white-carpeted apartment is full of park paraphernalia, her daily breakfast mouse-shaped donuts. She watches cartoons on repeat, especially the old ones. She has not masturbated, ever, as she is saving herself for a Ben or Jake or Paul who will undoubtedly be a virgin himself. Maybe not Jake. Jakes are sometimes fucks. I don't know. I'm riffing. I want another bump before we have to go back on shift.

Liz says to me, sincerely, "I don't know why you go along with her. You're better than this." She has always categorized Kate as the mean girl and me as the weak-willed sidekick, and there's never been any need for her to believe otherwise.

"We going to Bab's tonight or what?" Kate says this to me, ignoring Liz. Liz's face has returned to its wounded bereft exaggerated image, and I can't help but wonder if she's ever trimmed her bush or if the thing just runs wild in her cotton princess panties.

"Yeah, maybe," I say, distracted. Bab's, short for Babylon, is the Old Hollywood–themed strip club in the basement of the pirate-themed strip club, the Gangplank, where all the visiting New Yorkers go. Kate and I go because those same visitors are almost always looking for California sweethearts to liquor up in hopes of relieving their jet lag and daily rage and whatever other vitriol is stored up inside them. Ready to be pumped out from between their legs into something willing, or even partway willing. It's usually a matter of perspective, anyway. And they always leave the next day.

"I'd like to finish my book," I say, "but maybe after."

Liz stares wistfully at Kate's dress, gives a long, shoulder-slumping sigh, then turns to gaze beyond us into the endless abyss of want.

"No, bitch, you promised, remember? My brother?" Kate leans in close enough that her hair brushes my arm, and I can smell her sweat and the sickly-sweet department store perfume she said she's worn since puberty. I just catch a glimpse of the hole in her tongue where her piercing lived before she took it out for this job. That tongue can speak five languages, one more than my own. It's how she got the job, likely how we both did. Over- or undereducated millennials, we're all a dime a dozen, but somehow, we both ended up here.

And so I do remember. Her brother just moved to town. I had forgotten. My mind has been . . . elsewhere as of late.

III

Just a short walk up the hill from the giant Western brothel–themed tourist bar on the Sunset Strip sits a large Mediterranean home crawling with vines and flowers that only open at night. On either side of the enormous imported wooden door sit mature cacti, a South African breed that one finds all over the city in front of beautiful homes like this one. This cacti's cuttings sell for something like twenty dollars apiece online. Its sap, known as a milky latex, when ingested or brought into contact with the eyes, causes severe rashes, blindness, and death in pets and humans. Almost no one knows this. But I do.

I arrive home, brushing my fingers against one of the cacti as I pass.

People say that no one is from Los Angeles. This is of course not true of all, or even most of the white people to whom they are referring, nor most of those in the minority groups that make up the vibrant and vital fabric of this town. However, it *is* true of me. Where I am from is not important, as where I am meant to be is here, and backstory is generally entirely overrated. Designed merely to sate our need to understand why someone is the way they are, to categorize and pathologize instead of simply accepting. But I am not completely lacking in generosity, so here are the bones of it:

My parents and I parted on bad terms a number of years ago. Their transgression was nothing more than bringing me into this world as something entirely different from and completely incomprehensible to them. But anyone who has truly experienced this domestic ostracism, not just the hormone-fueled tumult of the teen years but the great lack of understanding and betrayal that is the total inability to *be seen*, will understand that this is no simple failing at all.

The only person who exists in my world besides Kate is the woman who took me in. My grandmother, Tallulah, was an actress back in the days of Hollywood's glory, not so famous that people hear my name and know who I am related to, but famous enough that when they see her face, when they used to see her face, they would often stop and furrow their brows and try to piece together why she was so deeply familiar to them. But her famous Halloween photograph adorns countless walls, is sold in prints that likely cost less than twenty dollars, on street corners or on chain websites. They used to say she was the most angelic of the starlets, her face eternally youthful and innocent, her natural nearly white-blonde hair a rare commodity in this town. And her eyes. Blue as ice, even now. Just like mine. The truth is that we look so much alike, we're nearly identical. But people have short memories. And they rarely care about anything beyond themselves.

Now here I am, her double, her ghost, haunting the Strip unseen.

Entering through the front door, the foyer greets me, opens up into the large living room beyond. My bedroom sits on one side of the house, and the master, my grandmother's room, on the other. Between them a series of open spaces: dining, kitchen, bar. Balconies wrapping around both the main level and downstairs, looking out over the Strip and up into the hills. Downstairs, there is a small movie theater and a guest suite that has never, as long as I have lived here, been utilized. And below that is the wine cellar. Only the wealthy have basements in Los Angeles. There is something unsuitable about them here, and to spend too much time underground in a city in which the ground routinely shifts is a sort of glamorous temptation of fate. We have no yard, no pool. Just the three stories attached permanently and precariously to the hillside. As fixed and fleeting as any of us will ever be.

I step into my grandmother's room. Hilda, her nurse, has just left, and the air still reeks of her disinfectant. I have never liked Hilda, not since the day she arrived and shoved me aside, shooed me out of the room as though I would ever do anything except help, as though I would not give all of myself to this woman I love. But Hilda has kept my grandmother alive, and that is more than enough to make up for her impatient European efficiency and vulgar sense of entitlement to our home.

But now it is my grandmother and me. Only us. I stand just inside the door. I do not approach her, and I do not say anything. The room, like the rest of the home, is tastefully decorated by a designer in an Old-Hollywood bungalow aesthetic, though the house is far larger than any bungalow. The velvet curtains are pulled wide, and the late afternoon sunlight spills in over her body.

My grandmother doesn't know I'm here. She is dying, has been dying, slowly and ungracefully, for months now. Cirrhosis of the liver that led to hepatic encephalopathy that led to hepatic coma. The failing body works in every way to remind us that we are nothing more than a series of fired impulses, a machine of biological compulsion that really has very little use after reproduction. A slight tremor makes its way through my grandmother as I watch her, and her lips quiver as though she is attempting speech. She is not conscious. It is too much to wish for.

I remember those same lips, with her signature red lipstick, meeting the rim of a glass, her Old-Fashioned swirling amber inside. The two of us tucked in a booth at Jones my first night in town all those years ago. Red-checked tablecloths, brick walls, low lighting from sconces and small lamps. She ordered us two plates of spaghetti. Neither of us touched them. I took a sip from my own glass, filled with the same liquid as hers, and set it down, my hand shaking just a little.

She sat back and tapped her long red fingernails on the table, studying me. She wore an ivory Chanel blouse, left undone to a scandalous degree, a black lace La Perla bra beneath. Bulgari diamond snake around her throat. She has never told me her age. I could ascertain it through a quick internet search, but if there is something she does not want me to know, I am content not to know it.

"So. My granddaughter." She said the word slowly, tasting its syllables, its hard consonants exaggerated in her haughty mid-Atlantic precision. This was the first day we had ever met. She and my father never saw eye to eye. It had almost everything to do with the fact that she took very little interest in raising him and left him in the care of a nanny for most of his childhood. His father was undoubtedly a movie star, but his identity has remained a mystery to my father for the whole of his life. I know, now, of course. But I will not tell him.

"You're beautiful," my grandmother said to me.

"I look just like you," I said.

The edge of her lip quirked up, and her nails fell still on the table. She considered me.

"What do you see, when you look around this room?"

Billie Holiday played over the speakers. Waiters visited tables unhurriedly. In the small pools of light in the dim space, faces leaned close in conversation, dipped down to take a bite of food or a sip of a drink. Someone laughed. The bartender shook and poured.

"I see . . ."

"Don't try to please me," she said. "Just look. Really see."

I drew my eyes away from hers and scanned the room once more. I saw humans. Humans trying so hard to make meaning, to create a space for meaning. An experience. Something to be desired. I saw walking corpses draped in finery meant to look not so fine. Expensive but casual. *I am not trying,* they said, *this is effortless.* But the trying, the striving, it poisoned the air, it perfumed it. It was everywhere. It was intoxicating. Everywhere, all the time, people are pretending. But here, in Hollywood, it is so much more. So much more that it renders it authentic. I wanted to drink it down and gulp it up and fill myself with it. I looked back at her, and I knew that my cheeks were flushed.

There we sat, the two of us, and I stared into her eyes, so like my own, this woman the picture of what I will grow into, what I will become. And the wrenching loneliness I had felt for the whole of my life, the simple fact of my being utterly and completely *different,* began to float away. We were two wolves in a flock of sheep.

She smiled then, as though she had read my thoughts. A wide and knowing predator's grin, and her eyebrow lifted. She brought her glass up above the plates of untouched food. "We are going to get along just fine," she said.

The bar fades from my mind, and I am staring at an unmoving woman, sunken in ways I never could have imagined.

Connected through translucent tubes and wires to machines that light up and seem to do nothing else beyond take up real estate in the room, marring an otherwise beautiful space. All of it, a dying dream. Her condition, usually brought on by alcoholism, I was told was likely in fact brought on in her case by a rare genetic disorder. *Hereditary,* they said. *You should be cautious yourself,* they said, to me. In my initial frantic research, I even turned (in perhaps my darkest moment) to the overly moneyed and inanely out of touch new age corners of the internet— largely broadcast from the west in Venice and the east in Joshua Tree—in which I was informed that liver disease is tied to an excess of anger.

My grandmother's familiar, a decrepit old Lester the Cat, brushes past my ankle and into the room to jump up on her bed. He bends down to nuzzle his face against hers, trying to get a reaction. Of course he does not. I can't be in here anymore. I close her door softly behind me and head out into the living room. The floor-to-ceiling glass looks out over the Strip on one side, the hills on the other. Props from her movies hang from the walls and sit in corners on shelves, preening and alive. A tiara, an old telephone, a vase of fake winter flowers. I pour myself a glass of water and strip my shirt off over my head, let it fall to the floor. Unlike my grandmother, I adorn myself with nothing. I wear simple clothing, keep my face and my neck bare other than the makeup I am required to wear at work. It suits me better. I sip from the glass, and my hand again shakes.

Here is what matters: my grandmother is dying, and Kate will soon find everything she wants and more, and I will not enter her brave new world of television stardom and Hollywood grandeur with her. But I have done the research. On average, it takes two years from the current stage of my grandmother's illness to claim the life of someone her age if she does not wake, which the doctors have said I should not hold my breath for. And, on average, from my own personal observations, it takes a young Hollywood actress about five years of nonstop pursuit in this town before anything substantial takes off, if it ever does. Kate arrived here three years ago, so she also has about two years before anything happens. So, I have determined that I have two years with the two people who matter, before I become a one. It is not exact, or even reliable if I am being honest, but it is enough to keep myself sane. My grandmother doesn't speak to me anymore, but she is here, and that is the core of it. She is everything.

I have the Strip, and I have the park, and I have Kate and my grandmother for two years. I know everything about this place, every crack, every facet, and I am its surveyor and keeper and master and appreciator. For the next two years, my life is perfect. And beyond that, I will live alone. The timer on my life as it exists now is ticking louder every day, culminating in that ultimate inevitability.

I don't have to face it yet, and in the meantime, there is so much pleasure in routine.

IV

Inside my room, I turn on Billie Holiday. There are only two kinds of music in my world: Billie Holiday and Halloween songs. Nothing else stirs me in the right way, produces the tingle from the ear to the breast, down through the spine. I have long been curating and developing what I believe to be *the* definitive Halloween song canon, and it is beautiful.

I flip my small TV on, an antiquated proper television that takes up space and depth and only plays VHS tapes. I love my old TV. I know that it will not endure forever, that one day its outdated technology and many years of dutiful function will be claimed by time and decay as all things are. Everything good fades and disappears.

I pop in a porno, man on man, light bondage, an old favorite. On my desktop, I open YouTube and pull up a video of a gray wolf hunting a rabbit. Like the porn, I've watched it before, and I know how it ends. It doesn't make the buildup any less exquisite. There are no spoilers in life. If you are observant and pragmatic, the endings of all things are easily predictable. In the most basic terms, human life is always punctuated with death. It does not cheapen the buildup to know it. There are many winding paths to an inevitable end, and there is so much beauty and pain in the *watching*.

I slide my jeans off and lie down on my bed just as Rick inserts the smallest of his plugs into Conrad and the wolf steps behind a thin gray-barked tree, his olfactory senses on alert but his eyes not yet having found his prize. Billie croons over the speakers. I open my phone with my free hand. I check the time. It's perfect. She is always most active on social in the afternoons, once her kids are home and needing her attention.

She is Susan Parker, and if I am able to smoothly execute this, her life is about to end.

I open my app, one of many fake accounts. Trixie Krueger. Thirty two years old, Orange County, *Pro-American and Proud!* You can get away with any name these days. All these children are Paxton and Austynn and Braydyn and Braydee. These will be the names of children's parents and grandparents. These names will be written in history books.

For months, Trixie Krueger has been conversing with Susan Parker, a fanatic NRA member and mother of five. Gaining her trust, becoming her confidant and friend. Susan Parker's children bear an uncanny resemblance to fleshy malformed dough, and not one of their names disappoints. There is Kayleigh, Karleigh, Chasen, Brantleigh, and my favorite, Boone. I have memorized them, have reveled in their now even bleaker futures. Susan and her husband drive matching H2 Hummers, but hers is pink. They have money, family oil. Susan's husband's entire wardrobe consists of casual camouflage, and he drinks Kum & Go's HuMUGous one-hundred-ounce sodas on the daily. I have not been able to ascertain the flavor, but I'd like to think it's Mountain Dew. Susan, on the other hand, does not drink caffeine or alcohol, has never smoked or imbibed any drugs, and keeps her body dutifully pure for her husband and Jesus. Perhaps it is her shunning of vice more than anything else that really brought me to understand that she was the most beautiful, the most perfect of targets. I don't mind so much that she is racist. Morally disappointing people exist everywhere. It is really just the holiness that kills me. Nothing in this world is so deliciously satisfying as watching a pious person go down.

So many months of work, and I think today might be the day. I am nearly dripping with the anticipation of it.

I open our chat.

The chat begins the way it does every time. Small talk about her children and the long sunny weekends we've returned from. I compliment her most recent Insta post, an image of Susan and two mom friends posed in beige and leather riding boots with the caption GOT MY PSL WITH MY GIRLS, OFFICIALLY CHRISTIAN GIRL FALL! I inquire about the latest PTA dramas. I mention an armed robbery somewhere that could be anywhere, but I know where she lives, her street number and the color of her mailbox. It's enough to get her going. It really takes so little.

SUSAN: It's just that with all these people moving into the neighborhood I fear for my kids safety. It's really disturbing all the things you hear and the police are worried too! My neighbors brother and also my sister-in-laws husband are both on the force God bless them and they both say we've really gotta watch out.

TRIXIE: It just isn't right. I know we've said it before, but they don't pay taxes. They expect all these handouts and then they make it unsafe for our children to live in their own God-given-rights homes!

SUSAN: Amen. Remember that robbery I told you about? Six houses down from me and someone stole his American flag too! And he's a docent at our church!!!

TRIXIE: Honestly I know it's not Christian of me to say it but I just sometimes wish we could round them all up and burn em.

I send the message, my heart pounding, and wait. She types. Rick and Conrad on the TV move on to the medium-sized plug. The wolf's eye catches movement. Billie croons. *All of me, why not take all of me?* I slip my hand beneath my underwear.

SUSAN: Frankly it's what they deserve. Every day I fear for my babies. Every night I go to sleep and I lie awake thinking what if someone comes for them when Joel and I are not around. Nobody knows what that feels like. It's not right and it's not the world I thought they would inherit from us. The one they were meant to inherit. It just makes me sick.

My heart pounds again, my breath coming in faster. I reach for a vibrator so I can use both hands to type.

TRIXIE: Look I know we haven't met in person but I feel like I know you. And it's just so nice to know there are good God-fearing women in this country, that you're keeping His spirit alive. I've been wanting to ask you something for some time but I needed to know what kind of woman you were first. I needed to know I could trust you.

Send.
She types. I wait. My heart is pounding. Conrad is moaning. I am so profoundly wet.

SUSAN: You can trust me.

I type.

TRIXIE: Well, I'm not sayin this is true . . . But hypothetically if I were to tell you that I am a member of an organization . . . the type of organization that has been around for some time and is still around even though they have to keep it quiet . . . if that organization existed and if I were a member maybe I could tell you that we've got a chapter in your town. Maybe I could tell you that they COULD do something about that little problem of yours. We do it all the time— take care of our own. We know how important it is to stick together to stand up for the country we were promised. So . . . if this hypothetical were real could you see yourself being interested?

I send it. I am sweating. Blood pumping to my clit. My skull. I send another.

TRIXIE: If you're not we can pretend I never said anything. It is after all a hypothetical.
TRIXIE: ;)

She types. She pauses. She types again. The wolf spots the rabbit. Rick is rock-hard. Susan Parker types. I wait. The vibrator buzzes between my legs.

Finally, it comes through.

SUSAN: I'm interested.

I exhale. I screenshot the conversation. All of it. One hundred and eighty-six messages from Trixie Krueger, one hundred and seventy-two from Susan Parker, age thirty-seven, Louisville, Kentucky. 251 Sherman Drive. I screenshot her LinkedIn, full of her volunteer Church work and Haiti missions. I screenshot her Instagram, her Facebook, and her PTA membership photo on the website. Conrad on the TV says, "Yes, Daddy!"

I open Reddit, and I post it all.

I run my server through a Ukrainian IP address, so Trixie

Krueger, fictional as she is, will not be found. I've done it before, and I know how to cover my tracks. But Susan Parker, on the other hand . . .

The Reddit upvotes and comments begin to arrive. She will be annihilated. Her life is irrevocably ruined, and she is about to lose everyone and everything she loves. I did it. I did this to her.

The wolf's jaws close. Rick shoves himself into Conrad. Billie sings.

I move the vibrator aside.

I come, violently, beneath my hand.

V

An hour or so later, I lean in close to the bougainvillea outside the tomb of Tower Records, still basking in the afterglow of the most delicious downfall of another, the demise of a woman who thinks herself chosen, who believes herself to be untouchable.

Bougainvillea are the ultimate microcosmic display of this city. Exquisite, exotic, erotic. The shock of their purples and pinks a transgression against the dusty green of the palms, the smoky slate sky. Like the city itself, the bougainvillea does not belong here. It is too vibrant, too alive, never meant for this desert at the end of the world. And yet, here it is. And beneath the dazzling colors and intoxicating scent, there are thorns longer than fangs and sharper than kitchen knives, waiting to cut us all open. I like to gather them all up in my fists, punctured and pleasured and raw.

The Sunset Strip was originally a stretch of dirt road built to connect Hollywood with Beverly Hills. A no-man's-land, a desert expanse of nothing. An absence to be traversed only when absolutely necessary. After some time, a few bars popped up, outposts for the traveler, and a gas station here and there. Then came the visionaries, the ones who saw the space for what it was and what it could be. Francis Montgomery. Arnold Weitzman and William Douglas Lee, the architects of the Chateau.

Over the years, the Strip has lived a life of extremes. High highs and low lows, heydays followed by periods of nothingness, of forgetting. The last great high, of course, was in the days of rock and roll. The riots in '66. Mötley Crüe, Jim Morrison, Tom Petty, Blondie, Jane's Addiction. The Roxy and Whisky a Go Go. The Viper Room.

Since the late nineties, it's been somewhat of a ghost town, certainly not the raucous strip of glamorous anarchy it once was. There is the bookstore with the other bookstore behind it. There is the luckless hotel with the fit young bellmen. There is the tower that used to hold Spago and has sat mostly empty ever since, and there is the Coffee Bean and the Bullwinkle statue. Places to get your pussy waxed and your eyelashes extended. The rock clubs of old, all the many billboards. But mainly, it is quiet. It is the best-known and worst-kept secret anywhere. And it is all mine.

I inhale the air of the early evening, the bougainvillea bloom perfume, the light slanting sideways, long shadows, late heat, and I revel in the glory that is some degree of certainty about life. That is knowing home and fearing no one.

I catch sight of something.

A foreign body, a small creature tucked away inside the vines. I blink, think perhaps I imagined it. But no, there is something here.

I lean in closer and squint to inspect it. There are so many needles and errant pieces of trash in this city, it's generally unwise to reach your hand in anywhere without having a good idea of what you're reaching for. This thing in front of me though, it is not trash. It is intentional, meaningful even. And I know it was not here before.

Unease spreads through me like a sudden-onset illness.

It is a doll's head, this newly arrived thing, without hair and with one eyelash missing, attached carefully and lovingly to a plastic toy alligator body by a dark red substance I know instinctively to be blood. I reach in, and gently extract it from its thorny nest. I cradle the little foundling as though it were made of glass or something even more precious and fragile. A single human hair is wound and tied around its neck. On its belly, scrawled in letters of the same red, it says "*In order to know virtue.*"

I blink, and a chill runs through me. The air is still. The Santa Anas soon will come, will shake the whole town. But now, it is crushingly quiet, stale almost. I pull out my phone and search it. I know I've read it before, I know— The quote is by the Marquis de Sade. I turn it about in my head, tumble it through the fissures and rapids of thought and hope and desire. I turn this most perfect creature one way and then another, the doll's single remaining eyelid fluttering open and closed as I move it. It is so lovely. It is so much more than the feat I just accomplished inside my bedroom. It is everything. This creature existing here, as if hatched from my own flesh and mind.

It is something *new.*

I am unsettled. Deeply disturbed. Because I know with a profound and sudden clarity that this foundling portends something dark and ground-shaking. It is just a doll, it is just a thing. But I know the Strip like the back of my hand. Every bar, every tree, all its secrets. And this little entity has crept its way in, right under my nose. Someone made this. And while this person may not be like me, they are not nothing.

I don't like it. I don't like it at all.

Time passes before I convince myself to unhand the thing and turn to walk away. My skin seems to thrum where I touched it. Stung, poisoned.

My step is maybe, momentarily, uncertain.

The Marquis de Sade's words tumble through my mind.

"In order to know virtue, we must first acquaint ourselves with vice."

The night stretches out before me, a great gaping maw.

VI

G ive me a Slippery Nipple!"
  Los Angeles' architecture is chaos, and the Strip is a prime example. A trend emerged in the 1920s of buildings erected that were shaped in cartoonish imitation of what they purveyed inside. A giant hamburger for a burger joint. A boot, a flower pot, a piano. Dubbed programmatic architecture, examples are found everywhere in this town. There is a reason so much of Los Angeles feels like the movies, feels like the park. It was by design. People come here for the beautiful artifice of it, for the extreme kitsch that makes life feel somewhat more endurable. We all seek the dream of beauty even as we know fundamentally it is only a façade for the decaying in the dark.

The Gangplank is no exception. On the east end of the Strip, between the Velvet Taco lingerie store and Pink Taco Mexican restaurant, there sits a giant pirate ship. One enters through the front of the hull, beneath the extremely sexualized figurehead bearing the name Starf*ck on a gold chain that hangs around her neck, no doubt a later addition to the 1959 building. Initially, the Gangplank was a themed restaurant for families, but in the nineties, Pedro bought the building and turned it into the magnificent double-layered strip club it is today.

I brush past the girl leaning all the way over the bar for her

Slippery Nipple and head through the faux shipwreck adorn-
ments to the door at the back that looks like it should lead to a
coat closet. It slams behind me. As I descend, the music shifts
from the upbeat pop upstairs to something moody and dark.
I am bathed in the red light of Babylon. A pool table, a bar,
round leather booths. Between and above the booths stand
stripper poles, three in total. I know all the girls. The owner and
sometimes-bartender, Pedro, pours generously for Kate and me,
and Kate has on multiple occasions inquired, only ever mostly
joking, about job openings on the poles. Pedro always smiles
and pours us a little more. "You two are such sweethearts. I
could not corrupt you! Especially you with that angel face," he
says to me and gives me a kiss on the hand.

Red lights. Red walls. The dancers sliding and writhing.
Leather, mirrors, shadows, smoke. Pedro pours me a glass of
whatever he can afford to get rid of. The foundling doll sits in
my brain and my chest, insistent and sharp. I should have taken
it. Or destroyed it. Done something with it. I down the glass,
and Pedro gives me another. I turn and search for Kate.

"Bathroom," he says. I nod my thanks and head over to my
favorite booth. Irene, the dancer on the pole beside me, says
hello. A man sits at the booth just beyond her. He is movie star
handsome, and I think I've seen him in things. My eyes slide
over him and to the rest of the bar. I turn back around in my
seat and swirl the liquor in my glass. I shouldn't have come out
tonight. I shouldn't have left the doll. I pull my book from my
bag and try to distract myself.

At first I was drawn to illicit, banned, or subversive books
because they were just that. But after a time, and especially since
my grandmother's illness set in, I've been using them as sort of
instructional guides. How to Exist, as told by misanthropes
throughout the ages. My grandmother is no longer able to guide

me, but these characters can, in their respective (admittedly occasionally imperfect) ways. *Story of the Eye* by Georges Bataille is an old favorite, and Simone is one of the sole examples I have ever found of a female character (even if she is secondary to the male narrator) who possesses and embodies true savagery with no tragic backstory or expectation of victimhood. Like so many male misanthropes throughout history, Simone simply is the way she is, and the reader accepts her without question. We do not fixate incessantly and exhaustingly on the details, we do not cringe at the deviance. Instead we accept. We obey.

But more on this later.

"There you are, ho!" Kate says, sliding into the booth. She wears a minimal coverage gold dress and victorious smile. A man lingers behind her and sits down as well. "Maeve, this is Derek. Derek, Maeve."

"It's nice to finally meet Kate's brother," I say.

Derek gives me a strange look. His suit is expensive, cuff links, platinum wedding band.

Kate grabs Derek's face and shoves her tongue into his mouth. He kisses her back and smiles, realizing, perhaps for the first time, what a prize of a potential mistress he has found. Kate turns and raises her brow at me.

"So, not the brother?" I say.

"No," a low voice says from over my shoulder, "I'm a much better kisser."

Kate squeals and springs out of the booth, leaping into the arms of a very large man standing beside me, planting a firm but mostly familial kiss on his mouth. "Yeah he is," she says. "The best. Everyone, this is Gideon, my baby, baby brother." She says this in a baby talk voice and ruffles his hair. He is a head taller than she is but somehow seems less huge with Kate beside him. She collapses back into the booth beside her man of the moment, one who is undoubtedly a show business exec for Kate to be fawning over him the way she is. Derek's face lights up.

"Oh shit, I know you," he says to the brother.

"You do?"

"Yeah. You're Gideon Green. From the Rangers."

Irene on the pole dips lower. Gideon's eyes flash to her and then back to Derek. Gideon shrugs. "Well, the Kings now."

"No way, that's crazy! I hadn't heard."

"You a fan?"

"No way, man, Islanders all the way. Sorry. No offense."

"None taken. Who wants drinks? This round on me, for abandoning New York."

"I'll drink to that," Derek says, and when Gideon leaves, he turns to Kate. "You didn't tell me your brother played hockey."

"You didn't ask."

"He's like . . . a huge deal."

She shrugs, moves her hair over her shoulder. There is a feeling there. Jealousy, perhaps. Something more complex.

Derek leans back in the booth and eyes Irene and the bar appreciatively. He is pleased with Kate, and she is pleased to have pleased him. I return to my book.

"Mind if I sit here?" Gideon is again standing beside me. I glance up. He is rugged, strong-jawed, tediously handsome. He wears a gray sweater and jeans. My face is level with the zipper of his pants and what lies beneath it. I slide over so he can sit, and I return to the page.

"So that's crazy, they just swap you in?" Derek says.

"Yeah. Been here a few weeks, training. Haven't gotten a minute until now though, with getting the new life set up, and all that."

"Giddee, you found a place, right? Nearby?" Kate says.

"Not too far."

"Where?"

"I'll show you this week," he says.

She rolls her eyes. I can feel it even with my own eyes on the page. She is tense, and perhaps that is why I am focusing on their words and not the words written in front of me. I am always painfully attuned to the mild to wild swings of Kate's moods. Perhaps it is because I know that one day she will leave me, even if that day is far off. Perhaps it is because Kate, while not quite like my grandmother and me, is different. Different enough. The tension continues through in her voice as she says, "Always so mysterious. And speaking of, don't mind my rude friend, Maeve. Who clearly thinks it's acceptable to read at a table full of people."

I lift my head and exhale, tucking my book away.

"Maeve is a genius," Kate says. "Well, actually Gideon too."

"And we all love Kate for her vivid imagination," I say.

"No one in this town has any imagination," Derek says.

"And what is it you do?" I say.

Derek is annoyed that I do not know. A muscle ticks in his forehead. I smile, kindly.

"I'm a director," he says.

"Ahh," I say. "I only watch porn."

"How much do pro players make in a year?" Derek asks Gideon.

"Derek, come here, I want to show you something," Kate says. "We'll be right back." She gives me a meaningful look to say that I should *behave*. She drags Derek by the lapel up and out of the table and whispers in his ear. He smiles and follows her to the handicap bathroom. I glance up at Pedro who shakes his finger at me and mouths the word "naughty." He always says I am the nice one. *You are so innocent,* he says, *so beautiful!*

Kate has been doing this more and more as she climbs the ranks of the ladder of Hollywood, as her dues are paid and she grows closer with each small part to *The Big Break.* Leaves early, arrives late. I can feel the tether between us straining with each new step toward her future, and I don't know how to bridge the gap. I don't know how to encourage her forward without moving her away from me.

We became fast friends three years ago, both pretending to be miserable working over the holidays but having the time of our lives. Hedonistic and deliciously willing to forget any troubles over spiked cider and a bender of nights we only half remember. It started on our first day at work. Liz had just been "promoted" to her supervisor position and had handed back her princess dress mere days before. Kate wouldn't step into her role for a while, nor would I mine, as we still had our fur character dues to pay. Cinderella and Snow White, who had inhabited their respective princesses for some time, were to step in for our coveted characters temporarily until Kate and I were ready to take over.

In our first meeting, Liz broke down into tears in the middle of her welcome speech upon relaying this information to us and had to be escorted out of the room. I sat in a folding plastic chair in the back corner, and Kate sat a row up and a few seats over from me. There were quite a few new hires, three rows, each five chairs wide. I would learn later that the park tends to hire, and fire, in batches. I didn't notice her any more than I did the others. Cinderella and Snow White sat at the other end of my row. I didn't notice them either. I was too busy breathing in the magic of the place, the slight spoiled-milk scent of the break room, the creak of the cheap plastic below me.

And suddenly I was drenched, and covered in ice. I didn't move, just blinked down at the iced coffee now seeping into

my jeans and long sleeve shirt. I considered it as I slowly moved
my head and looked up into the imperious face of Cinderella.
I took her in now for the first time seriously. Average, perhaps
a little tight-faced, eyes a little dull. I suspected she came from
Missouri, maybe Arkansas. She had that look about her that
said she grew up reigning over the aisles of Superstores with her
girlfriends and visiting that homophobic chicken place every
Saturday night, as they would naturally be closed on Sunday,
and she would be eating Christ flesh then anyway. She wore flip-
flops or boat shoes daily to her high school, saved up for them
for many weeks to be able to fit the implied uniform of all the
other girls. It was safest to never stand out. Bully or be bullied,
and all that. She attended or cheered at every sporting event,
her boyfriend on the team (not the quarterback), and smiled
through the deep unshakable knowing that her life would always
end up right back there. It would never amount to much more
than this.

"Oops," she said, looking down her little sloped nose at me.
"Guess I tripped."

I didn't say anything, just looked at her, saw the slight caking
of her makeup and the imperfections it covered. I realized she
was waiting for a response, so I smiled, slowly, holding her eyes.

The smile dimmed on her own lips, and her brows furrowed.
After another second, she took a step back from me. Gooseflesh
raised on her arm. My smile deepened. This job, *the* job, was
already so much better than I ever could have guessed, was so
real as I sat here now with my wet clothing and the linoleum
floors and the flickering lights above us. It was so . . . perfect.

She stood leaning back, staring down at me. I just watched
her and smiled and thought, my life before Los Angeles didn't
matter at all. I had now found my grandmother, and I had
found this. It was perfect. Just . . . meant to be, if there were

such a thing. I thought all this as I smiled and looked at this girl and her empty iced-coffee cup in her nail-bitten hand. I held her eyes and did not blink.

"Jesus," she said after a few seconds. She backed away further, and she knocked into the chair of a fur character. She stumbled and averted her eyes from mine. She hurried back to her seat. My eyes followed her the entire way, and she glanced back at me twice as she tried to tilt herself away, as she tried not to feel me watching her.

"Well, she's fucking weird," she stage-whispered to the girl beside her, who sat with her jaw open, watching me. My eyes flicked to her, Snow White, and she turned her head away. I took in the fifteen-dollar green juice in her hands, her willowy frame beneath her gauzy beige linen dress, imported beads wrapped around her wrist. She likely lived west of Bundy or Centinela and used words like *wellness, cleansing,* and *fresh* on the daily. She worked this job solely to fund her ayahuasca healing retreats and constant supply of crystals and herbs necessary to her therapeutic TikTok account in which she spurned measles vaccines and promoted beverages brewed with high frequency sound vibrations for maximal *benefits*. She likely kept this job a secret from her wellness community but secretly loved it, the shiny American fantasy that it promised, the same one she daily scorned in her other life. Cinderella glanced back at me again. I watched her shiver. I continued to smile.

Liz reentered the room, her face red and puffy, but mostly composed. I swept my eyes over the rest of the cast members. No one was looking at me, I suspected some might even be actively avoiding me given the stiff set of their shoulders. But one girl was. The one who would end up playing the sister to my princess, the one with the bloodred hair. She was turned around in her seat watching me. She winked when my eyes met hers, a small smile of her own playing on her lips, and turned back around to face the presentation.

We were eventually released for the day, and I left the lounge to stroll through the park. Cinderella and Snow White did not speak to me as I passed. Cinderella even flinched away. Outside, I inhaled the sugar, pavement, and sweat. I had never cared or thought much about the park, or its overarching brand. But what Tallulah and this city had taught me, what perhaps had always been inside, was a deep and ever-growing appreciation for pretense. For the lacquered kitsch of our town and the hidden proclivities it brings out and encourages in its visitors and denizens. To witness people giving themselves over fully to fantasy, to *participate* in it. When my prowlings around the city did one day lead me here, I knew instantly. I went home and flipped through the movie catalogue, and I settled on the ice queen. And as I watched, it was as though the world had fallen into my lap. It all came together for me, as much as it had when I first appeared on Tallulah's doorstep. This was it. I knew my ice queen was the one.

Now, my first day on the job, I twirled in the sun and decided I might hop next door to the original park to take the teacups for a spin, just once, before heading home. It was one of the great perks, after all. I could be here now whenever I wished. It was, from this day forward, my extended domain. I had done this. I had given it to myself.

"Hey!"

I turned, and the red-haired girl was following me, jogging slightly to catch up. Her face was bright in the afternoon. She looked about my age and height. But of course she did. The park's character height restrictions are followed down to the half inch.

"Hey," she said again as she slowed beside me.

My eyes swept over her, and though her tight clothing clearly indicated she liked attention, likely male-variety, I wasn't quite sure what I thought of who she was. I couldn't pinpoint a location or a story. An aspiring actress, certainly, that much I could feel. I don't know how to explain it, but even a few weeks in this town, and one just knows. But beyond that, who and where she was from, what she did with herself and her time, I didn't know. I didn't have any ideas. Strange. She didn't present enough to give any one impression. I only knew that she stood before me when everyone else had flinched away, as I had intended for them to. And that was . . . interesting.

She pulled a cigarette out of her bag and slipped on a pair of mouse-shaped sunglasses that I suspected she had stolen off a distracted child.

"So we gonna go get a drink, or what?"

A beer is set back down on the table.

"Please tell me not everyone here sucks as much as that guy," Gideon says, then takes another sip.

I blink, am ripped back to the present. Kate's brother sits beside me. We are in Bab's, and Kate is in the bathroom with Derek, and I have the strangest feeling that I do not know how I got here. And then I remember the doll in the vines. I think I might be sick.

Gideon is talking to me, is sitting close in beside me, close enough that I can feel his heat. I move so that there is more space between our bodies. He is drinking his beer, and he smells of a light cologne. Citrus, clean. He is beyond wholesome. Kate's mentioned him before. Parents disapproved of nearly all her decisions, but Gideon was the golden boy, the apple of their eye.

It's because of them that Kate is the way she is, a rebel but not an outsider. Ultimately, all Kate wants in life is to be accepted, to be a member of society, but celebrated, elevated. She wants to win the game, and she likely will. It's the main thing that sets us apart. She is able to fully participate in this world, she is not so far removed from it that she has to pretend. Her only pretending is that she does not intentionally play, but that is the same as all the rest of them. The pretense of not trying, of ease and effortless allure. Je ne sais quoi. Feathers and lace.

"I don't know what you're talking about," I say to Gideon.

He snorts and aims his broad shoulders on me. "So you're Kate's best friend."

I sip my drink and set it down. "She's a good one," I say.

"She is," he says.

"Are you two close?" I know they are, and that it's complicated. Though I'm not sure exactly how. I also don't really care to hear his answer.

"Mm," he nods, sips his beer. "Been a long time since I've seen her in person though."

"Yeah, she stays for the holidays," I say.

"So you work at the park too."

"Yes," I say, wondering how long is appropriate before I can exit the conversation.

"Let me guess, an actress as well?"

"Everyone's an actor."

He nods, and his eyes wander. I haven't kept his attention. Irene takes her opportunity to slide down the pole upside down and brush her hair down over his shoulder and up the side of his face.

So this is Golden Boy Gideon. Kate may have called him a genius, but he's clearly a nonspecific athletic male. It's incredible the diversity of creature produced from a single womb. They look alike a bit, I can see now in his face, but he is so substantial compared to Kate's small frame. He is so of this earth. And she is infinitely more interesting. But I promised her I would behave tonight, and that I would be *nice* to him.

"What do you think of LA so far?" I say without enthusiasm.

Irene lifts back up and does something very intriguing with her leg for a man sitting at the table on her other side.

"I don't know," Gideon says. "I'm not sure I like it."

I take a beat. "Oh?"

"Yeah, I mean, I know it's cliché to say, but it's a town built on the idea of artifice, of a more beautiful world than the one that actually exists. I don't know. It's fake."

"And what is real? Sports? Games between men that were created by men?"

"I offended you."

"When people first arrive, especially New Yorkers, they think they see everything. They think they understand it all because, to their minds, there is not much to understand. You're seeing the surface because you're looking at the surface."

"So if it's not a city of artifice, then what is it?" he says.

"It is. But it's not fake. It's a city of secrets, of discarded and fresh identities, of hidden depths, and I'm sorry to have to say this after one conversation, and I love Kate very much, but if I had to guess, I'd say you're probably not going to make it here."

The words leave my mouth before I am able to think them through. My tongue doesn't normally get the better of me like this. I am destabilized by the foundling doll, by this whole night. I open my mouth to apologize, for Kate, when Gideon narrows his eyes at me, one side of his mouth tilting up at the corner. Intrigued, charmed. I can't imagine by what. But I've piqued his interest, and I didn't mean to. This is all happening wrong.

"What are your secrets, Maeve?" he says.

His eyes catch mine, and I realize I was mistaken. His face is not as perfect as I initially thought. His nose, up close, has been broken, it looks like in multiple places. Perhaps that is standard for someone in his line of work. He has nice lips, I'll admit, the adjective *filthy* briefly comes to mind. Not that I would indulge it. It's too dark to make out the color of his eyes, but I think they might be two colors. Or maybe it's the way he's sitting, half in the dim light.

There is a jolt, sudden and brutal. My stomach seems to fold in on itself. I lose any sense of equilibrium I had up to now. He pins me with his eyes, and I am stuck there, as the floor shakes, as I shake. I don't know what—

I sway, try to get my vision to focus. I look away from him and steady myself with a hand on the table. A disturbance in the atmosphere, a hiccup in the fabric of reality.

"Holy shit, what was that?" Gideon says.

I don't know what to say. My mouth is dry, and the room feels too close. I glance to Pedro behind the bar who is preparing to clean up broken glass. Pedro calls to me, asks me if I am okay. I blink, nod, wait for understanding. He says, "That was a big one!"

After a moment, I inwardly laugh at myself. How stupid I was to have not immediately known it for what it was. Earthquake. I breathe a sigh of relief. I glance back up to Gideon, and there is nothing there beyond an ordinary male. I am more shaken than I thought. I raise my drink to him.

"A proper welcome to town," I say.

Kate and Derek stumble out of the bathroom. Her hair is a mess, and the strap of her dress is down over her shoulder. Derek is pale enough that I think he might faint.

"Fucking huge!" Kate yells to me.

She might mean the earthquake. She might not.

VII

There are many definitions of insanity in this world. One could argue that spooning a man's eyeball out of the socket and performing carnal acts of religious desecration with it is *insanity*—we will revisit this later—and perhaps you'd be right, but I would argue that *true* insanity is far simpler than that. True insanity is driving in Los Angeles. There is no rhyme or reason to it, no code of conduct or set speed. Half the drivers are pretending to star in a drag racing movie, and the other half are driving a quarter the limit. Simply leaving the house for a gas station run can be treacherous. And the *rage,* the *rage* of all the drivers. Especially toward me. I smile and drink it all in.

In 1967, Ford put out a custom-ordered color for their Mustangs called Playmate Pink (often mistakenly referred to as Playboy Pink, even now when so many collectors covet it). It was initially called something different, but allegedly was gifted to one or numerous of the Playmates of the Year, and the name stuck. There is very little data on how many exist, but they are very rare and hardly ever come on the market. My grandmother bought one at auction in the seventies and famously attended a Halloween party at the Chateau Marmont in it dressed as a dead Playmate. The photo of her lying on the hood of the car, splayed out as the sexiest of corpses, is framed in my bedroom, grainy color and old quality. The photograph is famous. The pink of the car, though, often draws the ire and contempt of said rage-filled driver looking for somewhere to *stick it*.

Now behind its leather wheel, I swerve with glee as I weave in and out of them all on the highway, and eventually pull into the employee lot at work.

I walk through the security checkpoint at the employee entrance and down into the tunnels below the park. They will spit me out in the miniature Hollywood, which is where our Nordic castle room is located, inexplicably. Two male fur characters, a dog and a beloved cartoon toy cowboy, stand with their heads off, sneaking in a last-minute morning smoke. Down the tunnel, a girl who will probably end up playing the Arabian princess, but is currently stuck with the duck fur suit, practices her dialect and diction to herself. They make us all go through extensive vocal training to suit our particular roles, require us to watch the movies again and again to get it just right. She won't be able to play her princess role until she has it down—the accent, the intonation, the knowledge, everything. She will be quizzed extensively on every aspect of her character and every film in which she appears. In the meantime, she is a lady duck.

Fur training is another rite of passage. No princess becomes a princess without first paying the dues of being a fur character, and the suits are hot, it's exhausting, and while fur characters don't have to meet the same quota of guests per hour as the princesses do, they still have to be on all day, without any ventilation, out in the Anaheim sun. It completely sucks. I give her a smile as I pass.

I love this park, its underbelly and its outer shine. I love this park as much as I love the Strip and the whole of Los Angeles. Four hundred and eighty-six acres of pure magic. There is the magic of the park itself. It is of course a place to escape the harsher realities of life, a world within a world, a fantasy with hidden depths like all fantasies. But one that became an empire, inspired and fueled so many millions or billions of people that it has become an inextricable part of the very fabric of our society. It is a happy childhood, distilled, a fantasy realm of possibility for the low cost of one hundred dollars a person per day.

And there is so much that is unseen, lurking just beneath the surface. Glorious and feral. At night, dozens of cats are released in the park to control the city's native rat population. They prowl the rides and the faux-rocks and claim the territory until daylight. Occasionally one escapes security and cleaning crews' notice before park opening and can be found milling about and mewing in and among the visitors. And there is the behavior of the guests. People become the most extreme versions of themselves here. It is amazing. The fantasy realm of Los Angeles and the park allowing them to indulge their strangest and wildest inner desires. It is entirely common for tourists to be caught scattering ashes of loved ones in the famed ghostly mansion ride. They come to us and tell us of their divorces, their losses, their house foreclosures. As if we are real princesses with the power and magic to absolve their problems. As though a princess, real or not, would give a shit. It happens all the time. Adults approaching us as therapists and not twentysomething-year-old baby boomlets who will lose the job if we so much as gain a scar or five pounds. I live for it. Their misplaced trust, their sappy, overflowing feelings. I draw it all in.

And then there are the mysteries, the secrets. Rumor has it that not all the skeletons in the pirate ride are fake, though I have ridden it many times over and cannot myself determine this to be fact or fiction. I of course hope for the former. And the absolute best secret of the park, another rumor unconfirmed but one that I suspect is true: if a guest dies in the park for any reason, the body must be removed from the property before the visitor is declared dead, keeping its seventy-year legacy clean and free of ever having to admit there was a death within its walls. Legends of Los Angeles, legends of the park, legends of a false Scandinavia. We're all just playing into stories created before our time. We're all just living and altering them, every day.

I push open the door at the end of the tunnel and prepare to greet them all.

During our lunch, we are summoned to the break room and sat down before a very smug-looking Liz in sparkly mouse ears. She has just finished a Bavarian cream–filled from Randy's that she ate in the break room while staring into a princess poster on the wall, sighing heavily between mouthfuls. I know this because it is how she eats her donuts every day, leaning her face against her hand, her brows drawn in a picture of exaggerated bereavement. It takes very little to imagine her as a child in the very same posture and clothing, similarly stewing in the stimulated aftermath of her afternoon treat and lamenting a birthday party invitation she didn't receive. A slight bit of glazing sugar sticks to the corner of her mouth, but now she stands before us with the smugness, and I know that things are about to get very bad or very good.

Not everyone is here, as most are currently working. Liz will likely have to perform this speech many more times today, whatever it is. In the room now are maybe six fur characters as well as five princesses, two princes, Kate, me, and the royal cunts, Cinderella and Snow White. Kate downs a meal replacement shake and pointedly avoids looking at the donut box on the counter behind Liz. She has an audition in the next couple days, and she generally prepares by partially starving herself.

"Okay, everyone, thanks for coming in today for this meeting," Liz says. "We have some VERY exciting news, and I've been just chomping at the bit waiting to share it with you!"

She lets out a little giggle and childish shoulder shrug, and everyone waits. Cinderella sips from a can of soda. Snow White averts her eyes from it, disgusted by all its processed cane sugar.

"So there have been complaints issued to Corporate. I'm not going to say what they were regarding, or who placed them. But Corporate LISTENED, and they have sent us the angel we need! And I of course mean angel in a completely nonreligious sense, as we of course do not subscribe to or discriminate against any one singular religion here! SO, without further ado, I truly cannot be more excited to present to you our new team supervisor, Andre!"

A slouching thin man who looks like someone's science class boyfriend wearing an all-charcoal velour sweatsuit and mouse ears emerges from behind the door, apparently having been waiting for his cue in this lackluster performance. He steps out and purposefully does not meet Liz's eyes before coming to a stop in front of the rest of us. Interesting.

"Hello, hello. It is very nice indeed to meet you all, and I look forward to getting to know each and every one of you more." He looks at Kate and me as he says this, and Liz crosses her arms over her despised bosom in triumph. So they've discussed us already. I am nearly certain Liz herself would have been the one to file the complaints, but there's always Cinderella. Really, most of our coworkers hate us. Still, bringing in the heavy artillery. Well played, Liz, well played.

"I am not here to come down on you, just to make sure our corporate values are being upheld. This is the most magical place on earth, and we want to keep it that way! We are magic makers!" He smiles broadly at all of us, expecting some kind of response that he doesn't receive. Pocahontas picks at one of her nails.

"So, uh, yeah, basically I'm just gonna pop in, check on you guys, oh, uh, excuse me, you *all,* and you know, provide feedback to you, and to Corporate as we go along. You'll barely notice I'm here! Great! So I hope you all have a wonderful rest of your day, and Kate and Maeve, can I see you both please?"

Cinderella laughs with Snow White, and they linger to see what's going to happen, but Liz shoos them out and follows after. She turns and gives me a victorious smile before closing the door. It's just the two of us and Andre. I picture us in a threesome. I picture Kate and me slicing off his ear.

"So. I'm sure you know why I've asked you to remain behind," Andre says.

Neither Kate nor I say anything.

"You two have a lot of responsibility in the park. The ice queen and her sister are still very popular. It's a coveted position, and I can tell by the looks on some of these other princesses' faces that they would gladly take your places if they were available to them." He leans back against the communal snacking table and clasps his hands in front of his elastic tracksuit waist tie. How can anyone take a grown man seriously in these ears? "Do you feel that your work performances here have been exemplary?"

We nod.

"And what is it you do that makes you feel like exemplary employees?"

Kate rattles off with convincing ease everything and more that a corporate enforcer such as himself would love to hear. After a moment, Andre turns his gaze on me, and I do not lie to him. "I love working here," I say. "I look forward to it every day."

He furrows his brow, bites his lip, and nods his head a few

times. He pulls his clipboard off the table behind him and taps it with his pen. "And that," he says, "is part of why Corporate sent me here. This park has been around for a long time, and we've had a lot of princesses. But we have never received as many satisfied customer letters as we have about you two. The kids just love coming here, and I don't know if you've seen, but parents rave about you in our Yelp reviews. So I want to congratulate you on a job well done and implore you to keep at it. And to further celebrate you two, here are two twenty-dollar gift cards to the food courts! Not to be used on any beverages. This world can always use a little more magic, and you are the valiant heroines providing it to America's families every day."

Kate and I don't know what to say. We stand there a moment longer, and Andre says, "Well, enjoy your day, and I'll see you out there!"

We turn to leave the room, both a little stunned. Just as we are about to head through the door, he calls out, "Oh. Just one last thing."

We pause, knowing this is our moment of execution. The man is clearly a sadist, and I have to say I deeply respect him for it. I brace for the worst, my heart thudding in my ice-blue dress.

"What do you two think of, uh, Liz?"

Kate tilts her head. "What, you mean, like, as a person?"

"Sure, as a person, but mainly as a boss."

"She keeps us on our toes," I say before Kate can speak. "She takes the job very seriously and very much strives to run a tight ship."

Kate shoots me a look of betrayal, but I ignore her. It would be unwise to denounce Liz to this man who adheres to rules and hierarchy just as she does. It would lead to questioning and perhaps a line of inquiry that would damn us far more than it would Liz. Additionally, I've spoken the truth. As much as I despise Liz, as much as she is merely a peon of the Grand Capitalist Regime and the largest pain in my ass to date, she is also an adversary, albeit a weak one, in a world frankly lacking in much excitement. Liz is part of the job. Frustrating Liz. Appalling Liz. It would not be the same without the ever-present threat of her try-hard do-good twitchy eyes catching us in the act of something we are not meant to do. I do not wish to see her banished from this place any more than I would us. I am sure Liz does not feel the same about me, but that's her issue, not mine.

Andre nods again and says, "Good. Very good. Thank you for your time. I suspect that she might be outside the door. Please send her in when you go."

Indeed, Liz is waiting anxiously on the other side of the door, clearly having tried to eavesdrop. Kate leans in close as she brushes past and says, "Careful, Liz, I think he might have a crush on you. Very improper in the corporate structure. And did you see his package?"

Kate's comment leaves its mark. Liz is destabilized, her face bright red, her eyelid twitching slightly as she plasters on a smile and heads into the room.

VIII

I am back on the Strip, late afternoon sun hot on the pavement, and I feel sick.

The doll is gone.

I have been avoiding revisiting the site of its apparition, have been avoiding looking into this particular bramble of flowers, passing by this particular corner. But today, I worked up the nerve to revisit the thing, and possibly to destroy it.

But it is not here. I stand, and I reposition myself, reach into the same spot I reached into before. A crow circles above me. An El Camino passes, bouncing on its wheels. There is no doll.

Was there ever?

I think it to myself, and as soon as I do, I unthink it. I inhale as though I can suck it back into my lungs or my treacherous mind. There is a tingle in the back of my skull, and I turn, slowly, certain I will find someone standing there. Watching. Waiting.

At home, I am restless. I watch the 2003 video of Michael Jackson fulfilling his lifelong dream of grocery shopping, his friends having rented a shopping center out for him so that he might, along with them, play pretend at normalcy for an hour or so. I loop the video and watch again. Three minutes and thirty seconds of this extraordinary happenstance. Initially, it is charming, endearing. This man who is so far removed from society experiencing something innocuous, taken for granted, and to anyone else, surely extremely disappointing upon final attainment. But the glee he expresses. The absolute pleasure in his pretend errand unsettles me. I don't know. I am sick watching it, and yet I cannot stop. I make myself watch. Again and again.

And then I am on my feet, and I am in my grandmother's room. Time has passed. The sun has lowered so that its light will only fill this room for a few minutes more. Just moments. Dust mites swirl, and Lester the Cat sits beside my grandmother's head, his tail flicking, once left, once right.

My grandmother sleeps. I listen to the ragged rise and fall of her breath, in and out, arrhythmic over the incessant whirring of the machines. It is still disturbing, even after these months, to see her bare face, free of her heavy armor of makeup. I have considered applying it, coaxing her image to rework and return to its natural form. But it would be a violation. A boundary irreversibly crossed. She has never allowed anyone near her. Even in her days of stardom, she applied her own makeup, styled her own hair. The act of intimacy required to enter someone's space so fully, for so long, has always been far outside my grandmother's comfort. Mine as well. In all our time together, we've never so much as shared a hug. Our hands have never touched. I do not wish to touch her now, only to return her to normal. To feel her watching me. To know I am seen, by someone.

My mind flashes back again. My first night here.

After our dinner at Jones, I couldn't sleep. I rarely sleep anyway, but usually I doze for a couple hours, at least. But that night, it wouldn't come. I was electrified, couldn't stop myself from trying to take in every square inch of the room that even then I felt would become mine. We hadn't discussed it, hadn't gotten much past the *I'm your granddaughter, and I'm here now,* but I felt it all the same. This house that existed as though it had been made for her. And her blood ran through my veins. There was such a feeling of rightness about it all that I felt if I closed my eyes for even a moment, it might disappear. It might never have existed at all. Too perfect to be real.

Tallulah was and was not what I had expected, had imagined from my father's limited stories and the films of hers I could find. But even if my parents' scope had not been so unforgivably limited, how could anyone possibly describe Tallulah? How could anyone do her justice?

In the thin hours of that first morning, I heard movement in the kitchen. I stayed very still, deciding what to do. Tallulah was everything and more, and I held no illusions as to what she was capable of. It permeated the air of the house. Her scent. Her domain. She was not warm, and she was not maternal, and for these things I was grateful. But here I was, a foundling in her lair, and my fate here was not yet determined. There was a slight air of danger about her, of instability, the type of woman who might every once in a while lash out with a slap across the face or claw marks left on a lover's arm. But only if it was deserved.

I cleaned myself up and decided to meet her. She did not acknowledge me as I entered the kitchen, but she was aware of my presence. She knew, and accepted, that I was there. If she had not, I would have known. This I was sure of. She had laid a square of dark chocolate and four almonds out for herself, which she picked at without looking. A stack of magazines lay before her on the large countertop, unopened. Lester the Cat jumped on the counter and climbed on top of them, leaning in close to her. He eyed me warily. I plotted my next move. I knew Tallulah would approve of assuredness and strength over polite reluctance. Civility so often a tiresome burden foisted upon the one it is paid to, requiring acknowledgment and reciprocation. Still, I felt my heart pounding as I opened cabinets until I found what I needed to make coffee. I tried to steady my hands and set it brewing. My grandmother said nothing, which told me I was right, and I like to think my shoulders relaxed, just a little.

After some moments, she reached up and relocated Lester the Cat to her other side on the counter, clearing space for me. I was surprised. As much as she felt like the person I had always been searching for without even quite knowing, I did not know this woman who wore my face, not in the practical ways. But still, it was an opening, and I knew it would only be offered once. I took my mug and came to stand in the proffered place beside her.

Through the enormous panes of glass, we watched her territory as it slowly illuminated. Orange, yellow, pink. It was the first time I ever witnessed the day breaking over this city, the indifferent sun preparing to cast its harsh glow upon the dirty hot pavement, piercing the thick cover of smog. How could I know on that first day that this would become our routine? Years of this lay ahead of me. Beautiful, too short years of convening wordlessly in the kitchen with my grandmother and Lester the Cat, bearing witness. Neither of us slept, I would later learn, a trait I had never shared with my parents but now understood. I was never theirs. It was all so clear.

"It's time to leave," she said, her voice cutting through the perfect silence the moment the light touched the glass. "Go get dressed."

Outside, I followed just behind her as she stepped over the various debris on the pavement as though she knew the exact location of each and every piece of trash. The homeless awoke, a few newsstand and café workers arrived, unshuttered windows and doors. The crows cawed, seagulls screeched, and a light chill pervaded the air that I didn't yet know would be gone within the hour. The vegetation, the signs, the colors, the fading stucco and stained sidewalks and sleepy monumental street. I couldn't take it all in fast enough, I couldn't absorb so much so soon. It felt as though I had dreamt of a place my entire life and never let myself believe that it could be real. Of course, I had seen Los Angeles in movies and on the internet, but it wasn't the same. It was the feeling of it, being here now, the dry polluted air, suffused with hints of orange blossom and jasmine. It was the grime and the shine together. My grandmother's black Prada boots stepping over dogshit and cigarettes.

Tallulah brought us to a stop outside the Rainbow Bar, the smell of stale beer and cleaning chemicals wafting out to greet us. She wore a large black-brimmed hat and oversized black sunglasses. She handed me a vintage Hermès scarf with monkeys and snakes on it. I debated various ways I could wrap myself with it, as I was clearly meant to, and as I was thinking, an enormous red double-decker bus came to a stop before us. The doors opened with a hiss, and the driver nodded.

"Good morning, Miss Tallulah, another beautiful day!"

The bus lowered to the level of the sidewalk, and my grandmother took one regal step and then another inside.

We settled in the two right back seats on the open upper level, Tallulah clearly having staked her claim to them long before. The tour guide nodded at her, and over the course of the next few stops, the bus filled with eager tourists, as new to the town as I was.

I watched them step on, the excitement in their eyes, some of them fatigued in the early morning, some of them overwhelmed, not city people, or perhaps not accustomed to the vengeful heat.

"We do this every Sunday," Tallulah said. "You should know that, if you're going to be here."

I turned to her, but she was looking out over the city, not at me. I didn't know if this meant I could stay, didn't want to think it, in case I was wrong. I took in the early morning Hollywood streets, the overly eager people who would sign up for a tour at this hour and their dragged-along families, the shine of our red bus.

I tied the fabric like a driving scarf over my hair, and Tallulah conveyed her approval with silence. She handed me a large pair of sunglasses, which I also put on. I listened as the tour guide pointed out celebrity homes and locations of suicides and murders. Everything was so monumental, so full of death and life. A part of me could not reconcile the idea of my immaculate grandmother and these pedestrian tourists, and yet it made complete sense. We chugged through this city that awoke ungracefully around us like the breath of life, and I had never felt that the world held such promise in it. There were so many possibilities before me, and at the same time, I felt I could never want anything more than just this.

A smile played at the edges of my grandmother's lips—*my grandmother,* even saying it to myself was so significant—and I tried not to let her see me watching. I wanted to know this woman whose genetic material made up such a significant portion of me. We stopped along Hollywood Boulevard for the tourists to admire the stars and the handprints, and a few of them got off to crouch down and pose. Kitsch. Clichés. Cheap thrills, replicas, the exploitation of out-of-towners, of those visitors who will never feel this place pulsing through their veins. All of it so wonderfully American, Western, Californian, Angelean. So very much itself. The studio set shine, the extra-coated polish, the pigeons and trash and fanny packs and cell phone cameras, the too-white teeth and Snapchat selfies. *Look, Mom, I made it to Hollywood ;)*

"Well, what do you think?" Tallulah's voice, commanding

and clear. Her eyes were closed beneath her glasses, and her head was tilted back theatrically. "Isn't it just . . . ?" She waved red-polished fingers.

I gazed out over the top of the bus, peered down at the glinting stars and the filthy streets, the Chinese Theatre and the Egyptian and the wax museum. But Tallulah wasn't looking at any of it. It wasn't the city bringing her such joy. Her eyes were on the tourists. And I understood. There was no difference between this city and the woman beside me. The tourists admired Hollywood Boulevard, and she felt it. Every street, every lamppost was a part of her, was so much a part of her in fact that I felt they must have been birthed in the same great seismic crack. A silent unknown god these mortals all unknowingly paid tithe and tribute to, observing them from the back row. Simply watching.

And I thought, even dared to hope, that I, perhaps, had originated there too.

"Exquisite," I said.

Tallulah there beside me, smiling now so that I could see her canines, inhaling all of them, the naïveté and awe of the visitors, their very spirit.

"You understand," she said, adjusting her sunglasses, her elbow resting on the guard rail's edge beside her. "Which I suppose now can only mean one thing."

I cleared my throat and watched a man in a visor rows ahead of us try to fight off an attacking pigeon. I held my breath.

Tallulah turned her canine smile on me.

"It's yours now too."

My phone rings in the other room. I close my grandmother's door softly and answer.

"Please, please, please! I'll love you forever and ever!"

Kate. Another party. Another career-making opportunity in the guise of a suited adulterous downer of a man. And she needs a wing woman. I do not want to go, I do not want to be anywhere. But I know how these men can be. And I owe her. Perhaps Kate will not always need me to watch out for her, but for now—

IX

So here I am, by myself, my thong creeping farther and farther up into the crevasse of my derriere, and the man with the champagne tray hasn't been by in almost six minutes, but even so, there is not enough alcohol in the world to distract me from the mind-numbing Beverly Hills crowd of dustbags-in-training I've somehow found myself enveloped in. Kate, meanwhile, is across the room talking up someone who looks a lot like Derek from Babylon but may or may not be an exact replica with a different name in the same line of work. He is not particularly handsy, but the night has just begun. All these men are the same. In front of me stands another, talking. I scan the room for another drink.

"Yeah, we met back at my first VC firm, it was his first job too, and he's really just such a *guy,* man, I really never thought he'd be the first one down the aisle, but I guess when you wanna lock it down you wanna lock it down, amirite?"

This is an engagement party.

"Mmm," I say, glancing at his girlfriend who I believe would also very much like to be *locked down*.

"And how did you two meet?" I ask as my eyes follow two suited good-looking twenty-year-olds retreating to the bathroom for blow.

"Get this, you'll never guess. Guess."

He waits and watches me, full of giddy expectation. There are two things I despise in this world above all others: the first is when a person forces you to *guess* something as though you are a psychic or a child or could possibly be interested enough in their lives to expel brainpower to feed their narcissistic tendencies, to observe them fully and regurgitate some aspect of that observation back to them to their ultimate satisfaction, swallowing it all down like a grateful little porn star swallowing a big heaving helping of—

"She's your proctologist," I say.

He freezes, huge smile, eyebrows raised, as though I have punched him in his face.

After a moment, he blinks a number of times and then finds his words. "Well . . . yeah. I mean she is. How did you—?"

I am as surprised as he is.

"So you probed him and knew he was the one?" I direct this question to the proctologist who I now realize looks as though she has truly seen some things. I wonder how many items she has had to remove from rectums, and I picture her momentarily naked in a sea of glistening butt plugs, Gatorade bottles, and various girthy vegetables.

"He asked me out after the exam. It happens more than you'd think. But I don't know, caught me in a weak moment I guess." She shrugs and takes a sip of her drink. "And he doesn't care that I spend my days with my hands up other men's asses, so there's that too."

"Yeah, you know, some buddies of mine and me," says the proctologist's boyfriend, "we have this group chat—"

"Don't get into the group chat," the proctologist says.

"Why not? We're already on the topic."

"Not here. We're at an engagement party for Christ's sake."

He ignores her and turns to me. She takes a long drink from her glass and beckons the server over for another. I try to grab for one, but I am prevented by the start of this enthusiastic story. "Okay," he says, eyes manic with self-pleasure, "so I've got this group chat with my oldest buddies, there's eight of us, and we send each other videos every day. Can you guess what they are?"

"I'm coming up empty," I say.

"So, every day when I sit down to take a dump, I put the camera down there between my legs and film it. And all my buddies do too, and we send them to each other. Here, I'll show you some."

"Tom, put that away," the proctologist says. "Sorry, he's kidding."

"I mean, I'm not kidding. See? She doesn't care. May doesn't care, do you, May? You like it. You've really got a nice face, sweet, you know? Anyone ever tell you that?"

I have seen four of the defecating videos when a throat is cleared behind me.

"Mind if I join you guys? You look like you're having more fun than the rest of the party." The voice sounds familiar, but I can't place it. I look up and into the visage of yet another Ken-doll dud. But this one I know, met in fact only a few days ago. I roll my eyes.

"Kate drag you here too?" Gideon says.

The couple holding me hostage introduce themselves. I am able to snatch another glass of champagne and down it. It is not enough. I glance over to Kate and her man, and she looks as though she is enjoying herself. The man's hand hovers just above her lower back.

"Anything good?" Gideon asks, tilting his chin toward the still-outstretched phone.

"Quite," I say. "I was about to show my new friends a video of my botched caesarean."

There is a pause, and then,

"Your . . . ?" Tom's proctologist begins.

"I was part of a study. Experimental, you know," I say. "So they filmed it, and I kept the footage. It's just one of these things. The kid's still alive, he's just deformed a bit. I elected to have him removed a couple months early, as part of the study. It turns out you can still eat the placenta, even if it's extracted through the torso. It's somewhat meaty, but you can blend it into a smoothie, and it goes down a little better. *Smoother,* you might say. Here, I've got the video somewhere."

They both pale.

"Um," the proctologist says, "we haven't said hi to the bride."

"Yes," her boyfriend says. "Yeah. Okay. Good."

They are gone, and I watch as the man sets his hand on Kate's back, moves in closer.

"I prefer the lasagna method myself," Gideon says. "Although, I hear placenta makes a fine chili too."

"And there it is, the sparkling wit that got you into Harvard."

He raises his eyebrow at me. "The charming amenability that got you into Stanford."

I freeze and look up at him. "I didn't go to Stanford."

"Kate said you did."

"I didn't."

"You went full ride on an academic scholarship, and you dropped out after two weeks."

"You don't know anything about me."

"Your parents disowned you, and somehow you found your way here."

I stare at him and then push past to find the bathroom. I will be having a word with Kate later about sharing privileged information. I pull my phone out of my bag to call a car as the ground tilts beneath me. My first thought is of the doll. That somehow that unholy *thing* has caused this.

But then I see, understand in slow motion. It is not me, it's everyone. Someone gasps. Glasses fall, the room sways. Of course. They tend to come one after the other. Earthquakes arrive in the attire of either rollers or shakers. The one we experienced at Babylon was a shaker. They are more violent, more sudden. But I have always found the rollers to be far more unsettling.

The ground undulates beneath us as though we are surfing, the room swelling and collapsing, enough to destabilize us all. I lose my footing, and I am falling. I reach out on my way down, for anything, and I brush against something and take hold of it. It takes too long a moment to realize what my hand is grasping. It doesn't matter.

I am falling.

And then I am not.

I am staring at the ceiling, and I am somehow suspended above the ground. The earth stills, calms. Kate's brother's face comes into view. His arms are cradling my back, and he is holding me up, no more than a foot above the floor. His package is still firmly grasped in my hand. I release my fingers and let it go.

"Thanks," he says. "Your grip was a little tight."

I clear my throat. I open my mouth for a reply, and nothing comes.

"Are you okay?" he says.

"Please put me down," I say.

He pulls us both up to stand and releases me. The room is laughing and checking for lost spectacles and much-feared nip slips. I am not the only one who fell, and a number of guests shake themselves off, recover champagne glasses. I reach for a glass of whatever's nearest and down it. I set it down on a now-disheveled table, and Gideon is standing with my phone in his hands, typing something. Or maybe he's not typing. Wiping it off. I don't know. He hands it to me and offers a smile.

"Thank you," I say.

I slip it back in my bag and walk away from this man who has attached himself to me, and who I would rather not interact with, preferably ever again. I don't see Kate and need to make sure she's okay.

And then I can salvage this night. I have a new target on social media. I bought an old VHS copy of *Sense & Scentability*, the 1998 apex predator documentary, and one of *Beetlejuice*, and both should have arrived today. A Sybian as well.

"Maeve." Gideon's voice sounds behind me. I turn, a rage building in me that is not appropriate to the situation. I breathe and demand it to quiet. To sleep. He holds my book in his hands. The copy of *Story of the Eye* that I've marked and notated and read ten times through, the same one I was reading when we first met. It's fallen out of my bag and opened to a page with my notes on it. I see that his eye catches one of them. I feel it as though he has set his eyes on my naked skin. This was a glimpse not he, nor anyone, was meant to see. He closes the book and holds it out to me.

"Let me drive you home," he says. "This party sucks. And it's the least I can do after that handy you gave me."

"No, thanks," I say, and take my book.

X

Kate is fine post-earthquake and isn't ready to leave the party. She seems to think that this man she is hanging on has pull in a movie for which she's been trying to get an audition. I watch him from afar, and nothing registers. He is harmless. As much as anyone can be.

Outside, my phone is glitchy from the drop and shuts down halfway through my ordering a car. I try to mentally calculate how long the walk home will take or if I should coerce some man inside to give me a lift. I don't feel like putting out though, not tonight, and it would surely be expected. A diversion would be nice, but the eye contact, the human company. I do not want the interaction. The exchange and subsequent depletion of energy that is interfacing with other speaking mammals. I am wearing my grandmother's black flat Prada boots, the dressiest I was willing to go for the occasion. They can take the beating.

Someone unlocks a car remotely, the lights flashing on. The beep of the machine coming to life. The car beside me, the one I am leaning on, I now realize. I stand so that I am not touching it. Of course, it is Gideon who emerges from the walk, but this time he is moody, as though something has happened. He seems . . . larger.

He looks up, and it is a moment before he recognizes me. He

blinks, and the expression is cleared from his face, replaced with that athlete arrogance I now know much better than I'd like to.

"So you want the ride after all?" he says.

I am about to tell him where he can shove his keys when I realize it might not be the worst option. Gideon won't expect anything from me sexually, and if he does then Kate will have something to say about it. I can survive twenty minutes in a car with him.

"Where do you live?" I say.

"Why do you want to know?" So his mood persists, even beneath his mask of contentment. Alright.

"Just drive me to where you live if it's in the direction of my house, and I'll get myself the rest of the way home."

He stares at me, flatly.

"Okay then," he says. "Get in."

I do. I drop down to the black leather seat, cold against my skin. Vintage Porsche 911, in good condition. He starts the car. If I'm honest, I've always loved watching a man slide a key into the ignition, triggering the purr beneath my legs as the engine revs to hot grinding life. Even here, with this least desirable of generic men, I can appreciate the moment. We don't speak. We sit in silence. After about one minute of driving, the car stills.

"Why have we stopped?" I ask.

"This is my house," he says, his tone still dark.

I look up at the house behind him, an expansive Tudor a little larger than my grandmother's home, with a long front lawn that has been well maintained. Too green. Unnatural.

"What," I say.

"You insisted," he says.

"This is your house."

"I know. It's excessive." He exhales. He rubs his forehead. "I've kind of been regretting it," he says, "but they say buyer's remorse

is common with a house. I've only ever lived in apartments before. New York, you know." His eyes as they stare beyond the
windshield are a little wild, fiercer than is necessary. Or perhaps
the dim light of the car only makes them appear that way.

"Why did you drive to the party? You could have walked in
less time."

He shrugs, eyes still fixed on the unmoving road ahead of him.
"I, uh, you know we don't drive really in New York. I just bought
the car, and . . . I mean, I just wanted to drive it."

I look at the dash and the wheel. To be fair, it's beautiful.
Not like my Mustang, but still.

"I'm just going to walk home," I say.

"Look, I'm headed out for a drive either way, so it's up to you."

I turn toward the window, the manicured and strangely exposed homes of the Beverly Hills Flats. I've never understood
the appeal of this neighborhood. The wide swath of Santa
Monica Boulevard with nothing but office buildings and the
city hall. The exposure of the homes. Nothing hidden. Nothing
removed.

"Fine," I say, and I surprise myself by saying it. I shake it off.
It's been a long night. "Thanks."

We get back on the road, and he flips on the radio. The Ven-
tures' 1964 surf-rock classic and theme song for the show by the
same title, *The Twilight Zone,* comes on. It is one of my favorites.
It's nearly October, I realize. Just a week away. The Halloween
spirit is reviving. Without fail, this has been and always will be
the most wonderful time of the year.

"It's funny. I remember LA differently," Gideon says.

"How?"

"Well, when I visited Kate before, there were these things
all over the ground, below the trees. Like husks. I thought at
first that they were trash, and then I remember thinking they

looked kind of like carcasses. Like big bird carcasses. They were everywhere."

"Palm fronds," I say. "They fall in the winds."

"Oh so you've seen them."

"The winds haven't come yet this year. They'll be here within the month, and the fronds will fall." I do not tell him that this is one of my favorite events, one of the most magical and overlooked happenings in the time-vacuum calendar of our home. That I look forward to it every year. And yes, of course I have seen them.

"I can't wait," he says.

"Winds mean fires too," I say.

"Beauty always brings destruction."

I roll my eyes.

After a moment, he says, "It's such a fucking waste. I mean, she's so smart. And she just throws herself at these idiots. I can't understand it."

"There's nothing wasteful about it. Kate is doing what she feels she has to do to succeed. She's chasing a dream."

"Some dream," he says.

"As opposed to knocking a puck around all day?"

"You don't like me," he says.

I tilt my face so I can bask in the pink and blue glow of a neon coffee shop sign, the towering offices slowly passing by. I hate that he would talk shit about Kate with me here, as though I would partake in it, even if he's right. Even if I harbor the same thoughts at every one of these inane events she drags me to.

"Hm?" I ask.

He pulls over and brings the car to a stop.

"What now?"

He turns in his seat and fixes his eyes on me. There is still that instability in him, that slightly unhinged quality. I wonder

if he took drugs at the party. If a professional athlete is permitted such things.

"You don't like me. You think you've got me all figured out."

"Are we in a romantic comedy?"

"Come on, Maeve. You think I'm an asshole."

"I don't know what you're on about."

He stares at me a long time and shakes his head to himself.
"You really don't see it."

"If I indulge this, will you start the car again?"

He stares at me still, as though he is really searching for something. Rage still radiates off his body for Kate, for what she will
inevitably do tonight. He doesn't move.

"Fine," I say after a moment, just to end this. "What do I
not see?"

"We're the same, you and me."

I can't help it. I laugh now, a sharp bark of a laugh that surprises me. I don't laugh often, not like this. I smile, exhale my
pleasure at various events. But this laughter is foreign. It's as
though the sound came out of some other throat. It laughed me.

He starts the car again and pulls forward. The engine rum-
bles beneath me, and I think about the Sybian in the Amazon
box waiting for me at the house and the videotapes and my new
online victim.

"I don't know," he says. "Maybe this town just fucking sucks."

Out the window, we pass more neon signs and mismatched
architecture, the palms loom dark and silhouetted over us with
the bruisy black sky, stars obscured by city light and smog hov-
ering over it all, sealing us in, preserving us. I can't imagine
anything more beautiful.

Someone swerves into our lane and nearly hits the Porsche.
Gideon slams on the horn. "Jesus! Like that. The people here."

"The people here what?" I say.

"I mean, everyone says New Yorkers are assholes. And like, it's true. Kind of. But the real thing about New York is that everyone is so crammed together, is so busy, that the city operates like this one huge organism. You have to be efficient ordering your bagel and know what you want before you get to the counter because if you don't then you hold someone else up. You have to walk fast on the street for the same reason. You can't disrupt the flow. It's *respect* for community, you know, the *whole*. But here . . ." He waves his large hand. "Everything is so spread out. There's no city center, just like a bunch of neighborhoods, and no one gives a shit about anyone else. This city is like the epitome of the individual. Land of the fucking selfish."

"Why is it that every New Yorker comes to LA just to tell everyone how much better New York is?"

"What is it about LA that people get so mad hearing it?"

I don't reply. We'll be back at the Strip soon, and I never have to see this asshole again. Next thing I know he'll say—

"There's just no culture here," Gideon says.

I take a breath.

I take another.

There is no culture here is the second thing I hate. Beyond the scale of what I deem anywhere near acceptable. Fucking New Yorkers and their insistence that theirs is the only culture that matters, that life outside their city is inherently less important. It is now the top of my list of deep hatred. Maybe it always has been. And I believe Gideon has joined it.

"You can pull over," I say.

No culture. What a fucking snob. We turn onto Doheny from Santa Monica, the Troubadour on our right. A building that has held so many musicians and comedians and artists it is difficult to even count. Imperative to the fabric of our recent cultural history. This city *creates* the culture for the world.

Also, just on an etymological level, *everything* humans touch is culture. Towns in bumfuck nowhere with populations under a hundred people have culture. Human life is human culture, and people who feel that the existence of one type is of greater value than another frankly seem to be the most *uncultured* of all. I close my eyes so I don't search for something sharp in the vehicle to stab through Gideon's ear and into his brain. I wouldn't, but the fantasy soothes me.

There is a sound, and my mind is slow to register.

He's laughing. Gideon is laughing at me.

I turn and face him.

"What?" I spit out.

"I'm sorry. It's just too easy to wind you up. I actually really like it here. It was my choice, kind of, to transfer out."

My blood is still pulsing in my ears, and I am slow to make sense of his words. I study his face. He is, in fact, fucking with me. No one does that. Not really. I feel a number of things, clawing at my insides, begging to be freed, but mostly,

"I know you're Kate's brother, but honestly, fuck you."

XI

There is a second bar in my Los Angeles, another in addition to Babylon. But this one hardly anyone knows about. I've never brought Kate here or anyone else, and you could drive by a hundred times and never even know it exists. All the way on the other end of the Strip from Bab's, between the Whisky and the Sweet James (*Your Accident Attorney!*) billboard, sits the Tata Tiki Lounge, belowground in an unmarked squat stucco square building. Inside is The Bartender, whose name I've never learned and never will because he is the surliest bartender who has ever lived. We might have sex one day, but I am not sure. His is a kind of low-level chaos likely incompatible with mine. He stands behind a slippery dark wood bar, in front of a wall lined with novelty tiki mugs and Polaroids of topless women. I have long held a suspicion that the women were all close friends of The Bartender, as I often catch him staring thoughtfully at the images, and twice I've seen him break into a fit of rage and tear one of the photographs to shreds, top it with whiskey in a glass, and knock it back down his gristly throat.

There is only ever one other person inside the Tata Tiki Lounge when I come in, seated at the far end of the bar with his face buried in a glass of expensive custom-ordered French red with a bottle beside it. I have never been able to determine if he is

Johnny Depp or an extremely convincing Johnny Depp impersonator. But it really doesn't matter either way.

I come in twice a week, always on the same days and at the same time. Johnny is always here, and The Bartender, and me. Fake shrunken heads hang from the ceiling, and there is a jar of teeth on the bar, presumably fake, but how should any of us know. The Bartender only plays ambient music or death metal, but I began paying him years ago to play Halloween songs at my regularly scheduled visits, and it's now routine. When I enter today, my piña colada is waiting for me next to the jar of teeth, and The Specials' "Ghost Town" sounds over the dingy speakers. The piña colada is, in my opinion, the perfect beverage. Cold, sweet, and orgasmically artificial. However, I only drink them here and only by myself, as it is far too intimate to consume one's true beverage of choice in front of others. The Bartender and Johnny, of course, do not count.

"Ghost Town" was released in 1981 by The Specials, everyone's favorite British two-tone group. *Two-tone* of course referring to the period of Jamaican-ska-meets-new-wave-meets-punk that was coined by 2-Tone Records (founded three years before the release of "Ghost Town" by Jerry Dammers of The Specials) as a means to defuse racial tensions of Thatcher-era England by bridging that gap in the punk scene, at least. The song was an extreme success but sparked some outrage in Coventry, England, the purported ghost town in question. Longstanding frictions in the band came to a head at the same time, and "Ghost Town" was the last song recorded by the original seven members of the group. A reminder that the good never lasts. It is also a fantastic song to drink to.

Johnny gives me a nod without lifting his head, and I tilt my glass to him in answer. He's not looking too hot today. Coming off a bender. I feel for him. As much as I ever feel for anyone. I take my drink over to my table and settle into my spot. I crack open my book.

To briefly revisit, Bataille's masterpiece is a ninety-some-odd-page piss-and-blood-soaked 1928 novella of debauchery, youth, and bicycle rides. I usually read it in its original French, *Histoire de l'Oeil,* but on this occasion, I am reading an English copy from the small rare bookstore behind the large bookstore a few doors down and across the street. The translation is pretty good. The novella begins with Simone, a distant relative and sexual partner of the narrator, dipping her pussy into a saucer of milk. The book has much to do with eggs and, as I said, piss, a bit of psychological torture, and finally culminates in a threesome-turned-murder of a Spanish priest and the insertion of his eyeball into Simone's vagina. It was heavily influenced by Bataille's relationship with his paralyzed father who often urinated in front of young Georges and forced him to watch, and his bipolar mother. It is, in every sense of the word, fabulous.

But there is the problem. The page the book fell open to at the party. The one Gideon saw. The page that I have studied too many times to count.

Eggs are extremely erotic, painfully so. Bataille got that right. Fill the tub with them, lay your naked body down and let them crack one by one, slowly, exquisitely against your skin, beneath your weight. Brûlée sugar giving way to silky white cream. It's simple, and it's real, and it is so lovely and pure and dissolute that my dreams are full of them, my thoughts preoccupied as children pose before me at work, as I feed Lester the Cat, as I stare out over the Strip.

But the *cul.* I have tried so many times. I will try again tonight, but I know already that I will not succeed. It is, among so many other disappointments of this universe, all too clearly impossible. There is just no way to hold the egg in one's asshole fully without it breaking, a central image of the book and one so taken for granted. Perhaps hard-boiled. But then there is not the squeeze and the ooze, the slow drip of the yolk, the aborted fowl, the unborn dinosaur, creeping down the leg, golden and glowing, catching light as it clings to the tiny hairs, the smooth pores.

I am full, thinking of it, this predicament, this riddle, with unimaginable rage. It blinds me. It is there, always there. Even now, with something as simple as this. I take a breath and sip the bottom out of my drink.

The rage. So much more real than the blood inside me. So much more powerful than love or fear or death.

My grandmother sitting with me, back at our same table at Jones. Once again over untouched plates of spaghetti and half-finished glasses of alcohol. Six months into my new Los Angeles life. My fresh start. Before I found my way to the park.

My first job in the city was with one of the studios, a contact of my grandmother's. Someone who needed an assistant. It is not worth delving into, but I may have thrown a prop lamp with all the strength I possessed at an actor's head. He suffered a moderate concussion and purported emotional trauma. It was a partial miss, and no one else saw it happen. Actors are notorious liars, and with my grandmother's connections, it was wiped from the slate. Additionally, it is perhaps worth noting, the actor never worked again. My grandmother, however, wanted to discuss it over dinner. I was terrified.

"Maeve," my grandmother said.

I sat across from her, trying and failing to hold my head high. I did not regret what I did in the slightest, but I wanted more than anything not to have to answer for it. At least not to her.

"Maeve," she repeated, and I raised my eyes to hers.

"I need you to listen carefully because I will say this once, and once only." The waiter set down another drink for each of us, and neither of us reached for them. She stared me down, those cool blue eyes that I had in my skull too. I wondered if people felt this way when I looked at them. Fear. Excitement. Too difficult to distinguish between the two. Too . . . disarming.

"When a big bad wolf stumbles upon the pasture and is found among the flock of little lambs, do you know what happens to it?"

I knew she didn't want me to answer.

"Hm?" she said.

Still, I waited. The dramatic effect was what she was after, and I knew better than to rob her of it on this night. I did not know what she would do. What she would do to me.

"The wolf is *put down*. That is what happens, Maeve, if it is discovered." She took a sip of her drink. After a long time, she said, "This is not a place for wolves. Ours is a world of sheep who believe themselves to be something greater." She picked up her glass.

I glanced to the exit. I cleared my throat. "I don't know what this has to do with—"

She slammed her glass on the table, and small shards of it broke off on the tablecloth. After a long hard look at me, she turned an actress's smile on the onlookers nearby, *How silly of me, How could I have set it down so hard, Oh waiter won't you please bring me another?*

When we were once again unseen, she leaned forward and held my eyes. "Do not waste my time. Do not waste yours." And I thought in that moment that she might kill me. She could, and maybe she even would. I saw it. I understood. I had not spoken my thoughts of wolves and prey aloud to her. She had known. Because we were two of a kind.

Something stirred between us. I had known from the moment I arrived that I wanted to remain here with her, that I needed to. And there were similarities between us, for certain. But in this moment of her rage, in witnessing the full power of her attention in response to the mistake I had made, everything changed for me. A critical piece fell into place.

A lifetime thus far of being alone. Of *knowing* I would be alone, forever. To stand in a full room and know oneself to be apart, that invisible barrier between *you* and *them* to be in every way uncrossable. To find the will to exist in a world so wholly unsuited for you.

And to have all that wiped away. To think there is another, and she is *like me.*

"So what am I supposed to do?" I asked. I was terrified, and I was elated, and I wanted to overturn the table and hide and run and scream and weep. This was something vital.

Her eyes found mine again.

"The wolf is strong," she said, "but there is one who is stronger. You will have to feed it, every day, forever. You will have to nurture it, Maeve, for the wolf can never be seen again. Not by me, and not by anyone. You cannot be what you are and survive. Do you understand."

"Yes, I understand," I said.

She took another slow sip of her drink and watched me. She raised her brow and lowered the glass. "What wolves need is a disguise. We need to be shrewder, quicker, ready to outwit and outmatch and strategize. We will never be like them. We will never truly belong here. But we can make it appear as though we do. We play this game from the *outside.* Remain . . . unemotional. Detached. *Clever.*"

"Okay," I said. I was not alone. Even as she said what she said next, even as I was reminded of how much I had never belonged, it was all overshadowed by the single otherworldly fact of someone being here, my blood, my family. She wasn't turning me out. I could stay, for now, at least. Someone who was like me. It was nearly too huge to comprehend. It was everything, and more.

I was not alone.

"You have to put your wolf to sleep, Maeve. Keep it sedated and secret and tucked away. It is the monkey's time. It is time, my girl, to learn to play pretend."

XII

Once a month I have a date at the Chateau Marmont with a famous director I will not name because I have signed extensive NDAs saying I will not do so. He begs me to piss and shit into his mouth, and I try to find it demeaning and debaucherous in a meaningful way, but ultimately it is stale and boring, and mostly I just imagine, while squatting over his head and looking down over the length of his body, what would happen if I took the letter opener from the desk and slit him open slowly, along the shin bones, up the thighs. I once tried a French delicacy in a Brentwood restaurant with my grandmother that was intestinal lining of some animal. One is supposed to take a knife and slit it open, the inner contents spilling out like confetti.

The director swallows a mountain of pills to sleep each night, and I often find myself standing over him with the letter opener in hand, fantasizing about going through with it. But I enjoy sitting by the pool and the breakfast he buys for me each morning after, so I tell myself I can do it next time. Tantalize myself with an empty promise. One more day by the pool, one more unfulfilling night, piled atop so many others. The monkey does not dissect without reason. The monkey observes. The monkey feels no rage.

The Chateau was built the same year Bataille's masterpiece emerged, and it opened in 1929 as a luxury apartment building. Modeled after the French Château d'Amboise with its iconic high Gothic arches and ornately painted ceilings, it was converted finally to a hotel in the early thirties. Home to overdoses, affairs, hideouts, and more scandal than I will subject you to here, the Chateau is a hideaway in the middle of the city, a den of iniquity and a tranquil reprieve from the world at large for those who need it. It is where everyone who is anyone goes to do just about whatever they please. To be unseen by most and seen by all who matter. The director always stays in the same room in the tower, the very same room that Howard Hughes used to reserve to have an uninterrupted view of girls in bikinis down at the pool.

I can't sleep. I consider leaving, sitting in my grandmother's room in the dark with Lester the Cat. I consider just slicing off a couple of the director's fingers. Just to see how much I can do before he wakes. I cannot stop seeing the foundling doll in the vines. Even still, I feel sick, violated. The beautiful little thing crawling without consent into my life and disappearing just as quickly. The director snores. I step out of bed still gripping the letter opener to feel something concrete, and I walk over to the window.

The sun is not up yet, but the sky holds the faint glow of the almost-light, of the in-between. There is someone in the pool. I can just make out the lines of a man's body. Tall, powerful. He pushes himself through the water, splashing, the pool not large enough for a small person to swim laps, nearly impossible for this man. He takes about a stroke and a half before slipping beneath the water and turning around. This man is too big for this pool. I feel suddenly, sickeningly, as though I am too big for this room. As though I am too big for this body, and I am suffocating inside it. Plastic pulled over a nose and mouth, a body bag zipping shut. I step into the bathroom and run the water of the shower, but I never get in.

The director wakes sometime later. We eat our breakfast downstairs, and he then accompanies me with coffee out to the pool. The swimmer is still at it. I don't know how many hours it's been. Up close I see even more how absurd his movements are, how ungraceful in the cramped space.

"Oh god," the director says.

"What?"

He is neurotic as all "artists" are, but he isn't normally so dramatic, at least not publicly. He's too easily recognizable and has learned to make himself small when outside, even in places like this. Pretenders pretending. His face is white, and he looks as though he might faint.

"Shit. Shit, shit, shit."

I turn in the direction he is looking and see a young famous actress. She is having a moment, is on billboards all over town. Now that I think about it, maybe I heard something about her having dated the director for a while. The actress looks up. She has spotted him.

"Fuck. Did she see me?"

"Yes."

"Are you sure?"

I don't answer him. She waves and beckons him over, and he slumps his shoulders and goes to her, a yo-yo returned to its owner's hand. She sits on a lounger by the pool, so I follow to claim my own. I wait to sit though, lingering beside the director to see if the exchange will play out in any invigorating way.

A whole display of how unbothered she is, how unbothered he is, she just moved in to one of the bungalows. She asks about me, and her eyes slide over my body. Am I another of his actresses? No? She loses interest.

The swimmer stops, finally, abruptly, with his back to us. He stands in the shallow water and steps out of the pool. His back is corded with muscle, tight thick ropes of meat. He is fit in a way that is normally repulsive to me, the tightness of him. The hardness. The idea that anyone should care about their body vessel so much that they devote themselves fully to it. To mistake the body for the self, a waste of a life and mind.

He turns and removes his goggles, walks over to us, and stops beside the actress. He shakes his hair like an animal, and the actress objects with a cute and highly practiced sound of charmed annoyance.

"This is Gideon. He plays for the Kings," she says, eyes on the director.

But Gideon's eyes are on mine. He regards me with the surprised and self-congratulatory smile of a man about to receive head. I imagine holding his skull underwater. It is perhaps the only imperfect truth about this town, the inescapability of everyone, especially those one does not wish to see again, let alone so soon. But especially here at the Chateau, I really should have expected no less.

"Gideon, this is . . ." the actress trails off, waves her hand to further emphasize the unimportance of me. I can't help it. I smile.

"Oh, Maeve and I go way back," Gideon says, that look still on his face. His eyes hold mine. The actress is now acutely interested in me. She asks what I do for a living.

"Murders and executions," I say.

She watches me and waits for the punch line. When I offer nothing else she says, "Okayyy . . ." annoyance clearly written on her face. I say goodbye to the director and abandon him to his miniature hell. I take a chair and drag it over and away from them, and I situate myself and open my book. It doesn't take long for another chair to drag over next to mine, and for Gideon to place his large self on it.

"Strange coincidence, seeing you here," he says.

"It's a small town," I say.

"I don't know. It almost feels meant to be."

I take a breath and set down my book.

"If your intention is to ruin my morning, it's working."

He laughs. The rage threatens to fill me once more, but I do not let it. The monkey observes.

"I've been thinking about our car ride," he says.

"Hm?"

"Maeve, I'm going to say something, and I want you to just take it for what it is," Gideon says.

What does a person say to that. It can't get any worse, anyway.

"We should have sex, Maeve."

I was wrong. I have imagined this. Try again.

"What did you say?"

"You and I, Maeve," Gideon says, "I think we should fuck. Do the horizontal tango. Bone. Plow. Have intimate relations. Die the little death. I think you want to die the little death with me, Maeve. I could be wrong, but I don't think I am. I'm usually not wrong. Not about this."

"I prefer to die alone," I say.

"Well, we all do, fundamentally. But I think it could be good for you. And me. I'm not wholly selfless."

"And why is that?"

"Well, I don't really believe in selflessness, as a concept, it's more—"

"Why would you think this could possibly benefit me?" I say.

"You know why," he says.

"Believe me, I don't."

"Because when I look at you, I see it. It's there, behind that *innocent* face." He is mocking me. When I don't respond, as he was surely goading me to do, he continues. "You've got a lot of people fooled, but I see it. The dark. The void. That thing behind it all, the one that threatens to fill and annihilate us, you've seen it, and you're trying to unsee it. So am I. We could be mutually beneficial to each other."

I pause, half a second. "You have me pegged," I say. "Bravo. Now please leave."

"But the thing is, I really do. You should think about it."

"I don't need to think. The answer is no."

He stretches out over the lounger. Water droplets drip off his body and fall to the ground, bead off his skin in the light. I do not notice them. I do not stare at them, glistening.

"Besides, I've got a solution to your problem," he says.

"My problem, at present, seems to be you."

He laughs again, his Adam's apple bobbing, his body taking up more space than I have ever considered a body could inhabit.

"Exactly what problem is that?" I say.

"I noticed in your book, your notes, at the party. I was curious. I had some free time. I went and got a copy, read it, and I solved your problem."

Rage. Curiosity. Rage. The monkey observes. I breathe.

"Okay. So tell me then," I say.

"You've been trying it all wrong. I assume you've been trying it on your own. That's your first problem. That's where I come in."

I snort a disbelieving laugh, and he continues, the sunlight shimmering on his man body. I try to focus on the surface of the pool, normally calm, now upset and roiled by this new presence.

"Secondly, I don't know if it's gonna work with the raw egg.

Not unless you got some kind of clamp in there or something to keep things open. Which works for sure, but I think you want a more authentic approach. But . . . a soft boil. Not so delicate on the outside, but a runny yolk. Chef's kiss, you know?"

I blink at him. I've never thought of a soft boil. It's not a bad idea, and I can't help it, I feel a certain something happening in the lower regions of my bikini, but not because of this man beside me. He is pretending, trying to impress me. I don't know who or what he thinks I am, but I know that he is wrong, and I know he is not the skin he wears at present. There are all sorts of reasons to try on a new personality. Moving to a new place to start a new life is a compelling one, and this city in particular encourages us to try on these identities, to inhabit someone new. And it's often difficult to know what we truly want to be. So many ghosts and legends here to possess us. After a while, it's easy to lose oneself to it. To become more an extension of the city than a singular mind and self. But I don't intend to be a part of this athlete's momentary slip into the life of another, and I certainly don't intend to be around for when he realizes he prefers his missionary style cocaine and martini banality to whatever darkness he hopes to access from me at the moment.

"I think you're wanted," I say, indicating the actress sitting on her lounger glaring over at us. Her last role was playing a misunderstood young stepmother to a child dying of cancer. The film was two hours long, and I think this actress cried for an hour and a half of it. She's nominated for some award. She will probably win.

"Usually," he says, eyeing me. He, like everyone, is blinded by what they want to see.

"I'm a virgin," I say.

"Great. Ideal, really."

"I have herpes. And gonorrhea."

"Who doesn't?"

"I suffer a rare and incurable blood disease that will claim my life in three months. It's going to be very messy. Hospital rooms. Weight loss until I'm barely a flesh sack. See-through skin. Vomit. Midnight tear-filled screaming phone calls. Very emotional."

"We better get to work then."

Pussy really is the one true prize.

The actress clears her throat, raises her eyebrows, and loudly drags her chair over to ours.

"Looks like you two are having fun over here. Thought I'd see what all the *hype* is about," she says. She's furious. It fills me with enough joy to counteract the frustration of an otherwise spoiled morning.

"Just chatting about death," Gideon says.

"I was just leaving," I say.

The actress flips her hair over her shoulder dramatically and drops her sunglasses below her eyes. "I was born dead, actually."

Silence. A crow lands beside the pool.

"What," Gideon says.

"Yep. With the umbilical cord wrapped around my throat."

The actress pauses, her head tilted so that her neck is exposed in the sun. Gideon and I both stare at this woman who is clearly waiting for a response, is clearly accustomed to getting one.

Gideon doesn't offer her one, so eventually I do.

"Who says shit like that?"

XIII

The Five Blobs were a studio ensemble put together by Bernie Knee (mistakenly referred to as Bernie Nee throughout the whole of his career) in Los Angeles to create *The Blob,* intended to accompany the 1958 Steve McQueen film. The song was written by Mack David and Burt Bacharach, and when Columbia Records released it in the same year as the film, it became an instant hit. Bernie Knee's name (spelled correctly or otherwise) was mentioned nowhere in the film nor the Columbia Records single, and his very vocal outrage at this exclusion led to a terminated contract with the label. The Five Blobs continued with Bernie at their helm on Joy Records and released a couple 45s, but they are nearly impossible to find now. I turn the volume up louder in my headphones and make my way home.

I pass by the site of the doll, and still there is nothing. I despise the feeling that comes over me, as though someone is watching. As though I have been spotted.

The house seems neat and normal as I approach, but once at the front steps I feel an unmistakable *off*ness that I can't put my finger on. Perhaps it is a holdover from the doll . . . but no. There is something different about the house. I stare at it.

After a moment, I realize what is so strange. Hilda's shoes are there, just on the front step. I check the time. She usually is gone for her lunch break by now. But her shoes are here. She insists on wearing an outside pair and an inside pair for reasons beyond my fathoming. But we have a routine, Hilda and I, and we almost never deviate from it.

I remove my headphones and step inside. It feels different inside. I am filled with sudden and complete certainty that something is wrong, and I am nothing but living terror. I force my legs to move me into my grandmother's room, and my eyes scan the space. She's sleeping, if not peacefully, then the way she always is. Everything is fine. I exhale, my heart slowing.

Hilda isn't here.

But there is a someone in the living room. I can feel it, sense it. An intruder in the den that is ours. I step out to find Hilda sitting on the couch, upright, hands in her lap, hair that is not quite any one color slicked back and secured in the tightest of buns. Waiting for me. Her habitual severe look of foreign sternness is replaced with a thoughtful one. This more than anything unsettles me.

I take slow steps into the room and keep my mind carefully blank.

"Hilda. What are you doing in here?" I say.

"Oh. Maeve. I didn't hear you. Sit."

This is my house. My grandmother's house. She doesn't tell me to sit. Why is she telling me to sit.

"I prefer to stand," I say.

"Please sit."

"I don't want to sit. Can you please tell me what's going on?"

Hilda clasps her hands together in her lap and inhales the quick breath of someone who is bracing themselves to do something they've done many times before and know they will do many times again. Efficiency, Hilda's specialty.

"Maeve. It is time."

"Time for what?"

"You do not hear me." She slows down, just a little. *"It's time."*

A Star Watch bus passes by on the Strip. A flock of parrots circles above the trees.

"No, it's not," I say.

"I am sorry," Hilda says. Her tone does not say she is sorry. It says that she is doing a job. Businesslike. Concise.

"She has two years left," I say. "It can't be time."

"Who told you two years?"

"I did the research. She should have two years left."

Hilda nods to herself, looking at me now with the worst kind of look a human can look upon another with, one I never thought I would see from her. Pity. It is worse than any insult she could have thrown at me. "The internet says all kinds of things," she says. And I am too full of panic to respond to that comment with the violence it deserves.

I sit. Fall. I don't know. I'm in the chair.

"No," I say.

"Her quality of life is decreasing. She is tired, and she needs rest."

"She is resting."

"Not that rest."

"No."

"She is in pain. As you know, her last will—"

"She's fine, Hilda. She's just . . . resting."

"Maeve." She leans forward, tries mechanically to reach for my hand, but I pull myself back. At my refusal, Hilda shifts her posture and takes on a stilted and clearly rehearsed air of sympathy. "Maeve, this is difficult news, but it is what she would want. It is always hard to lose a loved one. It is a hard thing," she continues, like a child reading a school play script, "to have to prepare yourself. But we do not need to go back to the hospital. We can do it here. And we can wait. Two days, maybe three. But that is it."

"Two or three days?"

She nods, and her performance is over. She is Hilda again, unemotional, bulldozing. "Okay. I will give the doctor my recommendation today." She stands. Hilda stands to go. She stands to go, to call the doctors.

"Um," I say, barely getting it out, "Hilda, I . . . um, could you help me with something, quickly, before you go?"

She is surprised, but after a moment, she nods.

"Okay," I say. "It's just . . . downstairs, in the cellar, there's—" My throat is dry. I'm having trouble speaking. "There's this sculpture she really likes, and maybe we could bring it up, so she can see it again? It's not so heavy, I just don't want to break it."

Hilda considers, then says, "Okay."

We take the stairs down together, Hilda beside me, and I keep my mind empty. Blank. Calm washes over me. Perhaps acceptance. Should acceptance come so soon? It's not acceptance. There are no lights on downstairs, and I reach and flip a switch to turn on the sconces.

"The cellar is just over to the right," I say. I think I say. I must say because Hilda walks in that direction.

"Oh right. I just have to get the key," I say. "One second. Sorry."

I run up the stairs and into my bedroom. I take the keys from their place in my bedside drawer and run back downstairs. "Okay, got 'em."

Hilda offers me another practiced, conciliatory smile, but I can see that behind it she is already thinking about the traffic on the way home, what she will cook for dinner and what she will watch while she eats it. She is gone from this house already, gone from this news she has delivered to me, this proclamation she has made over another life. The only life.

I slide the key in the door and turn it. The lock clicks, and I push the great door open. It is dark inside, and cold, the way it always is. "The switch is further in," I say.

Hilda and I step inside, and I reach around on the wall until I find what I'm looking for. It hangs alongside her other props, and the weight of it is heavy in my hand. I flip the light switch at the same time to mask the sound of it, to distract Hilda. I watch her face as her eyes adjust to the light, as she begins to register what lies in this room before her, and the object I now hold in my hand. I can almost feel the adrenaline pumping through her system. Run, run, run, it says.

Too late, I say.

I swing the mace into the top of Hilda's skull.

XIV

Hilda is down in a single swing, but I rear back and hit her again, splitting her chest open, my breaths coming in hard and fast. I leverage my foot against her stomach to retrieve the medieval weapon, bring it up over my head again, and crack her collarbones. Nothing of her can remain alive, nothing of this woman who would end my grandmother. Nothing. I hack, and I bludgeon, until she is no more than meat, until she is no longer a person who can speak words to doctors, who can send people here to take away the one thing that is mine. She lies in a masticated red steaming lump on the cellar floor, and I wait for my breath to come slower again. I wipe the blood spatter off my face and replace the replica medieval mace on its hook on the wall, one of my grandmother's many props gifted to her postproduction. The cellar is full of them like the rest of the house. Movie props. Wine bottles. And then, of course, the bodies.

Well, they're not all bodies anymore.

My hands are shaking. I did not plan to kill Hilda. It wasn't something I wanted to do. Hilda has, up until now, cared for my grandmother, sustained her. But she betrayed me. She betrayed us. She would take from me the one thing that was mine. An

emotion pushes itself through me, overwhelms me. I can't identify it yet, I can't—

I steady my hands and prepare myself for the work that must
now be done.

Having stripped most of the flesh down with chemicals and
the slow cooker, and having worked my muscles to a place
beyond fatigue with the hacking, I now have to dry the bones
outside in the sun, so I decide it's as good a time as any to
pull out the Halloween decorations. Tomorrow is the first of
October, so I have pushed it as late as I can anyway. Usually
this is a task that fills me with great joy, but at present I feel
sick. I string up the cobwebs and the spiderwebs, and hang
the witches and the possessed girl and the skeletons and the
vampire and the werewolf and the mummy and Frankenstein's monster and his bride. Inside, Hilda's clothing and
hair burn in the pizza oven. Still, this new feeling in my
body, distracting me.

I have killed three times before, but I'm not quite sure if I
ever exactly . . . enjoyed it. I also did not dislike it. Perhaps the
closest experience I can liken it to would be preparing meat
for dinner. One simply *does*. I suppose the first time I did feel
something. In hindsight I would call it disappointment. I felt
disappointed to have watched the light leaving someone's eyes
and to have felt so little about it. Disappointed to have wielded
the ultimate power of death and felt nothing.

But with Hilda, when that mace collided with her body, I
felt something. As the weapon slammed into her flesh again
and again and pounded her body to a pulp, just for a moment,
I forgot what she had said about my grandmother. I forgot that
my grandmother was ill at all. I forgot everything.

For just a second with Hilda's blood on my face and the squelch of her flesh as I pulled the mace back to hit her again,

I felt . . . good.

Several hours later I am sitting out front, attempting to untangle string lights and listening to Don Hinson and the Rigamorticians' "Riboflavin-Flavored, Non-Carbonated, Polyunsaturated Blood," when the cops arrive. They park their squad car across the street. No siren, no lights flashing. I take a deep breath as they cross toward me. One of them is more senior than the other— tall with graying hair, he walks with confidence across the street. The other looks like he just graduated high school. He carries a notepad, no doubt in training. I turn the music down, slightly.

"Hello, officers," I say.

Cop Senior speaks first. "Hi, there. Is this the Tallulah Fly residence?"

"Yes, that's my grandmother. How can I help you?"

The officers' eyes roll over me. I am covered in Hilda's blood. The sixties swinging rhythm of the music plays through the speakers.

"Impressive decorations you've got here," the rookie cop says.

"Thank you. We do it every year. Normally my grandmother helps, but she's been ill."

"I'm sorry," he says. "That's always hard."

"Mm."

"We actually got a call from the hospice agency. They said you called them and told them a Hilda Swanson didn't come in today, is that right?"

It was sloppy of me, I now realize, to have called them so soon, but I was rattled by Hilda's proclamation. I give my best concerned smile.

"Yes. She's supposed to come every day at eight, and today she didn't show up. She's never even late normally. I'm sorry, would you like to come inside, or . . . ?"

Cop Senior waves the question away. "It's way too soon to even be looking into anything, she probably just skipped work," he says. "I just owe a favor to someone at the agency, they took care of my mom before she passed, but she's a little, uh . . . paranoid. So . . . Now we can say we came by anyway."

"I can give you a ring when she hopefully shows up tomorrow."

"That'd be great. Thanks."

The rookie cop snaps his notepad shut. "I love this song," he says.

XV

With my tasks completed, I don't know what to do with myself. Hilda's words are a mace through my own skull, and they are bludgeoning me again and again.

It's time.

It's time.

It's time.

Lester the Cat circles my feet and mews for something. I walk slowly and deliberately over to my bathroom and try to throw up, but I can't. I open my phone and search online for Susan Parker. As predicted, she has been eviscerated. Beyond ostracized. Blogs. Reddit, Instagram, Twitter, Facebook, local news. Her husband speaking out against her, saying he had no idea he was living with a bigot all this time. Canceled. Internet trolls saying they will come to her house and make her pay, saying her children will not be safe. Saying they will string her up and hang her and her family as her organization has done to so many. I have succeeded. She is alone. And yet in this moment her demise brings me no joy. It brings me nothing.

I am covered in Hilda's blood, but I do not shower. I try to masturbate, but I can't do it. I try to read, and I don't understand the words. I don't understand any words.

Distractions. Distractions for a life. Finding ways to live

exquisitely alone. Because alone is all I will ever be now. Alone and full of this rage.

It's time.

It's time.

It's time.

I pick up my phone. I'll call Kate. We'll go get into some trouble. Hilda doesn't know what she's talking about. Who is she to make the call on the end of a life?

My hands shake as I open my contacts and try to scroll to Kate's name. My eyes unfocus and focus again, and I see that there is a new contact here, below hers.

KATE'S HOT BROTHER.

I did not put this in my phone. How did it . . . and then I remember Gideon with my phone in his hand at the party. Lester the Cat meows in the hallway. Beyond that hallway is my grandmother's door. Behind that door is my grandmother.

I don't think. I have lost the ability. I stare at the phone. I stare at it, and I see Michael Jackson in the supermarket grabbing hold of food and placing it in the cart. Such a look of glee.

I click on the contact and make the call.

After a moment, he answers. He sounds out of breath.

"This is Gideon," he says. He's probably exercising, like at the pool. Maybe he's just finished a practice.

I realize what I'm doing and what a stupid idea this is.

But that doesn't keep me from saying, "Hey. It's Maeve. You know, from . . ."

"I know who you are, Maeve." I can hear the smile in his voice and am certain now that this is a mistake. But I need a distraction. I need to be here and not be here. I need . . . so much. So much more than I will ever get.

"About your offer."

XVI

I wake to a bed covered in blood, though it is not Hilda's, and it is not my own. I pull back the covers and step out from the sheets, following a steady trail of it through the house, over the wide wood planks, up onto the couch, back down, down the hall, and finally into my grandmother's room, through the open door.

The blood is on my grandmother's bed. I run over and find that it is not hers. I turn to Lester the Cat who sits on her pillow, staring intently at me. He meows, once, forcefully. And then he collapses.

Panic. I wrap him in towels and load him into the Mustang, chanting over and over, *Please don't die. Please don't die. She would never forgive me. Please don't die.*

I run into the vet's office and just manage to get out, "Cat! Shitting blood!"

They take him back. I watch his limp body bob up and down as he is carried away.

I sit in the veterinarian's office waiting room, reading, trying to read, Dostoyevsky's *Notes from Underground*. Somehow in the race to get Lester the Cat out of the house, I had the wherewithal to grab my bag, though I have no memory of doing it. I've switched to this book because Gideon, while perhaps having solved my problem, has tainted Bataille for me. At least for now. But at the moment, it really does not matter what book I hold, as I am unable to read even a full sentence. I am seeing him, and Kate, tonight. I want to cancel, likely will cancel, but I can't think about it just now.

Across the dismal, fluorescent-lit sick den for quadrupeds sits one old male, human, and one youngish male, canine. My heart races, and I breathe the way my grandmother taught me. The words still don't hold my attention. I look at the dog. Thick layers of skin droop from the animal, rolls of fur and hide and fat. The bulldog has an underbite. The dog pants heavily, producing a kind of noxious hot meat fragrance that circulates throughout the room. The human male attached to the dog by a leash loosely dangled in his Parkinson's-rattled hands has been holding a vigorous staring contest with my breasts for the better part of a half hour. His eyes, behind his glasses, are somewhat wonky. He is *significantly* old. Perhaps a screenwriter or composer in retire, the bulldog having been foisted upon him by concerned children following the premature passing of his wife, their mother, to be taken back in by them upon his own passing, not premature. Some part of their father to hold on to. Some desperate attempt.

My phone rings. The hospice agency.

A calm, or a semblance of it, settles over me.

"Yes, Doctor. This is Maeve. Thank you for returning my call. Hilda has still not come in yet. Have you heard anything?"

He hasn't. They're looking into it. They will assign me another nurse as soon as possible. Today even.

"Well, actually, that's why I called," I say. "You've been won-derful, but with this mishap, I've decided to make the switch to another agency. It's nothing personal, I just need the best care for my grandmother. If you could please just send her charts and care protocols, I will pass it all along to the new nurse. No, there's nothing you can do to change my mind."

I end the call.

The old man blinks. The bulldog drools, thick ropey spools of it dripping down to the linoleum. I reach down to the hem of my shirt, take hold, and pull it up to my chin, displaying for him my unbound breasts. The old man produces a sort of feeble grunt or groan at the unanticipated flesh sighting. The bulldog snorts through his drool, closes his mouth, licks his chops, then resumes his panting.

I set my shirt to rights, and the vet tech enters.

"Lester's mom?" she says.

"I . . . yes," I say, though the affirmative feels not only false but also cumbersome. "It's Lester the Cat. His name."

"Right," she says. She doesn't tell me if he is okay. I am too afraid to ask.

I follow the girl in. Messy bun, purple and pink scrubs bear-ing multicolored pawprints. Like nurses in hospitals, nurses in homes, these drab, tired, wrung-out sweat laborers who wel-come daily the barrage of bodily fluids not their own, the most thankless of jobs, and they wrap themselves in cartoonish rain-bow abominations, the frailest attempt to lift the spirits of their patients. Or perhaps themselves. I cannot think of anything more depressing.

The rainbow-scrubbed sleepwalker leads me into a room in which I wait and stare at a small metal table. I have brought Lester the Cat here once before, and I now remember the same tech giving him his once-over on this very table. Squeezing his little cat joints, listening to his organs, deftly avoiding the claw swipe while inserting the rectal thermometer. I have the insipid sense that if I remain very still and keep my mind free of thought, then everything will be alright. If I do not think the worst, the worst cannot happen.

She would never forgive me.

She would never—

"So you are Lester's mom!"

A small man stands at the door. Again, the meaningless impulse to correct him. I am not Lester's mom, and that is not his name. I can't speak. I do not move.

"I'll tell you right now, he's okay," the vet says. "But it's good you brought him in. Very good." He produces a manila folder from beneath his arm, and from it, three black-and-white images that he affixes, swiftly, to a whiteboard on the wall. "These," he says, flipping a switch that illuminates the whole thing, "are Lester's X-rays." He smells faintly of corn chips. His words sink in, slowly. Lester the Cat is okay. He will not die.

What I see before me is a triptych of *Cat* in black and white: long white spine, grayish sacks of organs. His spindly cat legs and skull. One image from below him, crouched in a near-pounce, and one from each side. It is difficult not to admire the perfection that is the feline shape. The predatory grace of even the domesticated. And he is alive.

But, there is, in addition to Lester the Cat's enviable countenance, clearly outlined in his abdomen for all to see: the proximal, middle, and distal bones of a human finger. Still attached. Still intact. There is a human finger in his intestine. Hilda's finger.

"As you can see," the vet says, "his intestine is punctured just slightly by the foreign body, which explains the bloody stool. If you had waited to come in, he might not have made it."

I hold myself very still. He waits for me to speak, though there is nothing accusatory or suspicious in his silence. I don't think so anyway.

"Will you be able to remove it?" I ask. "The foreign body?"

"Oh yeah, we've got him all ready for emergency surgery, but we wanted your approval on cost, and signature on liability release."

"Sure. Yes. All of that is fine," I say.

"Would you like to review the costs, or our resuscitation protocol?"

"No, I'll sign whatever," I say. "He's . . . very important."

"Aren't they all? Well, I'll just send our tech back in then."

He leaves the X-rays pinned to the board with the light on, glowing through the body of this little rapacious creature, one I did not know meant so much to me. My responsibility. He is my responsibility now. The weight of that realization settles heavily, nearly crushing.

At the door, the veterinarian turns and says, "Uh, Lester. Do you allow him to roam?"

"Um. Roam?"

"I mean outside. Does he go outside?"

"Yes," I say. "Sometimes."

He nods, once. "I know he probably loves it, but cats get into some pretty weird stuff when they're out and about on their own. I would, uh, maybe limit that in the future."

"Okay," I say. "Sure."

He nods again and reaches for the handle.

"Doctor," I say. He pauses and waits. I try to find my words. "Is this pretty bad? I mean . . . you're sure he'll be okay?" I ask. "There was a lot of blood."

He scrunches up his face, bestows upon me a career-cultivated reassuring smile.

"This? Oh no, this isn't a lot. He'll be just fine after surgery. We get animals in here, just spraying blood. *Gushing.* Like a fountain. Or a spigot. I mean, really. Just pouring."

XVII

They are able to remove the now-flesh-stripped finger from Lester the Cat's stomach, and they afford me the option of taking it home in a bag, which I accept. The rainbow-suited tech gives me a long look as I take the finger bone bag from her. I smile and thank them all for their help.

I lay Lester the Cat's limp sedated body on the small cat bed in my grandmother's room. His cone prevents his head from resting fully against the bed, but he seems alright enough. I have medication to administer to him twice a day until it runs out, and he must eat a restricted diet.

I have also received the care instructions for my grandmother from Hilda's agency. Pages upon pages documenting her as though she were never a person at all, simply a series of protocols. I shall have to keep track of her vitals, administer her medications, change and clean her catheter and bedpan, wash her body, roll her periodically, tube-feed her.

I knew. I knew what it would be, but maybe I also didn't. I watch my grandmother, this woman who I have not so much as touched in all our years. What would she say to this? I can't ask her.

I reach out and place my hand on the pulse point of her throat. Her skin is cool, crepey, so thin. Her pulse feeble and erratic. I pull my hand back immediately. Like touching the doll in the vines, I am stung, and I should not have done it. Like touching a divinity, a hot volcanic rock. It should not be attempted. It isn't right.

I read the pages again in case by some miracle they have decided to shift their letters and change what is written there. But they do not, and this is what she needs to remain alive. To remain with me. And so I must.

I take a long shaky breath.

And so I must.

XVIII

There was a night a year ago at the 69 Bar, before my grand-mother fell ill. Before anything began to change. In Little New Orleans in the next-door original park, there sits a speak-easy for a dues-paying membership club of extremely devoted park guests called the 66 Bar, located between a restaurant and a faux alligator skin purveyor, demarcated only by a 66 above an otherwise blank door. It is decorated the way one would imagine a park-version New Orleans speakeasy might be. Old timey, a little sexy, more colorful and free of obvious branding than anything would be in our world. It is the only place in the park in which security and staff will allow a patron to get wasted. Below the 66 Bar is an employee-only bar that someone long before us lovingly dubbed the 69 Bar. A watering hole for all the park employees, it is less extravagantly appointed than the upstairs 66 Bar, but it is significantly wilder.

Kate and I made our way to a couple empty seats next to Pinocchio and the Scottish girl. At least I thought those were their characters, it is difficult to remember everyone out of cos-tume. We'd had a long day; a woman came in to tell us of the death of her child, and she was sobbing too hard to leave at the appropriate time. It was nearly an hour before security finally came in and escorted her out. Then there was the teenage boy who not only invited us to "ride him instead of those dumb reindeer" but also attempted to expose us out of character for his entire time allotment, asking us about gaming consoles and airplanes, phones and social media. Luckily a Code V came and got us thirty minutes extra break time. A Code V means we got vomited on. That day, but not always, by a child.

Beside us was slumped a new fur character, sweat plastered to his forehead, swaying on his seat and slowly sipping what looked to be a lemonade, trying to rehydrate. On our other side, a new princess trying and failing to talk to one of the princes through a sort of makeshift sign language. It's happened to all of us at one point early on. Most of the princess voices are much higher than any normal speaking range, and the vocal cords are always initially strained.

We ordered sugary colored drinks, the same ones served upstairs, but these in thin plastic cups, and leaned against the wall in our chairs, facing each other. We'd sipped from flasks on the way over and we were both starting to feel the effects. Kate was dieting again for another audition, and her face was flushed from the alcohol. She seemed upset, still bothered by the crying woman today.

A few tables over sat our doppelganger sisters, the ones from the other park. We don't mess with them, and they don't interact with us, as a general rule. Behind them, one of the multiple ducks made out with a girl who I think plays that boy scout from the movie with the balloons. We're supposed to watch all the movies, supposed to possess encyclopedic knowledge that will allow us to jump into any role at a moment's notice, something we are often asked to do, but honestly I can't be bothered. My princess is the only one worth my attention, and I already have the gig.

The truth is that everyone here loves this job, has to, to some degree. It's a grueling process, even auditioning in the first place. The day begins with five hundred people who look just like you and ends, after hours upon hours of scrutiny, with just one. There is the multi-month fur training and the derision from the other princesses, there is the toll the job takes on your mind and body, in the suits, in the poses, staying in character at any cost, holding a smile for hours upon hours, speaking with a voice not your own. Sure, it's a great stepping stone to an acting career, and many people are in it for just that. But it's not easy. It takes dedication, and indeed a love for the place. A belief in it.

"That was fucking rough," Kate said.

I nodded my assent and took a deep pull. We were both exhausted.

Kate was about to make a joke at the crying woman's expense. It is Kate's way, to recapture a good mood lost by comparing her miseries to greater ones of others. Some perceive it as cruelty, a lingering habit of the high school mean girl, but it is a survival mechanism like any other, and it is an effective one. Kate wields it adeptly.

But she surprised me. When she spoke she said, "Do you ever think about it? Like *really* let yourself think about it? Where we all go, you know, when it ends."

I studied her, tried to ascertain from her posture and presence whose death she could be thinking about, or if it was only her own eventual demise.

"That bothered you today," I said.

"I mean, fuck," Kate said, running a hand through her hair. "It was like she wasn't even a person anymore. Like she was just the grief. That's it. Like, forever."

"Maybe forever," I said, though I knew she was right.

Kate leaned her head on the wall, her eyes glassy and pained.

It was not a look I'd seen often in her. Had I ever seen it? It was grief, sorrow. But for whom?

"Have you thought about it?" she said. "What happens when we die? If we go somewhere or if we even know what's happening? Or if it's just like . . ." She waved her hand in a despondent messy gesture. "Poof. Nothing." She closed her eyes and then opened them again. "Have you thought about it?" she repeated.

I hesitated because I knew what she needed, because there was something in her history that she had not shared with me and might in this moment, but I also do not lie to Kate. So I gave her the only truthful answer I had.

"No," I said. "Not really."

XIX

I slide into the front seat of Kate's mint green Thunderbird. Late afternoon sun stretches the shadows long in front of my grandmother's house. The possessed girl hanging from the tree and Frankenstein's monster are both beautifully illuminated.

"What's wrong with you?" Kate says.

"Long day," I say. "Cat got sick."

I violated my grandmother. I violated—

"House looks good," she says, nodding at my decorations. I do an impression of a smile and thank her. Her eyes search my face. "Okay," she says. "We're gonna fix you right up."

She searches on her phone and selects a song, connects it to the Bluetooth and turns up the volume. She's picked David Bowie's 1980 "Scary Monsters (And Super Creeps)." She's picked it for me.

We head down the hill and over to the 405. We drive with the top down. Kate's hair blowing in the wind, golden hour sun glinting off the cars, the pavement. A gleaming city and a smoggy blue-gray sky. A friend to whom I owe much. And while we are not the same, can never be, there is so much between this girl in the driver's seat and me, our shared time these last few years binding us together, it is almost enough to make me forget.

Almost.

We pull up to the Toyota Sports Performance Center in El Segundo, and signs tell us where to park. Our Hollywood denizens of glamour and style giving way to uniform sweatshirts, shorts, and even flip-flops. Ocean salt permeates the air and my nose; I draw it deep into my lungs. Seagulls dip and dive overhead. Kate seems excited, perhaps a little anxious. She checks her phone, does not find what she is looking for.

Today's training camp scrimmage is not open to the public, but Kate or Gideon got our attendance approved. In the stands are a few wives or girlfriends, half-interested in what is happening on the ice, one young boy who watches intently. Coaches prowl the lowest part of the stands where the waiting players sit.

Half the players on the ice wear black and half white. The arena is expansive, the air crisp and sharp. I watch as these men shove themselves against each other, dodge, slash, and battle with their sticks, as men are generally wont to do.

One of the men in black is smaller than the rest and seems to be doing a repeat dance of inserting himself right in front of each of the opposing players' faces, perhaps . . . talking, though from the other men's casual postures, it seems innocuous.

"That guy is called an agitator," Kate says. "Or pest. It's his job to do that, instigate fights. Find weaknesses and probe them to force key players from other teams into doing something stupid, once they're playing for real. They don't normally do it in practice, but some of these guys are crazy. Who knows."

It is, I have to admit, something incredible, to watch these enormous men move with such speed and grace, the only things holding them up two single blades of sharpened metal. I shiver in the cold of the arena, and Kate explains the rules to me. I try to find the patterns to their movements, but this is a world I know nothing about. It occurs to me how little I do outside the places I know so well, and I feel . . . perhaps less steady, here. I have exited my den and entered another. One belonging to these men, to these fans, to Kate.

Gideon is not yet out on the ice.

I find myself mesmerized by the tracks their skates make beneath them, the way in which the surface is ever-changing with their movements. I wonder if any other sport operates the same way. And presumably the ice needs to be repoured or frozen or set or however they do it. A living, shifting surface. A frozen artificial lake, and these men who own it.

I read once that sharks are thought to be an example of evolutionary perfection. They have been honed over four hundred and fifty million years into simple, efficient, optimum predators. They may not outsmart some mammals, but who needs intelligence when one is a sharpened and biologically perfected killing machine?

Eventually, patterns begin to emerge. It seems most of the players avoid one man, a colossal hulking figure in white. At his approach, almost all the opposing players divert or back away, leaving him a wide berth.

"Who is that," I say.

Kate follows my gaze. "Those guys are called enforcers, or sometimes tough guys, or heavies. They're pretty much on the team so that when he," she tilts her head to indicate the man mouthing off, "starts shit with another team, or if anything gets started in any way, the enforcer finishes it."

"He's enormous," I say.

"Yeah. He just got traded in too, from Chicago. His reputation is sort of insane. Like, he barely has to do anything because his past fights are so legendary, guys don't want to even get near him. He'll be a crowd favorite. Gideon will be too." Her tone is casual, but beneath it runs a current of disapproval, perhaps. Or jealousy.

"This is just training camp, right?"

"Yeah, but they have to train like it's real, know what the others on the team are made of. Gideon has friends on other teams, and he has to be ready to take them down without a thought. The game is what matters. Winning."

I take this in. A new player enters, and Kate nods her chin to him. GREEN is clearly written on the back of his black jersey. So this is Gideon in uniform. He moves with a steady grace that I find . . . maybe a little intriguing. I think of our phone call, his proposition, what might lie before us.

"What kind of player is he?" I ask.

"He plays left wing, but he's what you'd call a sniper. Basically, he gets the puck in the goal. That's Gideon, the crowd-pleaser."

She is looking out over the rink, and her face is hard and thoughtful.

"He's always been so good at it," she says. The deeply tangled web of *sibling* creeps out from her every pore. Competitors, teammates, friends, and not. His presence here making her more complete, but also something else. I wonder what she thinks he could take from her.

"Have you googled him?" Kate asks.

I turn to her, but she is not looking at me. "No," I say. It's the truth.

"I imagine unless you've been living some secret life, you don't know anything about hockey?"

"Not really."

"So, my brother's got a reputation. There are a lot of social rules to this game, and he started his career already having played at Harvard. He's not the only one, but a lot of these guys come from small towns in Canada or Finland or Slovenia, never went to college, and there's a sort of pride and camaraderie in that. All the guys who play, there's a set of unspoken rules, and there's not much worse than acting like you're better than someone else. Gideon's been good about leveling that out. Like, he used to do art, paintings and things, but with his background, if he flaunted that sort of thing, it would set him apart in a bad way. But now . . . I don't know what's changed. He's been different ever since he moved here. Or maybe before, and this is just my first time seeing it."

"What do you mean?"

"Like he bought this huge house in the Flats when the other guys are living in the South Bay, at least until the season starts. And he got a massive contract. Like stupid big, and some of them are still paying their dues. Obviously, that's out of his hands, but he just seems a little . . . erratic to me lately. I don't know."

There *is* envy in her words, but also concern. I turn back to the ice, and we both watch as he glides up and down the rink.

"I never told you. About Jared," she says.

I turn and watch her. She is somewhere far away, and yet her eyes are glued to Gideon. I have never seen Kate hold herself so still. Not a practiced stillness, but the sort that occurs when the body will permit nothing, shuts itself so no single thing might penetrate. She works her mouth as though she has forgotten how to make use of it. After a long moment, she speaks.

"My high school boyfriend. I mean, he was like . . . my *first,* and my first love. I don't know, it . . . Um, anyway, it's not worth going into the whole thing, but he was Gideon's best friend and my first love, as I said. And . . . he died."

She tucks her hair behind her ear, and a muscle twitches in her forehead.

"So, it was this horrible thing that I went through, and Gideon did too. We both lost our most important person, and we grieved him together. I don't know if Giddee and I would have been close, or even friends at all, otherwise. We weren't really before that, not since we were kids. But. It's kind of hard for us, some-times, to be in the same room, I think. I think we both remind each other of him."

I knew, from that night at the 69 Bar, that there was loss in Kate's past, but as she didn't share it, I didn't push. It tied many loose ends together, including the question of Gideon's self-diagnosed darkness. They both experienced loss, and both when they were young.

"I'm sorry," I say.

She swallows and checks her phone again. "It's the past," she says.

Out on the ice, the agitator says something and then im-mediately stiffens, clearly regretting it. Even from here, we can see. Everyone on the ice seems to pause. It seems the joking has crossed a line, that the agitating has become, well . . . real. The enforcer, the recipient of whatever insult was thrown, stands still for a long moment and then begins to skate with purpose toward the smaller man. The coach yells at him. There is a full foot of height difference between the two men, and the coach yells again, but the huge man keeps coming. Everyone is watch-ing, and even as Gideon hits the puck into the net, no one besides him and the goalie notices.

The enforcer grabs the agitator's jersey and pulls back to swing, and suddenly Gideon is no longer at the goal. He is there. His body shoves at them sideways and wedges between them, knocking the smaller man out of the way. Gideon's helmet is thrown off, and he catches a huge, skull-knocking fist to the face by the enforcer. His head is thrown back, and someone yells again. There's blood on the ice, and the enforcer takes a step back and looks at the coach, still shouting. The big man turns back to Gideon and offers what looks like an apology. The agitator saying something over and over, seemingly also in contrition.

Gideon clutches his face, hunched forward, and Kate is up and standing now, tensed, beside me.

After a long moment, Gideon stands up straight, puts one arm around the enforcer's back, and with the other, throws his fist in the air, a huge bloody smile on his face. He whoops, and the coach shakes his head as some of the other guys call out with him.

Kate sits back down.

"And there it is," she says. There is so much feeling in Kate's few words. Relief, disappointment, annoyance, and resignation. She feels that she is perpetually second best. Because Gideon is the type of man who can get away with anything. Despite the house, despite the money and iniquity of status, just like that, he's won them over, perhaps for good.

"Maybe he's jealous of you," I say.

She turns to me with a look that says I am an idiot and that she is insulted that I would try to placate her. But I continue, and I mean it.

"You get to live the life you want. You don't have to play stupid games to win people over," I say. "You're you."

She looks at my face for a long time and then reaches over and squeezes my hand, and because it's her I allow it, perhaps even let myself enjoy it. There is a form of charity in her tenderness, and it veils that same disappointment she feels for Gideon. But it is shifted toward me. I have let her down by saying this. I have not measured up. And in an instant I feel as though we are worlds apart, as though our planets collided by some remote miracle but are beginning to drift back into their respective homes, away from each other. And she can feel it too. She knows it's there. It's too soon. Everything is happening so fast.

"Kate—" I say.

A whistle is blown, and the game is over.

XX

We sit at the Kings Cove bar inside the sports center, and drinks appear before us. Some of the other players drink and eat at other tables, but most have headed out, slumped, tired, a couple limping.

A few of these large newly showered men, some bloodied, all exhausted, wired, famished, clap Gideon on the back. A few glare at him sidelong. There are some dynamics at play that I cannot from the outside begin to discern fully. I am not sure how long they've trained together before this, as a team. Still, after tonight it seems he has been accepted by most of the pack. And having enemies is always a sure sign of strength. One does not bother competing with another of little significance.

At the edge of the bar, girls wait to speak to him. They must have snuck in after the practice. He ignores them.

Kate, Gideon, and I sit around a high-top table. I can almost feel the testosterone and adrenaline pouring off him even after he has showered off his sweat.

"That was quite a show," Kate says.

"Don't want to disappoint the fans," he says.

"Speaking of," she says, "you want to go deal with them?" She means the girls who still haven't left. The Doors' "People Are Strange" comes on. It plays everywhere in October and is often considered Halloween-adjacent. I accept it in the canon. Music can make a place feel your own, and this time of year, for one month without fail, my music plays everywhere. The world becomes a little more mine. The bar has a few cobwebs hung and a light-up plastic jack-o'-lantern on the bar top. I suppose I sway, a little, to the music.

Gideon makes a face of exasperation at his sister, something he might have done many times over the years, and turns to me. "Would you like to go somewhere else?"

His attention so directly on me in this moment is . . . unsettling. He has broken the unspoken agreement that the two of us speak only through Kate, at least while she is still here. "I'm good here," I say.

He gives Kate a *there you go* look, and she rolls her eyes. "Maeve will hang out anywhere with Halloween stuff," she says.

"Hm." Gideon takes a sip of his beer and follows Kate's eyes to the decorations. "I learned once where the whole jack-o'-lantern thing came from, but I can't remember now."

"It's what they used to call phantom lights over the peat bogs in Ireland," I say, finding my voice again. "Jack-o'-lanterns, or will-o'-the-wisp. There's also a story, Stingy Jack, Jack o' the Lantern."

"Maeve's sources on everything are Russian literature or Reddit, so grain of salt."

"Excuse me," I say.

"Sorry, Wikipedia too."

Kate doesn't normally turn her jabs on me. She's upset with me, from the way I disappointed her in the game. She won't stop checking her phone. I do not want to feel it as much as I do. It doesn't mean anything. I try to shake it off.

Kate's phone rings. She immediately picks it up. By the look on her face, this is the call she's been waiting for. She's nervous, excited, hopeful, terrified. It is so much feeling all at once, too much. She stands and leaves the table, heads over to a quiet corner of the bar.

It's just Gideon and me now. He wears a black sweater and black pants, and his canine tooth is bloody and knocked back at a wrong angle. It will have to be pulled. I am destabilized, by Kate. By all of it.

"Does it hurt?" I ask.

"I don't feel a thing," he says. It doesn't impact the sound of his words, but maybe the way he moves his lips around it. The rest of his teeth are white and straight and well-tended, but I suspect now that not all of them are real.

He leans back in his chair and watches me, the expectation of what I have agreed to by meeting him hanging between us. He looks good. It is difficult not to respond to him like this, bloodied and triumphant. Powerful and dominant on the ice, and here. I do not fault myself for the bodily response. It is why I came, after all.

"So," he says.

The word hangs between us, a question, a promise. And I think that perhaps this is a bad idea after all. I feel a stirring. A restlessness. An ache. Perhaps I—

"Holy shit. Holy shit, holy shit, holy shit!"

Kate is back, and her energy bulldozes us. I turn to her, slightly stunned. She is bouncing on her toes beside our table, and she jumps on me, pulls me into a forceful hug, even as I stiffen against her. She's on Gideon next, jumping up and down as she holds him, screeching. When her face emerges again, it is flushed and so bright and so full of joy that she is overflowing with it. Tears leak from her eyes, and she shakes her head, looking at her brother and at me. Her chest is rising and falling, and I can nearly feel her heart pounding.

"Fuck," she breathes. She leaves us, goes to the bar, comes back with six shots. She takes three of them, in quick succession. She swallows hard, makes a face pained from the burn of it, closes her eyes, and then turns to me. She is really crying now, shaking her head, the tears shining on her face.

"Maeve. I got it. This is it. I got the part. A *movie*. A real fucking movie. Not an indie, not some experimental B-movie bullshit. I'm talking red carpet. Oscars. Sixty-million-dollar budget MOVIE."

I cannot muster the response she desires, or any response, but she does not register it. I might as well not be here. She hugs me again and then touches her chest and her face to ensure she herself is here, and that this is real.

"I . . . I have to go," she says. "I have to go meet Derek. Remember him? He's directing it. I'm . . ." She stares off somewhere beyond Gideon and me, somewhere far beyond what we can see, or will ever be able to. After a long moment, she says as though in a dream, "I love you both so much." She does not look at us as she says it.

She turns, and I watch as Kate walks through the bar and out the door, away from us. Away from me. A tether stretching thinner and thinner with every step. And me, just sitting here. No words. The door slams closed behind her.

When I return to myself, Gideon is watching me. That anger is there again in him, the same anger he felt after the party. For Kate. For the things she does to attain what she desires. For what she will surely do tonight. In thanks to Derek, in gratitude.

He growls out the words, "Back in a minute."

When Gideon returns, he is stuffing his wallet into his pocket. "Come with me," he says.

My hackles raise at his use of the imperative, but the deep rumble of his voice awakens the untamed and female in me, and curiosity outweighs rage for the moment. Both are welcome relief from the reeling terror of Kate's news. We walk silently out of the Kings Cove bar, through the lobby to an unmarked door. Inside, we are only inches from each other. We take the long nondescript corridor to a locker room full of the scent of male sweat and ball sack and steamed shower soap, and I perhaps momentarily allow myself to watch Gideon as we walk, the movement of his shoulders, the broad mass of him, the hint of that strength beneath his clothing.

I feel him watching me too.

The locker room leads to another corridor, and again we are pressed in tighter together, side by side. Two bodies inches from each other. I can smell the recent shower on him, the detergent of his clothes. Feel his heat. Closer and tighter. The air crackling, just a little. Full of uncertainty and too many feelings. Full of promise. Both of us silent. Without meaning to, I hold my breath.

And then we are spit out in a bullpen in the arena. The same one in which the waiting players sat during the scrimmage. Gideon steps away from me, and I take in the space.

The sheer enormity of even this practice rink is significant, inspiring, I will admit, even to me. It hits immediately. The size, the cold, the scent. One can't help but imagine all these seats filled with bodies, the volume that must swell from the crowd, and this is only their training arena. The artificial feel of the rink, the cold and the slightly acrid smell of the damp rubber flooring surrounding the ice. I know instantly that I like it here. Just as I like any place in which it is apparent, the way we humans have imposed ourselves on our world, and dominated it. Summoned ice where there was none before, created a raw and original environment that we might adjust or even destroy however and whenever we wish.

Such power in kitsch, such power in men. My eyes finish their sweep of the stands and settle on the one before me.

Someone has unrolled a long thin carpet leading to the middle of the ice, and as he gestures me onto it, I suspect that someone was Gideon. I walk forward, wondering at the power of the place, taking in what gods it must make of men. All those eyes, all those screams and cheers. The sweat. A thousand heartbeats, humans gathered in their fragility and mortality hoping to find or create significance or meaning. Follow a team for purpose, align yourself with them to feel a sense of belonging, to feel that any of it matters at all. Imbue it with every desire. Feed it.

Gideon finishes tying his laces and skates up next to me on the ice. I wasn't paying attention to him, didn't realize he was putting them back on. I also did not realize that we are alone in here. The arena is silent save for the low generator-hum of what I suspect is the constant refrigeration of the rink and the clean grind of Gideon's skates cutting through the surface.

I walk to the end of the carpet. Gideon must have bought our solitude. Now the question hangs heavily between us as to what we shall do with it. What we will do to get away from what we both just learned.

Here we stand in the middle of the rink, I on the carpet, and Gideon on his skates on the ice in front of me. We are alone, the lights in the stands have been doused, and we and the ice are all that are illuminated. That crackling pulse suffuses the air. I inhale.

He sets a puck down on the ice just beyond the edge of my temporary ground. He hands me a stick, and like the stadium and this man, the scale of it surprises me. The large and substantial but surprisingly light object. Weapon, even. In the right circumstance.

"What was it about me that said *sports* to you?" I say.

He smiles a still-bloody smile. "You hold it like this." He positions himself behind me, straddling the carpet, and wraps his arms around me to adjust the placement of my hands on the stick. "And this will be the basic motion of your swing." His arms, and mine, move back and forth in a practice swing. His body is significant. His chest against my back, his arms over mine, warm even through his sweater. Hard, obscenely.

"Obviously, you want to hit it into the goal," he says, voice low and clear beside my ear, his breath against my neck, "but it's more like . . . you want to feel it. The moment it collides, the speed and distance it's going to travel."

He steps back, lets me go. I feel the loss of him instantly. I shiver, once.

"Okay," he says. "Now try it."

I stare at him to ensure he is serious, and when it seems he is, I grip the stick harder. This is not what I came here for, but I humor him with a swing. I miss the puck and am filled with sudden rage.

I close my eyes and quiet it.

"Again," he says. I look up at him, and he returns my look with one that says the only way I can get from this point to distraction is to play along with his game, for the moment. I want to tell him he is going to miss out on something extremely worth his while if this continues, but the threat would be empty. I need a release. I need . . . something.

I reposition myself and try again. This time, I hit the puck, but it doesn't go very far. Gideon skates over to retrieve it and sets it back in place. The sound of his blades cutting through the ice. Precise. Razor-sharp. The effortless and lethal movements of his body, so fast, so thoughtless. The sense, again, of having jumped into unknown water.

But then, I am so much more than a shark."

"Now this is the fun part," he says.

"This really wasn't what I had in mind when I agreed to meet you," I say, the anticipation of what was promised me building, clawing at my insides.

"Maeve, tell me. What do you do with it all?"

"What?"

"I wonder about this sometimes. What nonathletes do with it."

I still don't follow, and the need inside me is building, and I am about to throw the stick at him when he says, "I mean your rage, Maeve. Your anger. Where do you put it?"

His question takes me off guard. My mind quiets.

"The thing is," he says, skating around me, his eyes never leaving mine, "you look down at athletes and sports and physical pursuits because you deem them something beneath you. You believe them to be for those who are not intellectually inclined, who have nothing beyond what their physical bodies can do. It's fine, a lot of people think that."

I should contradict him, I suppose, but of course he's correct, so I do not.

He smiles again. "When we were kids, Kate and me, someone broke into our house one time. It freaked our parents out. So, in response, they got this dog, this Doberman. He was a retired police dog, I don't even know how they found him. But he was completely terrifying. He could kill a grown man, no problem. I mean, he did, before we got him, according to them and whoever they got him from. Anyway, he just had this rage built into him. It was part of his build, his DNA. And as long as we gave him a place to put that rage, he was the sweetest animal you'd ever meet. So, we exercised him, and we gave him tasks, every single day. Because we knew if we didn't, if he didn't have somewhere to put his intelligence and his fury, he would find a place to put it. And that would lead to a lot of blood and death, which would lead to losing him."

The wolf is put down.

I grip the stick tighter.

"And you believe that by hitting this puck," I say, "I will have a way to channel the rage you think I carry in a productive and meaningful way for society."

"Who gives a fuck about society," he says. "I'm just saying it feels good."

Those simple words, *it feels good,* spoken in his baritone, and just like that, my need for distraction awakes again. I don't want to talk about life with Gideon. I need to forget life. I *need.* I don't want to talk at all.

"Just try it," he says, closer to me now, looming before me. "Hit it once. Hard. Like you really fucking mean it. And then we can get out of here."

Despite all that moves inside me, I stand the way he stood, the way he showed me to, and I look back at him.

"Now eyes on the puck. When you see it, you should think of that thing. Whatever it is that's fucking up your life, just see it. Feel it. Breathe it in, all that anger, the injustice, all of it. And when you're ready, you bring that stick back for the swing, and you hit that thing with every ounce of strength and rage that you possess. You fucking crush it and anyone who stands in your way."

Hilda. My grandmother's failing body. Kate's part. Kate leaving me. Now. Too soon. All of it happening too soon. This life stretching out before me so full of nothingness that I want to scream. I see it. I feel it to the brim. Gideon continues to instruct me as I rear back preparing for the swing, but I do not listen. All I hear is the sound of Billie Holiday in an empty house. All I hear is nothing.

I swing the stick, and it collides hard and fast with the puck. The crack of it reverberates through my arm and into my chest. I watch as the puck flies over the ice, so fast, gliding so fast away from me.

It slides into the goal and hits the back of the net.

I am thrumming. My heart pounds blood through my body, and I experience the same release I did when the mace collided with Hilda's skull, as it broke and splintered her leg bones and her arms and her spine and her chest. As her blood sprayed upward and painted my face and my body.

I feel amazing. I feel . . .

Gideon is standing in front of me, watching my face, his powerful arms and broad chest, his eyes alive too, with what I have done. And there it is between us, undeniable and vibrant. *Want.* Thick and powerful and thrumming. He closes the distance between us, just as I grab for the back of his head and shove my tongue in his mouth. Blood and spit and his hands on my back and my ass, and his hard huge body. I grab for his sweater and yank it up over his stomach and his chest. He pulls it the rest of the way over his head, discards it to the ice.

He reaches for mine, has it off in a second. I kiss him hard, shove myself against him, his skin and my skin, but not close enough. I undo the button and zipper of his jeans, grip them and pull them down. He meets me, matches my heat and my need. He takes hold of me and lifts me off the ground, and the world tilts as Gideon takes us both down to the ground. I am lying on my back on the carpet, shirtless, breathless, bare above the waist. He bites at my lip in a dare. I unbutton my own jeans in reply.

He is half-clothed, unbuttoned, the distraction I so desperately need visible and impressive as I suspected it would be. His lips trail down my neck and over my breast.

"No," I say. "Wait."

He pulls back, a question in his eyes.

"On the ice."

His eyes rake over my face, and then a hungry appreciative grin spreads over his own. He lifts us up and off the carpet. I suck in a hard breath at the shock of the cold on so much exposed skin. I arch my back, the ice burning my shoulder blades, and he hovers above me. I grab the back of his head and shove my tongue hard against his loose tooth. He groans and laughs into my mouth. He pushes himself into me in reply.

And it works. God, it works. I forget. I am not a person, I do not have fears or hopes or rage. I am only blood and skin and burning ice and a tight vise for a searching organ. The contact points between our skin, so hot, so excruciatingly hot compared to this cold, and my wrists are pinned to the cold by his hands, and I am here. There is only this. Need and want and breath and blood.

Hilda's blood.

It's time.

I close my eyes and feel the crack of the puck and the man moving inside me. The ice and the heat. His body, my body, breath and motion and heat.

It's time.

I twist my wrists. Gideon releases me enough that I am up, and he is down, and I am shoving him to the ice now, and my knees dig into it, and I hold my hand against his throat and move hard and fast until the image slides away, until I am here again, and his eyes are on mine, this sharpened blade of a body, honed and chiseled and powerful. He is living stone, granite and muscle and blood, hot and hard and pinned beneath me. I bend down and bite at his neck.

It's time.

I move up his throat to his lips, kiss him hard. Bite at his lip and his nose and his ear, pushing, grinding against him, pulling him into me. He lets out a growl. Maybe I do too.

It's time.

My breath coming faster. I need. I need to forget. I need to not hear her words. I need—

Gideon grabs my hair in a fist, pulls me away so that we stare at each other, so that our eyes are locked together. And I . . .

There is ice beneath my knees and a pulsing throat beneath my hand.

There is Gideon beneath me.

There is Gideon.

I—

Something moves in me, and it is not rage, and it is not fear. It is something else, something *new.*

Gideon.

Time, suspended. I don't know . . . I don't—

My heart is pounding. I cannot breathe.

I reach down into his mouth and rip out his tooth.

XXI

Fyodor Dostoyevsky wrote his 1864 existentialist *Notes from Underground* amongst liberal reforms and the restructuring of tsardoms in Russia that were done with the hopes of working toward something like Utopia. The book serves as rebellion and treatise against Russian (and perhaps all) collectivism, against this newly hatched and broadly promoted idea of *Utopia,* of, to his mind, unattainable perfection. The Underground Man, a misanthrope, an unreliable narrator, one could argue *the* antihero of all antiheroes, shares with us an excerpt from his diary and then a series of painful events as he interacts with others. I suppose some find his baseness and endless disdain to be laughable. I do not. Not in Russian, and not in English. I find it comforting. Reassuring. The Underground Man is an orphan, he does not partake in loving relationships, or many human relationships at all. But he derives his knowledge of the world through books and drama, uses them as a guideline for interaction. And if he cannot find love, he sows discord. And he enjoys it.

Since my grandmother's illness set in and I turned to books for the life guidance she had previously provided me, I have found only the misanthropes will do it. And it really is only ever men who have truly known how to discuss misanthropy in any meaningful or truthful way. Sure, there are the Anaïs Nins and Sylvia Plaths, but their depravity is either solely sexual or entirely too *sad girl.* Where is the savagery in women? Where is the barbarism? And yes, there is our glorious and aspirational Simone of *Story of the Eye,* but she too had to be written by a man, and the story is ultimately the narrator's, not hers. I have never understood, and still do not understand the notion that a woman must first endure a victimhood of some sort— abandonment, abuse, oppression of the patriarchy—to be monstrous. Men have always been permitted in fiction and in life to simply be what they are, no matter how dark or terrifying that might be. But with a woman, we expect an answer, a reason. But why would she do it? Why, why, why?

This societal and literary failing has only bolstered my knowledge that my grandmother and I are two of a kind, and that it is only the two of us. If there are exceptions, they do not show themselves, and I do not believe they ever will. I do not say it as a lament, only a fact. So I try on these characters as one would a costume. Turn myself this way and that to see how they feel, to see what I can learn. I have done this with so many fictional men in these recent months, but the unnamed narrator of *Story of the Eye* and the Underground Man have felt good. They feel, for the moment, right.

I sit in the Tata Tiki Lounge with my piña colada and my book. Days have passed since my bout on the ice, but my skin is raw and blistered all over from it still, and I shift in my seat. I do not dislike the feeling. I am sore in gratifying places, but my mind is erratic. My grandmother and Lester the Cat have been tended to, and in the moments I am unable to keep from remembering the details of the transgression of violating my idol's body, I find I have an appetite for nothing.

Today I struggled with her feeding tube. I googled it. It is surgically implanted in her belly and held in place by some kind of balloon. I thought I connected it right, but when I attached the pieces and started the flow, her stomach swelled, and there was bruising and discoloration over the whole of her abdomen, spreading out like a plague. I had to call a hospital and pretend to be a patient who couldn't reach her normal doctor to find out what to do. Still, her stomach has not returned to its usual shape, size, color. To have seen my grandmother's stomach at all. The pale skin, the lines. To have marred it and distended it. I can barely hold myself upright.

The Ramones' "Pet Sematary" plays over the speakers, and Johnny's head is swaying and jerking either in protest or appreciation of the song. He refills his glass to overflowing and leans forward to slurp the liquid from the top. The song, featured on the album *Brain Drain* and in the *Pet Sematary* film, was written, supposedly, in a spontaneous meeting between Stephen King and the Ramones when the author invited the band to stop by his home in Maine during their New England tour. The story goes (and Stevie always denies it, but I suspect it is true) that he handed Dee Dee Ramone a copy of his upcoming new book, and Dee Dee disappeared down to the basement, reappearing a short time later with the song written. The music video was filmed in the cemetery in Sleepy Hollow with cameos from members of Blondie and a number of pets, as well as some extras wandering slowly around the graves in costume. The band meanders in all their scrawny unkempt glory, ultimately to a headstone on which is written *The Ramones,* and I find myself returning to it. Knowing it was Dee Dee's last video with the band. Knowing that everything changes.

My phone sounds in my bag, and I fish it out slowly. I feel not entirely here, or perhaps too much here. KATE'S HOT BROTHER has sent me a message. I debate opening it.

I finish the page I am on and then set my book down and lift the phone. I open the text.

Rematch? Tomorrow night.

I indicate to The Bartender that I need another. He blends it, loudly, haltingly. The blender is perpetually on the fritz. I stare at the screen of my phone and tap my fingers on the bar top. Johnny mumbles something, and The Bartender hands him a cup full of maraschino cherries. Johnny takes hold of the cup, turns it back and forth, removes one of the cherries and examines it closely. He sets it back among its comrades and, with a growl, hurls the cup across the bar where it collides with a perpetually unused table near the door. The Bartender pauses, momentarily, then hands me my drink.

My phone sounds again.

Unless you're not up for it.

The wolf rears its blood-dripping head. And something else awakens too. I roll my eyes at myself. Rage and desire, how typical. I down the ice and sugar and alcohol as the song plays on: I don't want to live my life again.

I type back. I delete it. I type again. The Bartender is watching me, curious. I can feel his eyes. I drain the rest of my glass, and, finally, I hit send.

Are your moves more creative off the ice?

I do not have to wait long. Seconds later, the reply.

It is generally considered unwise to reveal one's plays ahead of time. See you tomorrow.

I chew on my lip and shove my hand down into my pocket. I pull out Gideon's tooth and examine it. It is white and nice. Distinguished, if a tooth could ever be called such a thing. I could keep it, but I have a better idea. I lift the lid off the jar of teeth on the bar and drop it down inside. An offering to the gods of piña colada. The Bartender raises his eyebrow and begins making me another. I turn back to my table, and my book, and I feel something. The distinct and unmistakable feeling of being truly observed, penetrated. I have felt it so few times in my life, and each time sits within me in such clarity that I feel I could relive every sensation, every millisecond. It is not The Bartender. It is not Johnny. I turn, slowly, and survey the room. Everything appears as it should, as it always does. But the feeling, the *wrongness*.

And then I see it. There, in a small alcove by the door, looming mocking and sinister, in place of the coconuts that usually sit there. My breath catches. I am full of something, but it is not rage this time. It is fear. It is terror.

I do not breathe as I take steps toward it, as I come face-to-face with this . . . abomination. With this divinity. I stand before it, and the song changes to The Cramps' "I Was a Teenage Werewolf." Every surface, every light, every floating speck of dust in this shithole tiki mecca, everything is alive, and everything is nothing because the only true thing is the creature across from me.

The doll.

This one, with bulging eyes, four of them, and teeth made of what I am fairly sure are human fingernails, one still bearing the remains of chipped red fingernail polish. A single growth protrudes from the top of its head, an oyster fork, the porcelain skin bloody and swollen where the fork has grown from the skull, pushed its way up out of it like something to be excised. The doll's body is the plastic body of a toy squirrel. At the attachment point between the body and head are wrapped a few fine strands of human hair, the parts sealed together with blood. It is so beautiful I do not know what to do with myself.

Time passes. The song seems to play on repeat. Johnny mumbles distantly.

Finally, I am able to make myself turn to The Bartender. The thing's four eyes bore into me.

"Who put this here?" I say. My voice is barely my own.

The Bartender squints in the direction of the doll, and he stares. He hadn't noticed it. After a long time, he shrugs. He sets my new drink down on the counter.

"Who else has been here," I say. "Besides us, who else."

He stares at me as though the question does not make sense, or perhaps the world does not make sense.

"Who else," I repeat.

He slides my drink toward me and says nothing.

Johnny slurs, "Where are my cherries."

XXII

One day every other week we get one extra-long break at work. I change into casual clothes and take a walk through the park. Kate usually joins me, but today she has to talk on the phone to Derek about the upcoming role. I spotted bruises beneath her collarbone that she shrugged off and said she did not remember receiving. I started to push the issue, but she laughed it off, and Cinderella entered so I left it alone. Kate likes rough sex, so it's likely nothing more than that. Still, maybe we'll talk about it later.

I walk through the faux Hollywood now, the miniature Los Angeles built here with the Theater, Backlot, and Farmers Market. This city built to feel like the park. This park built to feel like the city. I stroll past the highest-end dining establishment of the adventure park, and to what I know to be the best section.

If Little Hollywood is Los Angeles in miniature, then the bear peak section is California in miniature. A small mountain wilderness here in the park with national park–themed merchandise, towering pines, real and fake boulders. It feels, insanely, as though the air is fresher here than in the other "lands." This is usually the least crowded section of the park and always the most beautiful. Sure, it attracts a particular brand of high-sock fanny-packed visitor, but it also attracts me. I nod my chin to one such visitor who is actually security in disguise. They place them all around the park, dressed as tourists, watching and noting nearly every person's every move.

The main draw, besides the enormous stone bear-shaped peak at its center, is the twisting and turning water ride that promises to soak its passengers every time.

I stand before it now, but the water is drained, the attraction momentarily down. Apologetic signs posted. Kate and I used to come and stand in a particular walkover viewpoint from which we could see the exact moment the families and solo riders were sprayed. We would place bets on who would laugh, who would squint their eyes, who would lean over and away, screwing over the people sitting next to them.

I am brought back to a particular moment, one that I am often reliving.

Standing on the viewpoint by myself. The day before, my grandmother had not emerged from her bedroom in the morning. I did not know if I should leave her or go inside. She had never failed to wake early, but she was capable and strong, and who was I to comment if she chose to sleep in a little? Hours passed, and by the time I found her and then the ambulance came, she was unresponsive. My grandmother, the pillar of my life, my entire foundation, lay in a hospital bed at Cedars in a sudden-onset coma while I stood on this viewpoint trying to contemplate what a life, even in the short term, without speaking to her could possibly look like. Contemplating whether I could go on living in a world without her in it.

I stood there a long time, and Kate at some point appeared by my side.

She had a big audition that day, and she was going to go straight from work. She was telling me about the part and all the exotic locations it would film and how she really thought she had a chance at this one. And eventually, she turned and said, "How are you doin'?"

And just like that, I was crying. I couldn't even form a sentence. I was crying above the people down below screeching and screaming in the spray. There were no words, only these pathetic stupid tears that I could not stop. Kate grabbed me and pulled me into a hug. I stiffened, but she did not let me go. She did not let me go as I cried and cried and cried.

I tried to tell her to leave, but she skipped her audition that day, to be with me, once I was finally able to get the words out about my grandmother's condition. I was hardly a person. I was no different from the woman who had lost her child and sobbed on two young strangers in costume. The truth is that I do not know how I would have gotten through that evening and night without Kate.

The part and the film ended up being bigger than anyone could have guessed. Kate had been in final round auditions. And she had skipped it because of me. She has never said that she regrets it, has never brought it up at all. But when we pass billboards with the lead actress who did get the part, when the film is mentioned in conversation, Kate always grows quiet. And I do not blame her.

I push back from the overlook railing, and I wander for a while longer, taking in the park visitors, the Anaheim sun, the miniscule breeze. That girl on the bridge a year ago had no idea that her grandmother would not recover from the coma, that eventually the doctors would just tell her that keeping her alive and comfortable was all they could do, that she would never wake again. She would never speak again. I can't even remember what our last conversation was, only our firsts. I comb through my mind, but nothing comes. Nothing.

Back in faux Hollywood, I watch as a little girl in my princess's dress trails behind her family, staring at everything around her. The candy and clothing and child tantrums and parental fatigue. I watch her for a while. Her parents have their hands full with a younger child, and the little girl falls behind. When the mother notices, she turns around and is furious with her daughter for not keeping pace. The little girl does not cry or scream, she only stares.

The park is half of what I love. The other half is my character herself.

Of course we know and understand the roles outlined in Western folk stories and cartoon movie narratives for girls and women: princess protagonist, matronly helper, young competitor antagonist (in the case of stepsisters), and villainess. We do not, collectively, have a stomach for the idea of a young beautiful creature to be anything but good. We do not completely believe her capable of it. If you possess both youth and beauty, you can get away with much in this world. You can get away with anything. We all know the types.

But with the ice queen, something different happened. These two sisters in their Nordic kingdom, and the older one just happens to possess a destructive power. She is fundamentally good and wants nothing but good for everyone around her. But when her power is repressed and quieted for too long, it overwhelms her, and she retreats to her own self-made castle of ice to live out her life away from society. She becomes the antagonist by embracing her power. By enacting the life of the crone— solitary, strange, powerful—as a young beautiful woman, she upsets the entire balance. And yet . . . she is perhaps the most popular princess, certainly of the last decade, and perhaps ever. We might say much of it has to do with the iconic and extremely popular song, but I believe it is more. She defies archetype. Can we even really call her a princess if she is also the villainess? Even in the sequel, her restlessness and call to a life unbound by societal constraints is much of the force working against the perfect domestic protagonist couple of her sister and brother-in-law.

She is magic. She is an anomaly and a wonder.

I catch sight of a purple dress, behind the little girl and her family. Liz is here, wandering around without a costume on, just like me. Playing tourist. She stands nervously in front of the park's most upscale restaurant, fiddling with the bottom of her dress, waiting for something. Or someone. She is not actively sighing, which is interesting enough in itself.

Her face lights up, a rarity for Liz, and I follow her line of sight. Andre is walking toward her, his mouse ears on his head and his clipboard in his hand, wearing a blue tracksuit today. He smiles at her, and she smiles right back. I wonder if I am imagining it or if there is something there between them. Something . . . more than professional? Intriguing. I store this piece of information for later. There is too much in me at present.

The little girl in my character's dress sees me and stops in front of me. She does a twirl in her costume and waits for me to say or do something. There is that spark there in her eye. A little girl who might be more than that, someone who might end up being . . . unique.

"That dress suits you," I say.

"Thanks," she says, and she shrugs a tiny shoulder. "I know."

XXIII

That night, Gideon and I sit downstairs in the Viper Room, and I am at war with the desire to do what we did on the ice again and the desire not to desire it. I've had another long day of newfound caretaking duties, sponging my grandmother down, cleaning her as though she were an incontinent child. My brain working to black out these moments of extreme violation, of desecration that cannot be undone. She's still alive though. I check again, and again. I cannot stop checking. She is still here with me.

I would really rather have skipped to the getting stuffed part, but Gideon insisted on taking me for a drink first and was willing to come to my part of town, so here I am. Here we are.

He leans against the banquette on the wall, the green and blue lights again giving the sense of two different color eyes, which perhaps he does have, though for some reason I am unsure. He wears gray and blue, and I suppose I will allow myself to admit that his size, and the muscles . . . they are not unattractive. It is a singular and predictable exchange, the first time alone and fully dressed with another, postcoital encounter. Finding ways to reconcile the images one now possesses and yet knowing very little about each other. Well, he knows very little about me. But I suppose very few people do.

"You never finished that story," he says.

"What story," I say. There is a single TV on the wall flashing with posters and announcements for upcoming shows. The bartender shakes her shaker, her eyes flashing to Gideon, to me, then back to her customers. She is attractive. Perhaps we will talk to her later on.

"Jack o' the Lantern," he says.

"Oh," I say. I had forgotten. "Just another man who made a deal with the devil."

"Will you tell me?" Gideon says.

I sip my drink and prepare to tell him we don't need to talk, but the TV flashes to a new poster, and my heart beats, once, and then twice. My grandmother is there. In her dead Playmate costume, sprawled, faux-corpse, over the Mustang. And over her image, words. A band name and: OCTOBER 30, VIPER ROOM.

The band used her image. An image I have always loved, have always found sexy and hilarious and wonderful, the faux lifelessness of it. But now, after what I have seen, after what I have done . . .

"Maeve? You okay?"

I come back to myself. Gideon sits next to me. The screen shifts to another poster for another band and another show. Gideon is next to me. He wants a story.

"Yeah, okay," I say. "I'll tell you. But it's not a short one."

"Even better."

He settles in with his beer, and the words draw themselves out of me as though I am the speaker and not, as though we are somewhere that is not this bar, but is just as dark. An in-between space. Still, my grandmother's body lingering before and behind my eyes. Imprinted, insistent.

"Stingy Jack was a drunk," I say. "And he was a liar. And he was known for his silver tongue that he could use to find his way in or out of any situation he pleased."

I close my eyes, and I lean into the story, lean in until I see only the players, only the creatures of the tale. Until I am not Maeve but a nameless faceless incorporeal voice, and that alone.

Now, one day, the devil heard talk of Stingy Jack, and he went for himself to see this man. Perhaps he was jealous, perhaps he was craving a new soul to punish. Perhaps he did not believe the rumors, that one such as Stingy Jack could exist in such a way as he was purported to, in a way that perhaps even rivaled the devil himself for his wickedness and cunning.

Jack stumbled drunk, as usual, in the middle of the night, upon a body in the road. At first he thought it was a beautiful, fortuitously pliant and unconscious, woman. So naturally, he prepared to mount her as he had done with many such unconscious women on many such nights. But, all at once, her figure transformed, and Jack was entangled with Satan himself. Terrified, and suddenly filled with the knowledge that this would be his last living night on earth, he pleaded with the devil to grant his one final request: to get truly and terrifically smashed, one last time.

The devil had prepared to turn down any request, as everyone makes them in the end, but he could find no reason in himself to deny the man a drink. So they went to a local pub, Jack and the devil, and they sat and they drank, the devil drank too, and despite himself, he found he liked this infamous Jack. They were, perhaps, kindred souls in a way, even though they were born of two different worlds. This liking would in no way change Jack's fate, but perhaps the devil would be especially glad to torture this particular soul, if to spend a little extra time with him. Perhaps they could learn from each other. Or, at a minimum, provide each other with the occasional well-deserved laugh.

Now, the rub was that Jack had no money to pay for the drinks, and their bill was substantial. And of course the devil didn't carry money, as he ordinarily had no need for it. "Hm," Jack said. "Well, it's true, is it not, that you can transform yourself into any shape?" And the devil said, yes that's true, of course I can, as you have already seen. "Well," Jack said, "then why not transform yourself into a coin and pay for these drinks, and then you can change yourself back when the barkeep isn't looking."

And the devil saw no flaw in this logic, so he accepted and transformed himself on the spot. Now, once he was a coin, Jack pocketed the devil along with a crucifix that he stole from the barkeep, and this trapped the devil. The devil was furious that he had been bested, but Jack had all the bargaining power. So when he proposed a new deal, one in which Jack granted the devil his freedom and the devil in turn granted Jack ten more years on earth, the devil could not refuse. And so the deal was done, and they parted ways.

Ten years to the day, the devil and Jack met again. Jack had injured himself a few years past, and he now walked with a cane. He agreed that it was time for him to go with the devil, to meet his fate, as fair was only fair. When they neared the gates of the underworld, though, Jack turned to his old friend and said, "I know I have asked so much of you already, but there is just one thing." And the devil prepared himself to refuse, but again, he could not help himself. He liked Jack. Some people just have that power. So the devil said, "What is it you want, Jack?" And Jack said, "Only a single juicy bite of pear. You see, I injured myself, and I can no longer climb the tree." And so the devil said, "I can climb, and I will get you your pear."

But when the devil climbed the tree, Jack surrounded it with holy water, and the devil was stuck.

The devil was furious, once again, and perhaps he was hurt as well, as this was his friend who had tricked him now, twice. He demanded he be set free at once. But Jack was Jack, and he could only ever be himself. He said, "I will let you go free if you swear to me that you will never take me into Hell, never in all of eternity."

And the devil was then certainly hurt. Because yes, he was to take Jack into Hell with him to be tortured eternally, but they would be together, as the old friends they were. And wasn't Earth torture already? But what could he do but accept Jack's terms?

Now, years passed, and Jack's drinking began to take its toll. Eventually, it even claimed his life. Jack passed through the in-between to the gates of Heaven, but the angels would not let him in. For Jack had been sinful and unkind, and there was no place for such a man as him in the kingdom of Heaven.

Jack had but one remaining choice. He descended to the underworld and was feeling alright for the first time in a long time, he realized. For despite the torture, he would be reunited with his old friend. Perhaps they could even, after some time, consider themselves equals. Perhaps the devil needed an assistant, and who would be better suited to the task than Jack himself?

When he arrived at the gates to the underworld, his old friend was there. Jack ran up to embrace the devil, but the devil refused. He was deeply troubled. "What troubles you, friend," Jack said. And the devil, aged by grief as Jack was aged by the drink, said to him, "I cannot let you in, friend. You made me swear, and that oath was eternal. You shall never enter my kingdom, and I can never allow you to. I cannot take your soul." They were both distraught. But a deal was a deal. There was no taking it back.

And so the two men prepared to take leave of each other, forever. "I can give you this, and this alone," the devil said. And what he held out to Jack was precious, for it came from his friend, but it was only a small token. A single ember to light Jack's way. At the gates of Hell were a few dying or dead plants, and one of them, a root vegetable, the devil dug up for his friend. Together, they hollowed out the turnip and placed Jack's single ember inside.

And there was nothing more to be done. Jack walked away from the devil, to wander eternally alone, not in the kingdom of good, nor the kingdom of evil, but stuck in between. With only a small turnip lantern to light his way.

I am still staring at the screen in the downstairs bar of the Viper Room as I return to myself. I did not mean to, but I have leaned in a little closer to this man beside me. The music seems to grow in volume, something loud and heavy that pounds against my skull.

Gideon says, "Is that why you love Halloween so much? That story?"

I consider him for a moment. And perhaps it is the music or the night or the story itself, but I can spare a truth, just one.

"I love Halloween because all the time, everyone wears masks.

But one night a year, they do it openly. The dark and forbidden things they wish to be but deny themselves, on Halloween they don't. On Halloween, they embrace it, all of it. The hidden parts of the world are exposed, if only for one night. And those things that are truly dark are a little less alone."

"And it is enough. It has to be."

XXIV

We find our drunken way back to Gideon's house, the Viper Room bartender in tow. The house is blandly decorated with high-end designer furniture and little else, but the walls, the ceiling, the floor, are all exquisitely elaborate, as though the place was meant to look like a medieval castle from the inside. If it were not so well maintained, it would make the best haunted house.

"Damn," the bartender, Claire, says.

"Work in progress," Gideon replies.

We descend to a basement level with a lounge seating area and pool table beneath even more intricate dark wood carved beams and ceiling embellishments. Music plays through speakers in the ceiling and walls, and Gideon pours us drinks from a corner bar. The lights are dimmed low.

"So . . . what is it that you do?" Claire asks Gideon.

"Murders and executions," he replies, smiling at me.

Claire lifts an eyebrow but doesn't push it. Her nose piercing glints in the low light. She is tattooed, bartender hot, as is to be expected. She likely makes more in tips than many people see in salaries. I would guess she is from Salt Lake City originally, or perhaps somewhere deep in Idaho. Come out here not for the fame but for the people, for the edge. For a life faster and rougher than anything she could ever find at home. Some come for the sunshine, some for the lights of the soundstages, and some for the dark. I think I like her. If nothing else, she's certainly good-looking. And in this town, that really counts for nearly everything.

"And you?" She turns to me.

"I'm a princess," I say.

She believes I am joking as well. We drink. My mind flashes to the image of my grandmother at the bar, and I sit up, perhaps too abruptly.

"Shall we play a game?" I say.

"What did you have in mind?" Gideon says.

"Well, what do you have?"

Gideon leaves for a moment, and Claire takes off her leather jacket. She leans back and looks me up and down. "I've seen you before," she says.

"I pop in the bar from time to time," I say.

"You an actress? You remind me of someone."

I know who I remind her of. She probably sees that poster fifty times a day on that TV screen. Before I can answer, Gideon returns with a duffel bag. He takes his glass off the low table and dumps the contents of the bag on it. Playing cards, matches, dice, a few poker chips, a guitar pick, dinner mints, a candle, two vibrators, a butt plug, nipple clamps, ball gag, lengths of rope, a whip, two dildos, handcuffs, condoms, lube, and an old box board game of *Pretty Pretty Princess*.

"Yeah," I say. "We can make this work."

We are all in various states of undress and further states of inebriation as Gideon finishes the knots on Claire's wrists and ankles, strapping her down to the pool table. Gideon has put on a Halloween playlist, and Sheb Wooley's 1958 "The Purple People Eater" plays now, plays on repeat in fact. We each wear some of the plastic princess jewelry from the board game but have left the winning crown on the table for the moment. I chew on a dinner mint. One of the nipple clamps adorns Gideon's chest, the other Claire's. When he first took his shirt off, Claire exhaled a *fuck,* and I can't say I blame her. He has a small tattoo on his side that I did not notice before, an eight in tick marks. He picks up one of the dildos as I step around and fasten the ball gag in Claire's mouth.

Across the pool table, Gideon holds my eyes as he slides the toy into her. She moans and arches her back. He moves it in and out of her, slowly, deliberately, watching me, the muscles in his forearm rippling beneath his skin. His eyes still fixed to mine as he dips down and tongues her clit. I observe from across the table, the way his tongue moves, the dip between muscle and bone in the tops of his shoulders. His hands gripping the pool table edges.

"Candle," I say.

He pulls away from Claire and walks slowly to the table to retrieve the candle and matches. His eyes on mine as he lights the candle, as he tilts it over her. As the wax drips down. Over her stomach, onto her free nipple, down her thigh. Claire moans. Gideon's eyes flick down to her, then back up to me.

"Vibrator," I say.

Gideon sets down the candle, walks slowly once again over to the table, and selects one of the vibrators. He takes a sip from his drink, his throat working as the alcohol slides down, and positions himself back between Claire's feet. He takes the vibrator, presses it to her clit, and she arches her back again. The dildo is still inside her. Her breaths are coming harder and faster. Gideon's chest beneath the *Pretty Pretty Princess* purple necklace beads. The hard planes of his stomach. I sip my own drink, taking him in, the girl between us moaning and panting. *Pretty Pretty Princess* is a children's board game in which little girls adorn themselves with plastic jewelry in turns until someone gets to wear the crown. In the case of tonight, I don't think anyone's earned it quite yet.

"Cards," I say.

Gideon raises an eyebrow in a question. But he listens. He pulls away from Claire, leaving the dildo but removing the vibrator. Claire's chest rises and falls. Her nipples pierce the air. Gideon returns, and I step around the table to take the cards from him. Our fingers graze, and he takes hold of my hand, for just a second, towering over me. I can count the breaths between us, the molecules that separate his skin and mine. All the blood inside us both.

He releases me. I exhale.

Gideon returns to his place by her feet, and I climb up on the pool table beside Claire. I tell her to lie still.

Carefully, deliberately, I lean two cards against each other between her hips, and another two cards at the base of her ribs. One more pair between them. Three lean-tos on a flesh foundation. I lay two cards flat on top.

"Now," I say to her, "I am going to build us this card castle. And if you're the true pretty pretty princess, you are going to remain very still, no matter what Gideon does with those toys. Understood?"

She nods, once.

"Good," I say. "Because if these cards fall, if our castle is destroyed, you will be punished."

I add a level to the card castle and glance to Gideon who repositions the vibrator. Claire sucks in a breath and squirms, and the card tower falls.

The rage wolf snaps, but the monkey says there is fun to be had. This girl who looks upon my grandmother's corpse so often in that band's poster on the screen. Who sees and doesn't see. If she came for darkness . . .

"We'll call that a warning," I say. "Practice round."

I rebuild the castle, and Claire holds very still, even as her breaths come faster yet again. Gideon pulls the vibrator away and then pushes it back, watching her, and me. I climb off the table and lean against the back of the couch, surveying them, swaying to the song. I pop another mint in my mouth.

Gideon takes the vibrator away and dips back down with his mouth. I admire his back and his shoulders as he moves. I watch his arms and hands and legs and ass. He is nearly a weapon himself, the beauty and the power of him.

Within seconds of his tongue touching her, she comes, her back arching sharply and a groan and whimper escaping her through the gag.

All the cards fall.

The monkey and the wolf are both at full attention.

I click my tongue and shake my head.

"Too bad," I say.

Gideon steps back. He is rock hard in his boxer briefs, and his mouth glistens. My body responds in kind. One would have to be dead not to respond to the image of this man. He looks to me in a silent question. I look around the room for something suitable, and my eyes snag on a bag in the corner.

"What is that?" I say.

"Some things of Kate's. From our parents."

I step over to the bag and pull items out, clothing, paperbacks in Japanese, Spanish, and German. And I find something that is just absolutely, positively perfect. I smile.

I carry my prize over to the pool table just as Claire comes back to herself. I hold it below her line of sight and ask if she is ready for her punishment. At the word, desire lights her eyes anew, and as I hold up what I've found, I watch that desire shift and molt into

Confusion. Disbelief.

And when I do not move or say anything,

Terror.

She tries to sit up but is prevented by the ropes. She looks at me as if to say, *You can't be serious,* mumbles and speaks unintelligibly through the gag, looks to Gideon for appeal. But Gideon only watches me, waiting.

"I said there would be punishment," I say.

She shakes her head and struggles against the ropes.

The song plays on. *One eyed one horned flying purple people eater!*

"I've always thought one of these would make a fabulous toy," I say. "I mean . . . so long as you don't turn it on."

She struggles harder.

I hold up the curling iron and lick it, slowly, from the base to the tip, my eyes on Claire's. I spit on it and smooth the spit so that it evenly coats the metal.

I wink at Claire, and she pulls against the ropes, struggles to free herself. I remove the dildo and push the tip of the curling iron into her. She shakes her head and tries to scream, tries to back away. But she can't. I spit on the curling iron again and push it all the way in between the lips of her, the soft tissue, the easy give of it, so primed already by this hulking man beside me, even with her attempted struggle.

I hold up the cord and flip it back and forth between my hands.

"I mean, I wonder if you would even feel it, really," I say. "Well, of course you would, but a burn all over at once like that, it seems the nerves might suffer a moment of confusion, that second of pressing fingers to a stovetop before the pain sets in. And I suppose it wouldn't take long for the tissue to melt. It would likely stick to the metal, I would think. But I suppose I really don't know."

I turn to Gideon. His face registers nothing, which surprises me. I narrow my eyes at him, dare him to try to put a stop to this. But he is only observing, leaning against the wall, sipping his drink.

"I read that these things can get up to three or four hundred degrees Fahrenheit," I say, my eyes still on Gideon. "That seems like a lot to me, but we could just try and see." Claire is crying now, loudly, still attempting to speak and yell through the gag.

Still, Gideon does nothing to stop me. He doesn't even tense. He just leans against the wall and holds my gaze. The wolf growls.

"How long do you think it would take?" I say, still to Gideon. "To melt the flesh. Probably seconds."

Still, nothing.

"They might not be able to remove it once it's melted in. I mean, I'm sure they could do it surgically, but can you imagine the mess? Your pussy will never be the same, that's for sure."

Claire screams through the gag. Gideon does nothing.

I take a step over to the outlet.

He tips the glass back and takes a hard bite out of an ice cube.

I take another step toward the outlet.

He swallows the ice. Claire sobs.

I bend down and pause. I hold the plug just outside the outlet. And all Gideon does is look down and adjust his nipple clamp.

I want to rip it off him. Rage burns hot and fast in the back of my throat. He's not even paying attention now.

"Gideon," I snap.

When he looks back to me, he looks . . . bored.

I drop the plug and stand up before him.

My eyes are even with his chest, and my own chest rises and falls as I breathe through my nose, looking up at him. At my approach, he is hard again, and I am furious and perhaps a little confused, but he has to be bluffing. This must be his attempt at keeping me from hurting this girl. It has to be. His face, just registering nothing. He looks down at me with a gaze that says, *This is tedious. Can we please get back to the fun now?* He does not think this is fun.

He is infuriating. Insulting. He is—

My eyes catch on the length of him, and I lose my train of thought.

I close my open mouth and look back up at his face. He smiles, smug, self-satisfied. Claire screams. He dips forward, to press his lips to mine. But I pull away. I am tighter than a drawn bow. I am cocked and—I am flustered. I don't know what I want.

"I want a grilled cheese," I say.

This, for the first time, seems to make Gideon pause.

He nods, takes one of the pretty princess earrings off my ear and fixes it to his own. "That just happens to be my specialty."

Upstairs, Gideon makes the food, and we eat it across the counter from each other. Once or twice, one of Claire's screams makes its way up to us, but they are muffled in the large house. We don't speak.

When we finish, I help him clean, stretching out the moments, trying not to touch him as we both stand before the sink, our hips inches from each other's. Which I do not notice.

There is eventually nothing left to clean, so we silently head back downstairs. I walk before him. It is clear that whatever will transpire tonight will not involve Claire. She has lost her appeal. I sigh at her continued screams and tears and remove the curling iron from inside her. Gideon works on her ankle and wrist knots as I pour myself another drink.

She is freed and sits up, tearing the gag off. "Crazy bitch!" she yells at me. Her makeup streams down her face. Her eyes are still frantic.

"And what exactly did I do?" I say.

"You—"

"With him," I say, "made you come."

She stares at me as though her brain cannot compute what is happening. As though none of this is real. Perhaps none of it is.

"You—the curling iron."

"What curling iron?" I say.

Gideon's face remains neutral as he works on the ropes. Claire blinks hard and tries to work out quite a bit in her head. Her eyes sweep the room and run over me.

"I thought . . ." She shakes her head, keeping back from Gideon and me.

"Anyway," I say. "Maybe we can do this again sometime."

When Claire is gone, I turn to Gideon. He is still quiet, and I suppose I am . . . wary, of him. I sit down and place the *Pretty Pretty Princess* crown on my head, monitoring his movements and expressions. I finish off my glass and brace myself. I am annoyed that he would remain so neutral, would not deign to play my games with me, and I am disappointed and intrigued and aroused and still wary. I find that I do not know what he will do, and it is unsettling. I adjust my crown and consider my next move.

"Did you feign indifference so that I would stop?" I say. "So that I would let her go?"

Gideon watches me. I can feel it. He is standing beside the couch, leaning on it.

He doesn't reply.

"Did you think I would do it?" I say.

"I have a surprise for you," he says.

I pause.

"You . . . what?"

"I have a surprise for you," he repeats.

"You didn't answer my question."

"What answer would make you happy, Maeve?"

I grip the glass tighter and take a long gulp. I feel off-kilter. On unsteady ground. After a long moment, I say, "What is it?"

"Your surprise?"

"Yes."

"I finished one room in the house. I want to show you."

"You . . . want to show me a room."

"Yeah."

"Okay," I say. And perhaps if I were any other girl I would think I might be murdered now. A shark may not be the most complex of beasts, but it is still lethal. Still, I am me.

Gideon turns and beckons for me to follow. I keep a few feet between us. We walk down a hall on this same basement level to a room at the end.

He flips a switch outside the door and says, "This was supposed to be a downstairs guest room, I think, or maybe a gym. But I just had this idea, and, well . . ."

He opens the door, and I step up to the threshold.

Now I am the one questioning reality.

I shake my head and try to take in what is before me, but it is too beautiful, too perfect. My mind can't make sense of it. I have to parse it out bit by bit.

Fog machine smoke rolls out from the room and over my feet, and before me is truly and completely a Halloween paradise from my dreams.

Purple, green, and orange illuminate different parts of the otherwise dark room through the fog on the floor. Gravestones emerge on one side of the space, bats and full dark branches hanging down from between the dark ceiling rafters. And on the other side, chains fixed to the walls, crucifixes, and blood dripping down all around.

And there, black and shining in all its glory, a bed in the shape of an extra-large coffin.

It is the Halloween room of all Halloween rooms. A professional haunted house chambre of macabre delight. It is . . . beyond.

He changes the song so that The Ghouls' "Be True to Your Ghoul" plays through in-room speakers.

"How did you . . . ?" I barely breathe out.

"You know, it's pretty easy to find a lot of weird shit in this town," he says.

I walk into the room and over to the gravestones. They are stone, or something very close to it. They look shockingly real, likely from a film set. Around them, there are fake body parts, some skeletal, some still with skin and blood. I turn, and Gideon is watching me.

"You did this . . . for me," I say.

He shrugs. "It was fun. It's nothing."

I turn and try to take it all in, try to take him in. He surprised me. Gideon surprised me.

"Do you like it?" he says.

With the fog between us and the song playing and the massiveness of him, I am overcome. Tears sting the backs of my eyes. There are no words. Even if it was a small gesture to him, even if he only wanted to set the scene for a killer fuck. Perhaps especially then. There is nothing I can say to convey how I feel.

I jump on him and show him just how much I like it.

We move with each other in the fog between the graves. We chain each other to the wall beneath the bloody crucifix. We bite, pull, whip, clamp, lick, devour. We shove his jar full of rubber Halloween eyeballs in every hole they can inhabit. And when he produces the eggs, soft boiled, I arch my back as he inserts one into me, as he swallows the yolk that drips out. Exquisitely, devotionally. For hours, and hours, I think of nothing. Nothing except this body, this room, and everything we can do to each other. In this room of my dreams.

With this man who is perhaps more, perhaps much more, than I gave him credit for.

XXV

Two trends emerged in the mid-1960s that would forever change the world and history of Halloween music: campy gory monster movies, and hot rod tunes. Writer and producer Gary Usher combined them both in his studio-only band The Ghouls, inspired by and hoping to cash in on the success of Bobby "Boris" Pickett's "Monster Mash," which had come out not long before and taken the world by storm. Capitol Records released *Dracula's Deuce,* the band's only ever album, in 1964, combining the expertise of seasoned LA session players and heavy influence from the camp monster craze. The best song on the album is "Be True to Your Ghoul," the very same song that Gideon played as we copulated beneath the faux foggy night sky and the string-strung bats. The refrain of *Rah, rah, rah, rah, hiss, boom, slash!* moves the tune along, giving it its undeniably catchy appeal, while Rick Burns sings about his Suzie Ghoul, the terror of the cemetery.

It is perhaps my favorite song, ever.

The song plays in my head, stays with me, as I change my grandmother's sheets, as I greet children under Andre's watchful eye, as I fuck Gideon in the tunnels beneath the arena, the tunnels beneath the park, the tunnels entered through the Hall of Records downtown. As I change my grandmother's catheter and give her a sponge bath. As Kate appears on the internet on Derek's arm on red carpets, as she watches me sidelong at work, more bruises appearing on her skin in more places. As I wash waste from my grandmother's body and turn her so she does not develop bedsores. As Gideon and I fuck Irene the stripper from Bab's and Aaron the bartender from the Kings Cove and four of Gideon's fans, or maybe five, or six.

The city explodes with pumpkins, spiders, cobwebs. Tourists come to my house to take photos with my decorations. The park begins its transformation into a Halloween paradise. Every theme park, every indoor and outdoor shopping center, every suburban neighborhood. The winds and fires still haven't come, but the nights arrive earlier, linger a little longer. I expose two pedophiles and an incel online, and frame two people who are completely innocent of anything. Lester the Cat recovers nicely.

And before I know it, there is only a week until Halloween.

Rah, rah, rah, rah, hiss, boom, slash!

XXVI

So what do you think now," I ask Gideon as we stroll side by side through the gravestones and tourists in the Hollywood Forever Cemetery.

The day is edging seductively into night, the bruisy swollen dusk clouds governing us as much as any actress's practiced pout, dictating the indescribable immortal mood. Gideon wears a sweater and jeans that I know take just about three quarters of a second to undo, and he smells of shower and hockey rink and fog machine water. I have come to know intimately the movements of his shoulders and elbows, hips and knees. The hard flex of his thighs and the exact measure of each hand. It is startling to think I could have ever looked upon his hands without picturing the various ways in which (and with what items) they might push inside me. My body pulses beside him, thrums. Something animal and undomesticated. I feel . . . present. *Here.*

We pass a flock of tourists surrounding the DeMille plot, snapping their photographs, basking, just this once, in the timeless luster of this city, savoring the taste so that when they return to their daily mundanity they can recall that *one time when,* the briefest brush with true greatness, once in a mortal life.

"What do I think of what?" Gideon says, dipping down closer to me, the low rumble of his voice nearly a growl as he grazes his teeth against the flesh of my neck. He moves behind me as we walk and comes to stand on my other side, edging in close again so that his arm brushes mine, so that his fingers skim against my thigh, heat flaring in their wake.

We walk, and I do not answer him, because we both know what I was asking. He understands that I meant the only thing, the one that will survive us all, the one that sustains us even now. If I took his hand and drew him toward one of the mausoleums, he would fuck me against the side of it until I could forget everything, until my shoulder blades were raw and I had left skin cells and blood scraped onto the surface of the stone as the only sign of our passing presence. As my sacrifice and tribute, as a territorial claiming.

He stops, perhaps having the same idea I do, and I continue forward until he catches my wrist and pulls me back toward him. I tilt my head up slowly, look up into his face. And just as I do, the last of the sun exits our scene. The cemetery lights flash on at once, momentarily backlighting Gideon so that I see only his silhouette before me. His features obscured, palm trees and gravestones outlined behind him. Looming over him, and us. Gideon and me and all the dead. Hollywood Forever. He draws us both into the shadows.

Our eyes adjust to the darkness surrounding us, cast by the large monument towering above, housing bones and memories we will never access. His face now materializes above me. Full smiling lips and sharp teeth, some fake, all functional. Crows settle and caw around us, as the cemetery forgets any last trace of the day. Tourists distantly trickle in for the night's event, but we are hidden from them here.

Faster than I can track, Gideon grabs the back of my skull

and pulls me in hard against him. I inhale sharply. He is so strong—even now, shockingly so. If I were to try and fight him, to attempt to break free, I would not be able to. He would best me. It is terrifying and thrilling, and I feel his heart's steady beat against my breasts. I feel my blood pulsing through my own throat. For this one moment, I have no power at all. I have no responsibility. I only exist in relation to this stronger creature, and I am fully at his mercy. The thought is . . .

He pulls back and grazes his teeth against my throat. I shiver in the night and lean in so they nearly puncture it, present my flesh to him fully. He inhales a growl and says, directly into my ear, "I love this city, Maeve." His breath heating my skin, his fingers digging deep into my hair, pulling it tight so that it's painful. Another shiver, a more violent one, rattles through my bones and touches an ancient part of me.

Gideon. He understands now. He finally sees.

The projector horror movie will start soon over on the main lawn. We can claim our place among the graves and movie watchers after. But for now, I lean in all the way as Gideon says,

"I love everything about it."

XXVII

Kate and I share a tradition of shopping at Century City together, as she always needs new clothing for dates or auditions or just living her daily life. Other than work, this is the first time she's been able to fit me into her schedule between contract negotiations, fittings, and naturally, extended and mostly late night one-on-one meetings with Derek. I need to get new sheets because I can't keep up with changing my grandmother's fast enough.

We stand on the upper floor beside a designer handbag store, and Kate surveys the other shoppers as though from on high, already trying on the new role of a woman who will be recognized in a place such as this. Perhaps she won't even come, her assistant will. She flexes this future identity as one would a newly discovered muscle, trying it out with this look, with that head tilt. With this delicate step down an aisle between clothing racks. Just as I do with the misanthropes. All of us shaping and molding ourselves all the time.

In the last week or so, she has had headaches on and off and has forgotten conversations we've had on the phone at night. She's been preoccupied, and perhaps a little more distracted than usual. Gaps in the memory, a distant look in the eye.

"Kate," I say, "is everything okay?"

"What do you mean?" Her head snaps to me as though she has just realized I am here.

"I mean," I say, "you know I've seen the bruises. You're blacking out. Is it Derek?"

She stands very still for a moment and then tosses her hair over her shoulder.

"How's Tallulah?" she asks. She never asks this, knows that it is not a question I am equipped to answer. It is a cruel thing for her to ask, and she knows it. We stop, between a specialty underwear pop-up and a vegan gluten-free Mexican restaurant. Faux spiders hang down above us.

I don't know what to say, so I turn and step into the underwear store. I open my mouth to tell her that my grandmother is fine, and maybe also to push the subject of Derek, but what comes out instead is, "Did you ever see that video, the one of Michael Jackson grocery shopping?"

She makes a face, not sure if she's going to let me change the topic, even as she has just done the same. "Yeah, I remember that one," she says. "It was so sad." She holds up a bra in front of herself before a mirror half-heartedly.

"Really?" I say.

"Yeah. I mean, his friends organized the thing, so like, he had friends. But, really, he was just so alone. He probably employs those people. I thought it was really upsetting."

I hadn't thought of it that way, but the idea and her casual manner of articulating it make me feel edgy and defensive. That can't be right. That can't be it.

"You might end up famous like that," I say.

"Maeve, are you comparing me to Michael Jackson?" She says it with an eye-rolled tease, and I smile, a little.

"Well, I mean, it's just that you two have such similar interests."

She bumps her shoulder against mine and says, "Stop it."

She's joking, but there is still a mood beneath the one she is displaying. She and Gideon are both mercurial in this way, both occasionally brooding. We wander out from the store and walk over to the escalator. Before getting on, she puts her hand on my arm.

Out of the corner of my eye, I see a flash of a girl watching me. Around my age, wearing black. I turn and she darts behind a pillar and then quickly into a home goods store. Goosebumps emerge on my arms. "Kate, did you see—"

"Hey," she interrupts. "I know I've been preoccupied, with my career and everything. But . . . I know it's hard with Tallulah. I'm sorry that she's sick. I'm sorry that you've been dealing with that all on your own."

And just like that, we are back. My friend is here, and I am not alone. Because I have her. A thought pushes its way into my mind that perhaps I have Gideon too. This troubles me, confuses me. I am sleeping with Gideon. I sleep with plenty of people. I put it aside, something to be sorted out later. Just as the Kate and Derek business will have to be sorted out as well. And for some reason I feel I want to see that girl again, the one in the home goods store, but she doesn't emerge, and I shake my head. I'm all over the place.

"Maeve," Kate says, "you and Gideon . . ." As if she read my thoughts. She chews the inside of her lip, her brow furrowed.

I clear my throat. "Yes?"

Her eyes search my face, and I can feel something I have felt on and off with Kate for the whole of our relationship. My heart stops in my chest. The singular momentous terrifying thing. The thing that I can't get enough of, that I pray every day will happen again and also desperately hope will not.

It happened for the first time at the tar pits.

We had been hanging out, passing time together in that initial holiday season of work at the park. It was logical, we had to work together every day anyway, and she seemed to like being around me. My grandmother had been filling her days on her own for the whole of her life and insisted I always keep myself busy. One of Tallulah Fly's hallmark lessons: never stop moving, fill your time, and fill it wisely. If you cannot fill it wisely, then fill it exquisitely. Though really, what's the difference? She mandated that we live independent of each other, that we share space and life but also prowl on our own. It suited me well. I had always enjoyed my own company. But there was Kate, and I suppose I liked being out with her. She was a bit shallow, petty in a way I found slightly distasteful, but nothing about her disgusted me. Nothing made me want to distance myself or destroy her.

One day we were drinking, and she asked what else there was to do in the city. She was dispirited in the wake of another bad audition, had been told now by multiple casting directors that she was presenting too old for the roles she was auditioning for, the roles that she wanted. The fur suit training was grueling, and Kate did not hold the same love for the park that I did, so there was little to sustain her there besides my company. She needed something new. I said I knew just the spot.

There is little better in this world than bearing witness to lethal ancient tar bubbling up from unseen depths as cars speed past on Wilshire Boulevard. I love the tar pits. I love the museum. I love the substance itself. Bitumen. Pitch. We began in the museum. We walked through the exhibits, the remains of the behemoths who used to rule this land in the Ice Age towering over us. Every single one of them having crept into the water on tentative or sure feet to drink, only to become instantly and permanently stuck in asphalt quicksand, to starve in the very place they had come to for sustenance. More than thirty-five whole mammoths, three hundred bison, two hundred fifty horses. But the herbivores make up only a fraction of it. The tar pits bubbling up even now all around and inside Hancock Park, the tourist traps, and museums—they are full of carnivores.

"Well, you weren't kidding, Maeve. This is kind of amazing." Kate stood below a Colombian mammoth, craning her head back to admire its tusks, far above her in the air. She wore a revealing red halter top and a leather jacket. Every outfit always designed to attract attention. In this way, she was a perfect complement to me. The eye was always drawn to Kate, and I could slip into the shadows. A man turned and pointedly admired her as he followed his girlfriend to the bird skeletons.

"They're still active dig sites," I said. "They find new bones all the time."

"This is like . . . actually kind of crazy. I mean, I'd heard of this place, obviously, but . . . wild."

I smiled, a little. *Wild* was not a bad word for it, after all.

We continued forward on our tour, the green-speckled light from the banana trees, palms, and ferns in the atrium dancing over the exhibits, casting their shine over all of us.

We read about the condors and the natives who used to live here. The extinct carrion birds and avian hunters. And then we arrived at the best part. The part I often return to on my own, and one that draws in many of the museum's visitors.

"Whoa," Kate breathed. It was the same reaction I had when I first saw it, though I'm not sure I said it out loud. Even now, I am in awe of this exhibit, of the sheer enormity of it, of the precision. The teeth.

The wall. A breathtaking, unforgettable showstopper of a display. Orange and yellow glow backlighting the jewel of the museum's collection: four hundred pristine, completely intact dire wolf skulls.

Across from the wall, and only about a corpse's length away, is a diorama of sculptural re-creations of the dire wolves, snarling and feral in interaction with each other. All it would have taken to lure countless predators to these lethal pools was one stuck and starving mammoth, one weak or dead thing already trapped. It was a draw too tempting for a predator to pass up, the opportunity to take down something so much larger than itself, so much meat for the seizing. More than two thousand saber-toothed cats have been found in the pits, but they are second to the wolves. The wall, the one Kate admired, as she leaned back against the informational display for the diorama, holds only a small fraction of them. More than four thousand have been found so far. This land was once crawling with wolves. All these ancient predators, and nearly all of them now extinct. Drawn to this place by the promise of blood and then trapped inside it forever.

"I went to that sanctuary out in the mountains, the one where you walk with the wolves and pet them," Kate said, her eyes still fixed to the skull wall, "my first week here. I went with this super high-pitched girl I met through my agent— trying to get us actresses to be friends and have community, blah, blah, I guess one of the girls he repped killed herself last year, so like, you know. So annoying, by the way. That voice, I just really couldn't do it. It'll be a miracle if she ever lands a gig that isn't playing a five-year-old or like a mentally ill person. Anyway, the place was a total Instagram trap, but I mean it was wolves. So . . . pretty cool really. But these are SO much bigger. God, I'd love to see them living. Can you imagine touching those jaws?"

I admired the wall with her, all the eye sockets and snout bones and teeth, just here before us. "It would be magnificent," I said.

"And they're just gone now."

I nodded, a feeling moving through me. "Seventy percent of species here died out at the end of the Ice Age." I wasn't certain of the number I had thrown out, but it really didn't matter. The core of the story was there. People so often get hung up on the facts, on plausibility or details. But every day in this life, we're all only telling each other, and ourselves, stories. We may as well make them good.

"Gone forever," I said.

"Except the bones."

"Yes. Except the bones."

Heat and climate had much to do with it, and Man did the rest. Because Man *understood* the tar, utilized it to strengthen their boats, hunted the giant mammoths to feed countless mouths, survived despite their frail bodies because of the minds they held. Even then, it was destined that this land would be shaped by Man's vision. Los Angeles was only ever going to become exactly what it was. Man's fantasy for Man's pleasure. Bent and shaped and broken to his will. Even when so much of this continent was covered in ice.

"So, worst death ever?" Kate said. "Just getting stuck there and waiting to die?"

I considered her words, and I tilted my head. I turned to her, the wall at my back, and said, "Not if the wolves came quickly."

I don't know what was in my face, what it was that I did or that she saw. But when she opened her mouth to reply, her eyes caught on me, and she stopped. The orange light from the skull wall reflected on her face, and she looked at me as though see-ing me for the first time. She looked to the dead things behind me and then back to me. And the color drained from her skin.

There was such an expression in her. Fear, understanding, confusion, maybe recognition. I've thought about it time and again, and it never quite tracks. I can't understand it myself.

But in that moment, I thought, No, she can't. But maybe . . . Yes. She does. *She sees.* Could she? It was dangerous, for both of us, if she did. But it was there. I saw it, and we both knew. It was a violation, a lifeline, a probe pushing somewhere tender and protected, fleshy and vulnerable. I hated it. I wanted more. I was shaken and confused myself, and perhaps I was terrified. It was different when it had happened with Tallulah. Kate and I were not the same. I knew it even then. But somehow, as though she had been given momentary lenses to penetrate the veil that separates me from other humans, she saw me.

She blinked a slow blink and averted her eyes. I watched her mind turning, saw her consider her next move as she kept her eyes cast down and away from me. She was afraid. It was an animal posture. She was deciding whether or not to run. My pulse throbbed. I could barely breathe. Something seen that should not have been, something witnessed that was meant to be kept hidden forever. How did she see?

After a moment, she shook her head, put on a teasing face, and said, "I was promised I'd see some pussy."

She flashed me a quick smile and headed off to the North American lion and saber-toothed cats. I didn't know what to do, so I trailed after.

As we finished the exhibit, she continued to act as though it had never happened at all. And I wondered if I had imagined the entire thing. But then milliseconds of tension, Kate keeping her body just half a step farther away from mine than usual. Holding herself just a little on guard.

Outside, the best bench was open for us to sit and admire the lake tar pit. Kate's performance was convincing, and if I didn't know her better, I would have thought I really had made the whole thing up. She was gossiping about work and one of the fur characters and how she had found Snow White's Reiki and singing bowls Instagram account, how she couldn't wait to show me. We headed over to the bench, and a new black gas bubble gurgled up out of the pit. It was lovely. I watched it through the people-proof guard fence, took in the sculpture of the mother and baby mammoth stuck and starving in the mud, clung to them for some stability even as I continued to monitor Kate.

Her voice trailed off. And I knew. Here was the moment. She *had* seen me, she had seen something that petrified her, or disgusted her, and it was all going to be over. She had nothing on me, not really, but if she knew, what would it mean? Surely at a minimum that we couldn't be friends anymore, or . . .

But her eyes were not on me. They were not on the mammoths or the tar. They were fixed on a single building, stark and imposing beside the park. Large letters printed on the side that everyone here has heard as many times as the word *hello*. SAG-AFTRA. She stared at it and breathed. She made herself look. Held herself very still and shook, slightly.

Then she turned to me.

Her eyes held nothing now, save for the glazed, starving desperation of a girl terrified her time may never come. If she had seen me, it did not matter now. Because the gods Kate worshipped were cruel and ever-present. Her eyes and thoughts were fully consumed, and always would be. And it had absolutely nothing to do with me.

Back in Century City, I remember this. I had convinced myself I imagined that moment, but then it happened, once or twice more over the years. Afterward, every time, I watched as she deliberately chose to forget what she had seen. Forced herself to forget. It is simultaneously the most glorious, needed exchange, and also gut-wrenching. But still, for it to happen at all. In these moments in which I can believe that she sees blood on my hands, glimpses the handle of a mace held tight in my fingers. This is what makes Kate so special, so vital. How rare and earthshaking and addictive it is to ever find someone who sees. Even if only for a moment. Even if she desperately does not want to.

We stand there a long time at the entrance to the escalators, this girl who is nothing like me but who I love as I would a sister, the one whose life is about to veer, permanently, I know permanently, away from my own. Toward the uppermost echelons of fame and splendor. Finally, toward her dream.

A woman approaches to step on the escalator and says, "Excuse me," but we do not move. She calls us cunts under her breath and maneuvers around Kate to get on.

Her too-long skirt catches on the mechanism. She trips and hurtles forward violently, dropping down the metal stairs at intervals, her hair catching in the side. Screaming. There is blood. People approach from below and stop to bear witness. A security guard stands, dumb and stupefied, before calling in for medical help. People yell.

After a long minute, Kate turns to me and leans her shoulder into mine, just once. She says, "I think we can find sheets downstairs."

XXVIII

K ate and I have said our goodbyes, she to go and see Derek, and me to stop in the small bookstore behind the large bookstore on the Strip for a rare first edition of *Fight Club*. I am just leaving the store when I see a girl, my age and wearing nondescript black clothing, and I freeze. She is the same girl from Century City. The one who ducked into the home goods store and who I now feel certain is, as insane as it sounds, following me. She has darker hair than mine and is lingering near some vines in a fence between Sushi Planet and the green flying-saucer music studio. I can't make out her face. I take careful steps toward her.

When I am maybe twenty feet away, she slowly turns to face me and smiles a Pennywise smile. She is pretty, perhaps even younger than I thought before. Neither of us moves for a long moment, and then all at once, she turns and walks away.

I do not tell my legs to hurry, they do it of their own accord. I walk faster until I am standing beside the vines where she was, even as my mind tells my body I do not want to see what I already know is there.

Dread hangs heavy in the air, and the girl's footsteps pound on the sidewalk. She's running now. Running away from me. I think I hear her laughing.

There is a doll. In the vines. A new one.

I jump away from it, involuntarily let out a sound that I did not know I could make. A new doll, another, this one with two heads and the body of a monkey, blood in its teeth. I am shaking, and I can barely breathe, but I force myself to turn and look for the girl. She did this. She made these abominations and thrust them into my life.

I swear, and I run.

I run after this girl who has infiltrated my realm. This girl who is horrifying. I run, and I run until I am panting and sweating and there are tears in my eyes.

I run until my legs will move no more and I am forced to concede, to admit to myself that I have lost her.

But I saw her. I found her. She is real, and I am not insane. This thought does not bring the comfort I thought it might.

I am shaking the whole way home, I ran blocks farther than I ever walk. My phone rings, and I can't deal with anyone or anything. I place one foot in front of the other, and I think of The Underground Man. I think of Georges Bataille being forced to sit and watch his father piss into a jar again, and again.

The phone rings again. I reach into my bag. Perhaps it is Kate and she has more free time or she wants to come over and eat takeout. A moment of normalcy, reassurance that everything I love isn't being ripped away.

But it is not Kate.

It is KATE'S HOT BROTHER.

I answer.

"I need to get shitfaced," I say upon entrance to Gideon's house, and he raises an eyebrow but produces a bottle of whiskey when we get downstairs. We drink the whole thing. We open another.

We fuck in the Halloween room, and he can sense that I do not want to speak, that there are forces rattling the inside of me so extremely that I would rather never speak again. But gloriously, mercifully, again, he makes me forget. He makes me feel . . . less. And more. So much more.

After a while, exhausted and sweaty and panting, we lie side by side in the coffin bed on the red silk of the inside, the top of it closed partway over us.

"This room is amazing," I say, looking out through the opening.

"I had fun doing it. I like decorating."

"Seems an unlikely hobby."

"I have a lot of hobbies that might surprise you."

"Do any of them involve using that wheel over there?" Gideon has brought in more toys, and it is true that certain parts of my body are ready for more, but mostly I am exhausted, and I believe he is too. He laughs softly, and I pull the coffin as far shut as it goes. I turn, allow myself the indulgence that is leaning into him. As if the dark can erase the closeness from truly existing. We are always permitted more away from the harsh scrutiny of the light. And I need this. I . . . like it, with him.

"Your tattoo," he says, his thumb brushing against the skin over my hip bone, even as I know he cannot see it now. "The fly."

"Mm," I say.

"I like seeing you, watching it all. The way you take everyone and everything in. I don't think Kate knows how much you see her," he says. "It sucks. I'm sorry."

I am surprised by this. It hits a nerve I do not want touched just now, but maybe he is right, at least partly. It should not make mc feel the sadness as deeply as I do. I clear my throat. "She . . ." I trail off. "She has been a good friend." And she has.

He makes a sound I take to mean he is not so sure. I don't want to fight about it now. I don't want to fight him at all. Perhaps this more than anything is new. I just want to be here. Feeling this. Forgetting, even for seconds, everything else.

"Yours?" I say, reaching up to touch the place on his side.

"My friend. Jared. Kate said she told you about him?"

"How did he die?" I ask.

Gideon pauses, breathes. "He fell, or maybe jumped, from a bridge. They never determined. It was a bridge a lot of kids used to jump from. But he was alone when they found him. He hit his head on a rock."

"I'm sorry," I say, and I find that I mean it.

"You didn't do it."

"You two were very close?"

"As close as anyone can be," he says, and there are decades of pain in the words. "In the end we weren't in a great place. He . . . wasn't good for Kate. And she was someone different with him. I've come to terms with the way she handles herself around men, but it's taken time. And I don't mean like protective brother weird sex stuff. It's just . . . she diminishes herself. And it's hard to watch.

"Anyway, Jared and I were in a bad spot, got in a big fight the same night he died, and I . . . regret it. He played hockey. I never . . . I thought I'd be something else in life, I don't know. But he died, and I wanted to feel him around again. I wanted to, sort of apologize in whatever way I could, for how it all went down with us. So I started playing. And . . . I never would have guessed, but here I am."

Life and all its choices and lack of choices propelling us forward, holding us still. I want to lie in the dark here forever, suspended and out of time. I want to stop wanting for so much I cannot have. For things to stop moving forward and spinning away from me with such violent indifference.

"Here we both are," I say.

I just want this.

We lie together in the dark, the warmth of him and the dark of the coffin. This thing spreading through me that makes me forget, that soothes the wolf and intrigues the monkey. This man who has the ability to bring me into this body and keep me here. I suppose . . . I like him. I like being with him. With his warmth around me and these walls full of so much that I love. This room that he filled for me.

When he speaks again, I have to blink and inhale to refocus. I must have slipped into sleep or something close to it. I have pressed my body into his. It is so unlike me, and yet I do not remove myself. If I move then everything is real again. If I can just pause and distill everything to this, then maybe nothing has gone wrong. Maybe I am not losing Kate or my grandmother or anything.

"You're not Jack, Maeve," he says.

"Hm?" I ask, holding very still, thinking perhaps I dreamt the words.

"You don't have to be Jack o' the Lantern, if you don't want to be."

I open my eyes fully now and stare at his chest in the dark, the faint silhouette of him, his words sinking in.

"If I am Jack, then you are, what, the devil?" I say.

I can hear the smile in his words. "I mean, the devil has the clout and the reputation, but Jack is the really devious one. Seems fitting."

I consider his words. I press my forehead to his chest.

"What is the alternative then? In this scenario, if I am not Jack, then what am I?" I say.

"I guess I just mean that if you are Jack, the story doesn't have to go that way. Maybe Jack doesn't need to ask the devil to make that last promise. Maybe Jack can just realize that his destiny with the devil is better than stumbling around alone and drunk on earth forever."

"So Jack should relent and allow the devil to torture him in eternal hellfire?" I say.

"Well, we both know you like a bit of torture." He locates and quickly nips at my ear, sending chills down my body. The wolf lifts its head. He continues, the rumble of his voice reverberating through his skin, into my skull. The steady rhythm of his pulse. "I'm just saying that life is torture, the afterlife probably is too, if there is one. Or maybe not. But to find a . . . kindred spirit in all this . . . I don't know. I don't think it happens all that often. Jack was a fool not to see it when even the devil did."

I pull back and try to see his face. After a moment, I say, "I think this is a bit of a stretch in terms of—"

"Hey," he says, reaching out and taking hold of me, his large hand in my hair. I can just make out his eyes in the dark, or where they should be. He is serious. Intensity boring into me, filling the space between us. He's powerful. He is, inexplicably, *not* nothing.

"I'm just saying," Gideon says. "You're not alone, Maeve."

The wolf whines, the monkey tilts its head. That feeling that is not rage and is not terror and is only partly made of sadness ripples through me, churns low in my belly and up through my breast. That something *new,* a different ache.

You're not alone.

And it might be the alcohol or the dark or my desperation to forget the girl and the dolls and my grandmother and everything that is unraveling in my previously controlled life. But here, in this coffin with this man, I think . . .

Just for this moment, I allow myself to believe him.

XXIX

I wake to a partially open coffin and a note.

Had to go to practice. Ordered breakfast for you. Text and let me know when I can see you again. Xxx

There is a quick but impressive drawing of a reclining devil in place of a signature. I sit up and realize that I am perhaps the most hungover I have ever been. I blink hard and force my body to exit the Halloween tomb, slowly, haltingly, tripping over a rubber werewolf hand and a crucifix. I squint my eyes and breathe through my nose. My phone and bag are over near the bar outside the room. In this basement level it is still difficult to know what time it is. But I never sleep past six, so I imagine it is around then. When I finally reach my phone, turn the thing on, and make out what is on the screen, my blood runs cold. I have sixteen missed calls from Kate, three from Liz, and five missed alarms of my own. It is ten o'clock. I was supposed to be at work at nine, and my grandmother needed her meds two and a half hours ago.

I sprint and stumble up and out of Gideon's house. I trip over the breakfast he ordered, sitting on the front step, and I have to stop and vomit in his hedges.

I drive. I do not let myself think about what I've done. I do not let myself think.

I run into the house and into my grandmother's room. I check her vitals. Her heart rate is elevated. She is paler than usual, and there is sweat on her brow. Her skin is yellow, jaundiced, around her eyes and mouth. I search through her medicine bag and find the syringe for her morning dose. I take a deep breath to try and still my shaking hands. They will not calm, and I inject her multiple times before I am able to get it right. Lester the Cat is agitated and mewing at me from the corner. I wait three minutes and then check her vitals again. Her readings are closer to normal. I exhale and check the rest of her. Bedsores mar the skin of her backside, deep oozing wounds that seem to have sprung up out of nowhere. Because I wasn't here to turn her.

I find my phone and shoot off a quick text to Liz. *I am extremely ill and cannot come in today.*

I google what to do for the sores and set to work. I am shaking the whole time, and I have to stop twice to go and evacuate the contents of my stomach in my grandmother's bathroom. I rinse my mouth in her sink and see a girl in the mirror who is cracking. A girl who believed she could hold it all together.

I sit with my grandmother for the rest of the day. The hours stretch on, each its own eternity. But I deserve this pain. I deserve this for what I have done. For what I have willingly forgotten.

I am a person with routines. I adhere to my routines because they make my life bearable and because I have responsibilities that I must uphold. Because that is the person I am, not the person who throws the few good things she has away on an empty promise. On a foolish girl's dream.

What the fuck am I doing.

When night falls, I stumble back to my own room. Lester the Cat has pissed on my bed. I have received a single text from

Kate following all the *Where are yous* and one that says, *I have insane news about Liz.*

They made me do my whole shift with CINDERELLA.

Liz saw my message but never replied.

This is my fault, and I need to fix it. I don't know how exactly I got here, how these distractions crept their way into my life, but I need to purge myself of everything that is diverting me from what truly matters. I need to be here. For my grandmother. For myself. For the scraps that are left of a life that is mine.

I send off two quick messages before I turn my phone off completely, and I do not allow myself to feel anything except renewed purpose. Even as a weighty, spiny, sickening thing claws itself through my gut and my throat, as it loudly protests what I am about to do. I force my fingers to obey.

The first message is to Kate: *I'm sorry. I fucked up. You deserve better, and I will make it up to you. I promise.*

The second is to Gideon:

Last night was a mistake. This whole thing has been. I can't do it anymore. Please don't call. Please don't text. Please don't try to change my mind.

I press send, and I am wrapped, completely, in silence.

XXX

I walk into work an hour early the next day, ready to swallow my pride and eat shit for Liz until she has forgiven my transgression. When I arrive, Cinderella stands in my dress, sipping a coffee imperiously as though she is about to host the ball of the break room.

"Oh, hello," she says.

"Heard you filled in yesterday. Thanks," I say. "Now get out of my costume, you plague-sore carbuncle bitch."

"I didn't *fill in,*" she says. "Oh. Oops! I wasn't supposed to say anything. Oh well." She shrugs and smiles behind her *Let It Snow* mug.

Before I can ask or say anything more, Andre and Liz enter, smiling insufferably, Andre carrying a large bag of Randy's Donuts, and Liz two coffees. They see me at the same moment, each of their expressions transforming. Andre's darkens, and Liz positively beams. My stomach drops.

"Maeve. Hello," Andre says. "Uh, could you give us a minute please?" He says this to Cinderella, who comically pouts then turns and saunters to the locker room, turning with a simpering smile to me in the last moment.

"Maeve," Andre says to me, and then lets out a long exhale. "We have to let you go."

"I . . ." I visit another realm. I sway on my feet. Just like that. He said it just like that.

I find my words, I think. "Because I missed a shift? I thought we were permitted a—"

"The missed shift was the final straw, but we would have had to let you go anyway," he says.

"Why?" I force out.

"Well, uh . . ."

"Oh my gosh!" Liz cuts in. "No, no, PLEASE let me show her the video. Please, please, please!"

She does not wait for Andre's response, which happens to be,

"Liz, let's not do this. I don't think we need to—"

"She made her bed," Liz says. She pulls up a video on her phone and turns it around so I can see. It is Gideon and me fucking against the wall in the employee tunnels, captured on a phone. It is undeniably me. Liz holds it out for far too long, making sure I see everything, ensuring her point is made. She then turns the screen back around to herself and admires it for a moment before pocketing it and leaning over Andre to plant a kiss on his cheek. "Isn't he so cute when he's firing someone?" she says to me. She is a new Liz. I have never seen her like this, so joyous. Victorious, smug beyond belief. Where are the insufferable sighs?

I take this in. I suspect this new romantic development is what Kate was messaging about. I have stumbled into someone else's reality. But here Liz is, beyond triumphant, and here I am on my knees.

"I imagine you two have found some way to circumvent corporate procedure?" I say, and I am disgusted with the defeat in my voice.

Kate enters the break room and takes us all in, standing here. She removes a headphone from one ear.

Liz leans even farther over Andre and ignores Kate. "I got promoted," she says, stretching the word out as though for a child's comprehension. "Which means Andre and I are equals in the company. Which means there is no rule against it. I've been meaning to thank you two." Now she acknowledges Kate. "If it weren't for you pointing out how attractive Andre is in the first place, I'm not sure I ever would have let myself entertain such . . . *naughty* thoughts." The word *naughty* still does not feel authentic in her mouth, and it seems as though she realizes this as well. Her face colors.

"Oh god, I think I might be sick," Kate says. "Like actually."

"Wait," I say. "So . . . you followed me? Into the tunnels, just to take that video? That was two in the morning, we were the only ones here."

"Oh, and that makes it okay?" Liz says.

"I'm just asking. You followed me at two in the morning to film this so that I would be fired?" The girl who was following me with Kate, and on the Strip. Liz following me. But it couldn't have been Liz, with the dolls. I mean, I know it wasn't Liz because I saw the girl, and she looked nothing like her. Liz took this video, and I am losing my mind. I am losing my job. My job that I love more than anything that isn't my grandmother or Kate. My perfect beautiful job.

Liz looks flustered for just a second then regains her winning glow. "I came in because I forgot something and I found you there and I filmed it because it is completely *illegal* and also against corporate *rules*." She pushes her hair behind her ear.

"What did you forget that you needed at two in the morning?" I ask.

Liz stares at me for a long minute and then says, "I'm not the one on trial. I haven't broken any rules. The real question is: What do you two have to say for yourselves?"

"Kate didn't do anything," I say.

"Oh no? Hm. What was it you did, Andre, before you got this job?"

Andre exhales through his nose and rubs his forehead. "I was a, uh, litigator."

"Right," Liz says, nodding. "So what was it you told me again about substantiated evidence?"

"We don't need to—"

"He said that your little flash drive, Kate, with those gross photos of all that kiddie stuff that you've held over me for all these years, saying you'd show Corporate and tell them I took those photos in the park and ruin me forever, he said that they could *never* prove that they were *mine*. So you have nothing over me. Absolutely zero. Diddly-squat. So next time you fudge up, which you will, you're out, and I am rid of both of you. *Forever*."

"Okay," Kate says. "Yeah, I can't do this. I quit."

"You . . . ?" Andre says.

"Yes!" Liz yells and throws her arms in the air. "Frick, yes!"

"Kate, don't," I say.

"You think I'm gonna stay for this shit?" she says, indicating the lovebirds. "I'd honestly rather have my own brains fed to me." She turns to Liz. "Anyway, I was going to quit soon enough because I got a big part in a big movie as a *real* actress, so suck on that you stunted fucking fur-suited freak! You know what?"

Kate stalks into the locker room and reemerges with her costume. She steals the donut out of Andre's hand and smears it, chocolate and all, all over the front of her princess costume.

"Do you see? Do you see this disrespect?" Liz says. She is happier than she has ever been. She is ecstatic, in the truest sense of the word, giggling like a child.

Andre just shakes his head sadly. "None of this needed to go down this way." I realize now he is wearing mouse ears. Before work hours and in no official capacity. He is just wearing them. He is barely heard above Kate and Liz and the now tearing fabric of Kate's former dress.

Kate walks up to Liz and shoves the ripped and donut-smeared fabric into her prominent tits. She leans in close and says, "You wouldn't have fit in it anyway."

This is the first thing that shuts Liz up. Kate stalks to the door and turns to me. "You coming?"

I nod, and when the door closes behind her, I say to Andre and Liz the one thing that is true that I can think of.

"I love this job."

It is a plea and an apology and more of myself than I ever intended to show Liz, but here I am. Here we are.

"Well, isn't that just too bad," she says. She smiles and bites into her donut.

Outside, Kate is leaning against the side of the building, her chest rising and falling. She is playing unconcerned, but she is rattled. She was not anticipating this. Neither was I. Decorations are being aired out and organized in the back lot for the upcoming annual Halloween party. It is my favorite event of the year in one of my two favorite places in the world.

"Stole Liz's coffee," she says. "It's all cream and sugar. Fucking gross."

"Kate," I say. "I'm sorry."

She stares at me long and hard and then finally nods.

"I can't imagine a whole day with Cinderella," I say, leaning against the wall beside her.

"She got pissed on by a two-year-old," she replies.

"She probably loved it."

"Were you with Gideon? Is that why you didn't show?" she says. There is weight behind the question, but we've been skirting around this issue, and I'm not quite sure what it is.

After too long a pause, I nod once.

She is about to say something, so I say it before she can.

"I broke it off. He's too good for me. I know." And the truth of the words as they leave my mouth hits me harder than all the insults in the world. I am winded and have to lean back against the stucco of the building for support. The sun beams down hard on us, unrelenting.

My words make Kate pause too, and I can feel her studying my face. She opens her mouth again but then seems to think better of it.

"Okay," is all she says. And she leans in to bump her shoulder against mine.

All at once, I sense that this is the last time she will do this. That here in this moment, Kate is gone, and there is nothing in her place except a memory of the feeling of her shoulder brushed up against my own. A stray rodent-seeking park cat saunters past us, having slipped past morning security. This is Kate's and my last moment here in the park together, maybe ever.

My heart beats frantic in my chest.

I try to take it all in, memorize everything, commit it to my brain for all time. But I can barely think or see. Our last moment here.

Our last—

Kate tosses the coffee on the ground and walks away.

XXXI

I somehow get myself home.

I stand in my grandmother's living room. She is dying. Lester the Cat has shredded six rolls of toilet paper and strewn them all about the house. I have lost the only job I have ever loved, and I am losing my best and only friend. Gideon is— was—a mistake I never should have made, and there is a girl running around injecting these hideous demonic beings into my life. It is three days to Halloween.

I thought that Gideon would call, even with the text I sent. I thought that maybe . . . but he doesn't. Which is ideal. Because I do not have to say we have to end it all over again. Because cutting him out is the right thing for both of us. It is undoubtedly the right thing, and my weakness at expecting his message only serves to prove it. How derailed I have become. How . . . *typical*.

I am here with my thoughts and my self.

I am twenty-seven years old, and a whole long life stretches before me. A whole blank and empty life.

I walk into my grandmother's room and pull a chair up beside her bed. I reach for her hand and then immediately drop it. It falls limp off the side of the bed, further showcasing the blue-purple of her veins, how thin her skin has become. Her arm is like a dead thing between us, emerging from sheets, and I hastily take it and set it back beside her, the cold feel of her flesh starting weak hot tears behind my eyes. Still, there is a pulse. I pull the sheet and blanket up over her arm and dry my face with shaking hands. She would be horrified to see me this way. She would be so disappointed.

Our first day meeting, hours before we sat at our table together at Jones, Tallulah answering the door in her silk robe, holding Lester the Cat, staring down her nose at me, though we stood at the same height. She was the most magnificent being I had ever seen. Larger than this life. So much grander than I knew any person could be. The sear of her eyes raking down and up my body, the careful studying gaze as she took me in.

"I thought you might show up one day."

Sitting at Jones. Sitting at the counter in the Fountain Coffee Room. (*Everyone goes to the Polo Lounge, Maeve. We sit at the Counter.*) Sitting on the Star Watch bus and at the Tower Bar and in so many different booths and banquettes and counter stools and side by side in the front two seats of the Mustang, on the 10, the 101, the 405. In black-and-white movies at the Egyptian and the Chinese. Always together, always her teaching me, showing me, helping me understand this world I was thrust into and was, like her, improperly designed for. Improperly designed to survive without subterfuge. The two of us, side by side or across from or near each other.

Never like this. Silent, often. But never inanimate. Never inert.

I clear my throat. I haven't spoken a word to her since she entered into the coma. I know that bereaved people do this, as was explained to me by the doctors, and I was told that perhaps she would be able to hear me. But I knew that if she could, she would be sickened by the idea that I would be so weak as to speak to someone who is most likely not here at all. No, in her

mind there is only nothingness—the dark empty void that will
come to claim us all, and the very same that we sprung up from
upon our savage entry into this world.

And yet . . .

"Grandmother," I say aloud. My voice is raspy and thick with
all I am trying to hold inside me, with everything that wants
to rage its way out.

"I know you—" I take a breath and push my hair back from
my face. I clear my throat again and only speak when my voice
is steady enough to merit being heard, even if only by my own
ears. "I need something. Please. I know that it is illogical and
useless, maybe, but I just . . . need you. Tell me how I can do
this. How I can live this life. This thing in me, it's too great.
It's too . . ."

Her lips flutter, and my heart stops. I lean forward, and every
shred or scrap or shard of hope I carry inside myself comes bubbling to the surface. Her lips, moving, trying to move, trying to
utter something, in response to me.

"Grandmother—"

Her lips still.

And there is nothing.

I sit beside her for so long that my muscles ache. Her lips do
not move. She did not hear me, and she did not try to speak. I
am a stupid useless girl with nothing.

My legs move mechanically, carrying me back into my own
room. I stand beside my bed and look around myself. The
curtains are drawn. The room is dark. The computer, the TV,
the videos, the music. Distractions. Diversions. Nothing. They
mean nothing.

I go to my bookshelf and stand before it. This is the final
place in which there could possibly be any kind of answer.
There has to be something. I am crying openly now, I realize

with horror. Tears leaking silently from my eyes now that my grandmother can't see. I do not even know myself if I am a woman who is crying alone in this house. If I am a woman who believes her brain-dead grandmother could speak to her or that this cruel fucked-up world would ever provide anything as generous as a sign.

I rip my books out one by one and throw them behind me, where they collide with lamps and tables and I do not turn to see what else. Stupid fucking Bataille and Palahniuk and Dostoyevsky. Marlowe, Goethe. Milton. James. Kant, Wilde, Sartre. Stupid fucking Sade. They can't help me. I have tried, I have been them all, and they do not fucking work. I throw the books, these useless men. I use every muscle I have. I scream. Oh god, I am screaming. Guttural and raw and terrible even to my own ears.

And then . . .

But no. It can't be. I am heaving breaths, but I force myself into silence.

I stand upright.

It can't be. But it is.

A single beam of light shines in now between the curtains from outside. A beam that was not there before, and it illuminates one book before me.

If there is any such thing as a sign, if there is anything compassionate in the brutality that is being alive . . .

I reach forward and brush my fingers against the spine. A book I had not considered before, not in any real seriousness, as an instructional. A way of life that is not quiet or secret or tucked away. How silly of me. How silly of us, to think we must do in shadow what men do in the light. What they have always done. How blind I have been.

I take the book from the shelf.

I do not scream now. My wolf is raw and agitated as always, the monkey screeching. But a new thought appears before me in this book.

I have tried the way of the misanthrope, the way of the deviant, the philosopher, the observer, the pretender. But there is one road I have not seriously considered walking down, have not permitted myself to. Perhaps it is time.

The monkey and the wolf stand at attention. And I think, why starve either when I can feed them both?

I hold up the copy of the book to the light, and everything changes.

Already it fills me.

"Hello, Mr. Bateman."

XXXII

It is accepted among most horror movie fanatics that the single most gruesome and appalling human to monster transformation is a title given to none other than David Kessler of *An American Werewolf in London*. Two minutes and thirty seconds of agony that radiates out through the screen into the viewer and stays with them long after. Screaming, sweating, bones breaking, suffering completely. Eyes bulging, limbs elongating and bending backward, muscles straining. In a stranger's apartment in a city across an ocean from his family and remaining friends. Alone. Hair sprouting, feet stretching, crying and calling out for someone, anyone, to help him. Teeth, spine, nails, torso, bloodshot eyes. Face elongating with cracking bones and tissue, ears stretching, eyes yellowing.

Screaming for help, and no one coming. No one even hearing.

An indifferent plastic Mickey Mouse toy looking on with a smile. The full moon silent and waiting, overhead.

The moon is nearly full tonight as I speed down the 5 in my grandmother's Mustang.

To visit the park one last time.

XXXIII

The annual Halloween party is the single greatest piece of art ever produced, and they hold it at the park. *My* park. A party after dark in October hosted by a menacing burlap sack of a villain with quite a lot of swagger. The park is decked out completely with Halloween decorations, and populated entirely by villains. Guests are encouraged to come in costume as well, though I suppose I receive some strange looks for mine. After all, the park princesses are not meant to be here tonight. But I have unfinished business to attend to. Besides, it felt so lovely to steal Cinderella's dress. The bitch stole mine. After a quick detour through a back entrance to the locker and break room one last time, I take myself on a little stroll through the party.

Throughout the park, there are a series of Trick-or-Treat Trails one can follow in which shows will be taken in, all manner of villain will be seen, and much candy will be collected. There will be a parade and children's shows and a giant fountain-smoke-light-video production in which a young girl must choose between donning a princess costume or a villainess costume. Spoiler: she chooses the latter, and subsequently is instructed by various well-known villainesses on how to be *bad*. I make a beeline for what I know to be the best part of the celebration.

In the wooded bear peak section of the park, they've piped the forest paths full of fog and colored Halloween lights and all manner of creeping crawling things. And the villains' wood is the best of all. A map is posted at the start with the various worlds of the films one will walk through, but they are all the dark underbellies of the fictional worlds. The sea witch's lair, the malefic sorceress's den. And at each, the villainesses themselves. Hollywood actresses in the making, striving, pouring their hearts out into their monologues here for the children and parents, wishing, hoping, praying for that phone call after the next audition. *The* phone call. Just around the corner, always just there. Giving it their true all. Perhaps an exec will stroll through the park tonight. Perhaps one of them will finally be *Discovered*.

I stop for a poison apple at one of the food stalls and meander among the villains and children. I check the time and shiver with the anticipation of what lies ahead. Whispers sound through the trees, bats fly overhead, haunting choral music surrounds us all, candelabras flickering. And right on time, there among the trees and smoke, I spot the two lovebirds I was waiting for.

Liz is dressed as a witch with orange and purple sparkly mouse ears and orange-and-purple-striped socks. Andre is dressed the way he always is, but his ears have been replaced with a set that match Liz's. They smile in awe as they wander along the haunted forest path. I watch them as they take in the villainess actresses, as they open their bags for candy. As they let their hands come together, their fingers intertwining. As Andre finally works up the nerve to lean in for a kiss. I slip through the shadows of the trees. Their bodies are so tentative with each other I wonder if it is their first embrace. Or perhaps they are in love. Perhaps this relationship is as real and magical as the park enveloping us. Perhaps every kiss between them is this exhilarating, this gentle and pure.

Andre buys Liz a light-up cauldron of popcorn, and they share a pumpkin spice churro, each taking a bite and then smiling at the words the other utters. Liz is blushing. Andre brushes his thumb over her mouth to clear the sugar. I take another bite out of my apple.

A little girl tugs on my skirt, and I bend down to her eye level.

"My, what a lovely little mermaid you make!" I say.

She smiles a bashful smile and buries her face in her mother's leg before turning back to me.

"Did you know," I say, and the little girl leans in closer to listen, "that in the real story of the little mermaid, she kills the prince? She stabs him with a knife again and again until all his blood and his brains and his guts are outside his body. All over the ground, and all over her. Because the sea witch wasn't going to allow their happiness. They were doomed from the start. As are most people in this world." I beam at her and tuck her hair behind her ear.

The sound of her cries doesn't come until I'm already walking away.

I toss my apple behind me, and my eye catches on someone waiting in line to fill her candy bag, a grown woman, one who I never thought I would see before me in real life.

I stop, frozen in my tracks, as worlds collide.

As I find myself face-to-face with Susan fucking Parker.

"No. Way," I say out loud.

She wears a YETI baseball hat pulled down low over her face to hide it, even here at night, but I know that face. I know those clothes. I approach her, slowly, doing my best princess walk.

She lifts her head and smiles at me. "Oh, hi there," she says, "I thought it was villains only tonight!" My eyes sweep her face.

More wrinkled than before, slightly. Dark circles, but smiling. She is sad, yes. Beaten down, a little. But her shoulders are thrown back, and even with the hat pulled low her head is held high. Susan Parker is not broken. I didn't ruin her. Susan Parker who I was certain I had thrust into the dark insurmountable loneliness of despair, the true horror that is having nothing and no one left. The worst thing a human can do to another, worse even than killing. I thought perhaps she'd end it all, or worse still, just have to live with it, find some way to endure on her own forever. I was certain I had done this to her. I was certain.

She is standing here before me, and she is okay.

"Well, I just didn't want to miss out on the fun," I say, my voice catching on the words as I try to synthesize this information.

"Look, kids, look who's here!" she says over her shoulder. She turns back to me and whispers, "My youngest loves your movie the best. She'll be so excited."

And before I know it, they all emerge. Kayleigh, Karleigh, Chasen, Brantleigh, and Boone. In various character costumes, even the older ones. All of them, here with their mother. And her husband, Joel, follows. He steps around their brood of candy-inebriated offspring and wraps his arm around Susan's waist, leans in for a kiss.

Susan Parker, whose life I was meant to have ruined, who I thought I had crushed, completely annihilated, has not been ruined. Holier-than-thou Susan Parker, canceled supporter of the KKK . . . *happy*. Life-worn perhaps, but fine. Not alone. Here she is with these children and this husband who, despite what I have done to her, stand by her. I have failed. I have not ruined her. She has family. She has people who love her. Even now.

And I . . .

"Well this is a Jesus blessing if I've ever seen one," Joel says. "Brantleigh, go get a hug from her." To me he says, "You wouldn't believe it, our daughter only wanted to see you tonight, and when we told her it was only villains, she cried and cried."

The little girl, indeed puffy from crying, throws her body at mine and suffocates my lower half in a sticky clinging embrace, her face pressing in desperately against my thigh.

"I told you there would be a sign. Is this a sign or is it a *sign*!" Joel says to Susan, planting a fat kiss on her cheek.

Susan allows herself a smile and says to me, "We just moved here. Fresh start and all that." She looks to Joel, squeezes his hand. There's an unsaid message between them, something like forgiveness. My stomach lurches. She turns back to me with teary eyes. "Thank you, this might be Brantleigh's best Halloween ever."

Perhaps they say more to me, and perhaps they do not. I am no longer taking in words or meaning. Susan Parker standing before me, smiling, living her life. Not ruined. Not deserted. Not alone. Just . . . happy.

Eventually, I come back to myself. Susan's family has departed, and I am left only with the smudgy remnants of the child's snotty embrace and a hollow and horrific ache. I wonder if I imagined the whole encounter but then feel the mess on my dress and the child's warmth sickeningly lingering on my skin. I have lost track of my mind, of my plan.

I check the time and swear. I scan my surroundings for Liz and Andre, but they are nowhere to be seen. I run for the employee lot, Susan's children's faces pressing in on all sides of my mind. Susan and Joel, as in love as they've ever been.

I make it to the employee exit and pause, turning back to the park and all its grotesque and wondrous magic, and I shove the images of Susan and her family away.

One last time I allow myself, force myself, to take in the

beauty of this place. The screaming children, the alcoholic or exhausted mothers, the distant or far-too-enthusiastic fathers. The stunted twenty-, thirty-, and fortysomethings who just love it here more than anything. Who cling to the softer simpler fantasies of their childhoods, ever harder as time goes on. As their bodies decay and wither, still that fantasy holds true for them. The pumpkins, the Halloween magic. I can't help it. I love this park. I love every sticky plastic inch of it. Perhaps Liz and I are more alike than we've ever admitted to ourselves. Perhaps Susan and I are. Both thoughts make me sick. I close my eyes and shake my head. When I open them, I look over my domain one last time.

This, my former kingdom.

Which has been taken from me.

I am not ready to leave, am not ready to let it go, but it is the turn my life has taken. And I have much I need to accomplish before the night is over. We have quite a lot of work ahead of us, and a newfound fury alights me. A greater rage than I have felt in quite some time.

For once, I do nothing to silence it.

The moon hangs fat and heavy above, spilling white light down alongside the parking lot lampposts, and I receive a bit of luck after all. Liz and Andre stand beside Liz's car, but she can't seem to get the keys in the lock. Perhaps because it's a fob she's trying to somehow insert, and they both seem to have forgotten that. Andre sways on his feet.

"Hi there," I say.

They are slow to register my words, but Liz lifts her head and squints at me.

"What are you doing here?" she says, even slurs a bit. "You were fired."

"I know," I say, leaning against my car, parked next to hers, with one space between us. "Isn't it so crazy?"

Andre takes the fob from her and tries, also, to somehow push it into the door of the car.

"Why are you wearing that?" Liz says.

"Oh this?" I say. "I took it as a parting gift. It looks good on me, doesn't it?"

"But you're not Cinderella," Liz slurs fully and then shakes her head.

"No," I say. "No, I'm not." I cross my arms in front of my chest, and after a minute say, "Well, you two have a good night!" I unlock my own car.

I am sliding inside when Liz says, "I don't feel good," and Andre grumbles in response.

"Oh . . . Do you two need help?"

Andre turns to me now, and there's a bit of drool spilling out and over his lip. He blinks hard. His mouse ears are crooked.

"Why don't I drive you home?"

Andre and Liz slouch in the back of the Mustang as we speed up the highway. As I swerve in and out of cars, their bodies jostling with each movement. Perhaps I veer and weave more than is necessary. Perhaps I drive just a little too fast. Turn just a little too hard.

"It sure is a shame you're not feeling well," I say. "You don't get sick all that often, Liz, and Andre, you seem hardy enough."

Liz mumbles something.

I gasp. "Wait . . . Oh no. You didn't by any chance happen to eat those donuts in the break room tonight, did you?"

Liz's brow furrows.

"I mean . . . I sure hope you didn't," I say. "Because I just have the darndest feeling that maybe those donuts had a good ol' heaping dose of Diazepam in them. Like . . . a *lot* of Diazepam. Oh, you don't know it? Huh, I thought you might have been familiar with your drugs, Liz. Well, it's a benzo, similar to Rohypnol, but it's perfectly legal with a prescription and widely used in palliative care. Isn't that just . . . *swell*?"

Liz gurgles something, and Andre's drool pools in her lap.

I turn up the radio.

"Do you know this song, Liz? No, I suppose you don't. To my knowledge, it is not a part of the park canon, though I suppose I could be wrong. Perhaps we could petition it?" I wink at her through the rearview mirror. "Leon Payne, the Blind Balladeer they called him, he wrote this song, likely with Eddie Noack in mind to sing it, which Noack did, in the late sixties. You know, those country guys. Yeehaw! The story goes that Payne was inspired by a conversation between his father and a friend about serial killers, but I prefer to believe he just wrote it about himself. Divine inspiration, we might say. The Eddie Noack version is the best known, but *this* version, this is the one."

I sigh, wishing I could run my hands over the singer, hear the voice right up against my ear, inside my bones. "Jack Kittel is his name," I say. "There's hardly anything about him, anywhere, and as far as I know, he never recorded anything else. But he recorded *this* song, the only song, in 1973 in Muskegon, Michigan. Have you heard of Muskegon? I hadn't, before. The way he uses his voice, the way he *feels* the notes and the lyrics, over that twangy, dreamy, lilting steel string." I shiver. "It just really does it for me. Gets me *hot*. You know, Liz? Yeah, you know."

Andre mumbles, tries to sit up, and slumps again.

"Oh, you know the song, Andre? I thought you might be a little cooler than you let on. You know what, I think we should sing to it. What do you say? Wouldn't that be just fun?"

Liz's head lolls against the window, connects with a dull thud. I turn up the volume and sing.

> *"You think I'm psycho, don't you, mama?*
> *I just killed Johnny's pup!*
> *You think I'm psycho, don't you, mama?*
> *You better let 'em lock me up!"*

Andre's drool dribbles down his neck and onto his crotch.

XXXIV

I picked up some supplies earlier today, at the hardware store, the pet store, the liquor store. I leave Andre and Liz in the car and head inside to tend to my grandmother and Lester the Cat. When that is done and I am satisfied they will not need anything for a while, I return to my friends in the garage. My plan was to get Andre and Liz down into the cellar, but Andre proves too heavy to move. Just getting him out of the car and onto the garage floor is nearly beyond my capabilities. He's too large for me in one piece. In any case, upon further reflection, I'm just not sure torturing a man who wears a daily tracksuit and mouse ears would really be all that satisfying anyway. Just . . . too sad.

Since I cannot move him, I settle for slitting his throat and leaving him in the garage. I take a quiet reflective moment to paint myself in some of his blood. I have to say, I do believe it has improved the look.

I give him a long, hard kiss on the mouth and, finally, steal his ears.

It takes longer than I'd like for it to, dragging Liz from the garage into the house and down into the cellar. Perhaps it's the boobs. I suppose I can use the exercise.

Downstairs, muscles aching and sweat marring my lovely bloody dress, I arrange her among the bones so that when she wakes they will be the first things she sees. I unpack the supplies I bought today, the little mice an impulse buy, a potential gift to Lester the Cat who has not yet forgiven me for the missed medication dose and bedsores. They titter and squeak, darting this way and that in their little plastic container with sawdust in the bottom. From the hardware store bag, I unpack the wrench and pliers. I needed new sets of both these items anyway, as well as the caulk, sulfuric acid, piping, cable ties, hooks, and copper wire.

From the liquor store, I got myself a bottle of birthday cake vodka. Because I deserve it.

Liz takes forever to wake up, so I watch some hentai porn and listen to the *Rocky Horror Picture Show* soundtrack. I release one of the mice in the living room for Lester the Cat.

The record is on its third playthrough, and I have come twice, when she wakes.

"Hello, sleeping beauty," I say. "You ready to have some fun?"

XXXV

Liz's eyes flutter open, and she sleepily takes in the room, brows furrowed, confused.

I grip the wrench hard in my hand as her brain makes the same journey Hilda's did. As she pulls against the ropes and tape I have binding her to the bolted-in wine rack. As she takes in the blood all over me. As she processes Andre's ears on my head. That is, I've sliced off Andre's actual ears and attached them to the mouse ear headband. I did this with ribbons of fabric from the bottom of my dress woven through holes I drilled in his upper cartilage and in the fabric mouse ears. I finished them with nice little bows. Liz screams from her immobile position, sitting on the floor, or tries to. It's difficult because her mouth is taped shut, so that she cannot speak at me, for once.

"I thought your former princess training would have taught you to better conserve your vocal cords," I say.

She bucks and rocks, kicks her legs, shoves her head back against the rack, toppling a bottle of wine that shatters on the floor. I step around the glass, reach down, and pick up a large shard that holds part of the label. I shake my head. "Liz, this was a beautiful vintage."

Liz is crying. I toss the wrench back and forth between my hands, do a little twirl in my pretty princess dress. "You know what, you're right, though. We deserve a drink. A toast, to a long overdue friendship." I twist the top off the vodka bottle and pour it over Liz's face until she gasps for air, and then I take some long hard gulps of my own.

Liz writhes and screams, her eyes fixed on my Andre ears.

A buzzing emerges through our party, and I step over to my phone which I suppose I have brought in here. I stare at the screen, and I am slow to comprehend what I see.

A call is coming through.

KATE'S HOT BROTHER is calling.

He is calling. When I told him not to call. When I thought that he would and then . . . Again, that thing, that spiny shredding thing moves in me, a feeling dangerously like hope, like want, like . . .

It turns to rage.

That I should feel anything but rage fills me with even more of it, fuels a fire that I now realize will never be extinguished. How dare he do this to me. How dare he think that he can.

I take the wrench and shatter the phone. Pull it back and pound down again and again until it is only glass and circuits and parts. Meaningless. Irrelevant. Laughable, even, that such an object should bear any value at all.

I am panting, heavily in the wake of the shatter. I adjust my ears. Liz is still struggling and shaking and crying, et cetera. But I am calm again. Calm in my fury. Calm in my bloodlust. The wolf, the monkey, and me. There is such simplicity in rage, such beautiful stillness.

But Gideon called. My chest. This pressure, clawing, pulling at me. Gideon, on the other end of that phone, in my mind, having infiltrated my mind and my world. Gideon—

A banshee's scream rips through the cellar, bouncing off the walls and reverberating back to us, deafening and full of violence.

Liz closes her eyes, whimpers louder. But the screams are not hers alone. I am the banshee. I am the one roaring out my rage in this unholy sound.

And then,

I am finished. I close my mouth.

I breathe in the room, clear my throat, and I adjust my dress.

I turn back to Liz, and I step slowly and purposefully toward her.

I sit down across from her, the bottle between my legs. "I'll tell you a secret," I say. "Since it's just the two of us here. It's been a long time since I had a girl's night sleepover. And I really didn't have all that many as a kid." My own voice is a little hoarse from the sound I just emitted. I lean back against the wall of wine racks opposite hers. "You strike me as someone who had a lonely childhood. Don't get me wrong. I had friends. But . . . it's lonelier, you know? When you have people around you, lots of people even, but they just can't see who or what you are. It's torturous, really. Kind of makes you question what the point is, if any of it is really worth sticking around for. I wonder sometimes if *you*'ve had those moments, Liz, between the limitless rewatches of the old cartoons and driving yourself into work at your favorite place on earth, not quite sure why the loneliness is still there, not quite sure what is missing. It's worse when you nearly have something. When you have so much you can point to that is good and yet you don't feel it, not really."

Liz whimpers, and I lean forward. She flinches back. "You want more?" I say, holding the bottle out to her. She shakes her head, turns away from me toward the wine rack and squeezes her eyes shut.

"You found real happiness with Andre, didn't you?" I say.

She looks up to my ears again, my Andre ears, and sobs.

"Here's the thing, Liz," I say, sitting back again across from her and taking a sip, wiping my mouth with the back of my hand. "Kate and I made things hard for you. Kind of. Sure, we did things we weren't supposed to do behind the scenes, but when it came down to the job, we showed up at every shift— except the one, and I really could explain that one—and we did a *good job.* We brought real joy to people, and there was *never* a customer complaint, ever. Kate and I gave it our all, and we never phoned it in.

"We all could have been friends, you and us, if you had just pulled your head out of your corporate-tightened ass and seen that, seen that we really were princesses in every way that actually mattered. And sure, Kate can sometimes be a little bit of a C-U-Next-Tuesday, but it's really part of her charm."

Liz is still crying, but silently now. She holds herself very still, as I sometimes do, anticipating that something much worse is coming. Praying on the unconscious level that the stillness will spare her from it. Knowing consciously that it will not.

"You didn't take Kate and me down because you thought it would be better for Corporate. We were good for the park. Management thought so, or they wouldn't have kept us around. You took us down because you were unhappy, lonely, and lacking in the kind of friendship Kate and I found in each other, and because you couldn't be a princess anymore. You felt that you could not participate so you set out to destroy. I understood all that." I take another sip and situate my dress around my legs so that more of the blood is visible. It's prettier that way.

"But then you found Andre," I say. "And what seemed to me, in the few moments I saw you together, to be real and true happiness. And *still* you wanted to take from us. Even when you had something of your own. We could have been friends, Liz. We could have created magic together."

Liz is staring at me now. The tears still stream from her eyes, but she is listening.

"That's always been your problem, Liz. You're just such a fucking victim. To be honest, it truly makes me sick. It makes me want to do terrible things, in fact. Makes me want to prove you right. Ah, well. We can't change any of that now. What was it you said to me, again? Do you remember?"

Liz is silent, petrified.

"I'll remind you. You said *I made my bed*. Well, Liz . . ." I pick up the wrench and hold it between my two hands, weighing it, turning it. "What did you do when *my* happiness was in *your* hands?"

She shakes her head now, tears streaming. Eyes pleading.

"Right," I say, stopping the movement of the wrench. Holding it tight in one hand. "You crushed it."

I crawl forward and slam the wrench against the side of her face. Her head knocks back against the wine rack.

She cries out, and I pin her legs with my own, nearly straddling her, but she's still drugged enough and restrained enough that she won't be able to do much with them anyway. I lean in close to her now-bleeding face and say, "I'll be honest with you. Maybe I owe you that much. You were horrifically annoying as a coworker, but you did your job well otherwise, and that is something I respect. Out of respect, I'll tell you the truth. It's going to be a long night. You see those tools over there? See that pipe? Can you guess where that pipe's going to go, Liz? I don't take you for much of a reader. But it only takes a little imagination."

Liz screams and tries to pull away, but she can't. I dig my knees in harder on her thighs.

"You're a virgin, aren't you?" I say.

Liz sobs and screams and knocks her head back.

"Yeah. I kind of figured you might be saving it for Andre," I say, shaking my head in pity.

Liz strains against her restraints. Another bottle falls and smashes to the floor. I release her, crawl over to it, and press my hand to the glass shards on the ground. I lift it up, blood streaming from my palm along with the faint tinge of a good pinot noir. I caress her face.

"That's obviously not going to happen now," I say. "Here's what is. If the literature is to be believed, that pipe at its size won't fit inside your virginal pussy without the use of some chemical help. That's where the acid comes in, naturally. We'll need to burn away some of your tissue to be able to accommodate it. At least that's what I have read, but we're going to just try and see what happens. I'm not too afraid to get messy. And what's a pipe without something to crawl through it, right? So we'll be letting a little something loose into the pipe as well, and once it's crawled up inside you, we're going to trap it in there so it can't get out, although I think it might suffocate quickly on its own. We have a few we can try it with. Again, this is all conjecture. Of course, I also have a lot of other tools that I don't quite know the purpose of, and maybe we could find out together. Like I said, it's going to be a long one."

Liz slams her head against the back of the wine rack, again and again, screaming.

"I know. It really sucks when you have what you love and someone takes it from you. It's really just the worst."

I step back and smile, lick the blood and wine and glass from my hand.

"Here. Maybe this will bring us both some peace," I say. "Music has a way of doing that."

When the song comes on, I close my eyes and take in the

piano melody. Liz lifts her head and registers what it is. Even a child would know. A child, especially, would know. I smile, sadly, and I mean it. It really didn't have to be like this. But then . . .

"Take my character," I say. "My beautiful ice princess, a true queen. Everyone in the whole of society told her to repress her power, shut her away in a castle and asked her to play pretend. But then she *learned.* Repression is not the answer. Fear of being feared means nothing. We have to *own* who we are, Liz. We have to, at some point in life, just be ourselves. And because we're being honest, because we're girl besties, I guess the truth is really this. You took something I loved from me, but . . ."

I smile the smile of a woman speaking her ultimate truth to another woman, owning her power, embracing the bonds of sisterhood, and I tell her.

"I really might have just done all this anyway."

The song plays in and through me and through her and through us and all around the space. It fills me with the same inspiration that it did the first time I heard it, the first time I put on that costume, the first time I was the queen with the power. The beautiful, misunderstood, restless princess who wanted, who *needed* more. Who defied the stereotypes, the archetypes of the princess hero, the evil or helpful crone. No, she was always more. She was a little of everything. And I was a little of everything, through her. Hero and antihero. Protagonist and antagonist. And she, ultimately, was accepted. She was seen and loved, even as she was.

"You know, we all have dreams in this life," I say, "but sometimes it just doesn't work out the way we want. I thought I'd be a princess forever, and you thought you'd have your cherry popped by Andre in a careful and loving night to remember. You thought you'd live out your life with him. But with your help, Liz," I say, "I've learned a big lesson."

The magnificent voice of the infamous song swirls all around us, filling the space like a fresh sparkling Hollywood sound-stage snow.

"We think we know what we have in life, and we think we get to keep on having it," I say, taking in the beauty of it all, marveling at it.

"But the world has other plans for us, and we have to roll with the punches. We are what we are. And we just have to . . ."

I throw my head back and sing.

"Let it go, let it go!"

I take another wine bottle and smash it into the rack right above Liz's head. She screams.

I reach for the pipe, and the acid, singing the song, letting the words flow through and in and out of me.

I pause in front of Liz, affected by the song, moved as I always am by it. Nearly brought to tears.

"Just one last thing," I say, and I bend down and tuck her hair behind her human ears and adjust her mouse ears so she looks extra pretty. I glance to the pipe and acid and then back to her, to make sure she understands exactly what I plan to do.

Liz shakes her head and cries. A snot bubble forms in her nose.

"We're gonna use a mouse, Liz," I say, and watch her face take this in. Horror, in its truest sense. She pisses herself. She tries to push back and struggle free, but we both know it is too late. I can see that she knows it is far too late.

"Get it? A mouse?" I smile at her and wink. Her head falls back, and she silently sobs to herself. Resigned, petrified.

"You look beautiful, Liz," I say. "Just like a princess."

XXXVI

I've cleaned myself up and left Liz in the cellar. The body formerly known as Liz. I need to clear my head, so I begin the slow dismantling of the body formerly known as Andre, and the work carries me through much of the remaining night. With the garage clean and Andre's meat parts cooking down beside his love in the cellar, I shower again and visit my grandmother.

I cannot sit still. I prowl the edges of her room, monitoring the rise and fall of her chest. The rage in my belly has not been quelled, not by Liz nor Andre. Fucking Susan. The man who called me. Who wasn't supposed to call me. Who isn't supposed to occupy my thoughts. Who isn't supposed to exist. The morning sun climbs over the horizon, begins its slow creep in through the windows, spreading over the floor, further and further until it envelops the bed and the woman lying in it.

This time of morning, she and I meeting silently in the kitchen, I for coffee, she for her morning meal of four almonds and one small square of dark chocolate. I never saw her eat more than what she could hold in her palm. I consider often the phrase *subsisting on vapors,* consider whether the vapors might belong to someone or something else. Perhaps she was sustained by Hollywood itself.

"Maeve," she said to me one morning, staring out over the

Strip, the early morning light on her face, startling me out of our habitual quiet, "people will try to take what belongs to you. As soon as you possess something worth possessing, someone else will inevitably emerge from the crevices to worm their way in and try to steal it."

I took her in, working to determine what it was that was nearly stolen from her, and wondering also what I could possibly have for anyone to steal.

She turned and pinned me with her stare, one I had learned not to flinch from but never lost the instinct to. Stillness was a lesson she had gifted me. The ability to mask, to fight instinct in every way.

"You possess much worth stealing," she said in that uncanny way of hers, knowing exactly what passed through my mind. As if by my existing in this house, no thought was solely mine. They were all shared with Tallulah, they all belonged to her. As perhaps even I myself did. This was her domain, and I was just existing in it.

"Come," she said, retying her silk robe around her waist. "I'd like to show you something. I'd like to tell you a little story."

I followed her, slowly, down into the cellar.

XXXVII

Back on the Strip, in the same spot between the sushi place and the green flying-saucer music studio where I witnessed the girl, I am tucked behind a tree and pressed tight against the back wall of the restaurant, the smell of fish and the caws of scavenging crows permeating and puncturing the evening air.

The dark-haired girl who placed the doll in the first location between my grandmother's house and Babylon came back and claimed it. She returned to the Strip, to this hiding place a few blocks away when I saw her, to leave this newest one. So at some point, it is a fair assumption she will come to reclaim it. I may have to wait for days, and it may not even work, but even if there is a small chance of taking her out, it will be worth it. I have all but stopped sleeping since the night in the coffin. I don't seem to need it anymore, not with all that is roiling inside me. Besides, I just have a feeling. She will come.

I knew I needed to ensure I could snare her, get her attention. And I am still shaking with what I have done. To have reached in and touched the thing would alone have made me sick, but destroying it, putting my hands on the doll and then casting it on the ground as if it were nothing, as if it would not curse me for the rest of my days—

I had to do it. The pieces of a destroyed doll before me on the pavement.

Even as I tell myself this for the hundredth time from my hiding place, my hands tremble and I am sweating. To have broken an idol, crushed it on the ground. Dried crusted blood and plastic. The double porcelain of the doll's head. The beautiful, significant creature.

I had to do it.

Hours pass. The sun travels its complete journey and is dipping down below the horizon. I spend the entire day unmoving. Silent. Waiting and watching. If she doesn't come, I'll have to touch the thing again, will have to reset my trap. Or I will just stay here. For days if need be. In such close proximity with the small being I have profaned.

And just as I convince myself this is a fool's errand, after hours of stillness, of near nonexistence, she relieves me of the stomach-churning thought. She comes.

I tense my muscles as she approaches, this girl who looks like me, but darker. I prepare my body for the pounce.

She reaches the broken doll on the ground, and she inhales a sharp breath as though stricken. She pauses, bends forward to take it, caress it gently in her hands, her horrid creation, her repulsive work, what is left of it. And in the space of a breath, her head snaps up.

Her eyes lock on mine.

I spring.

She bolts, leaves the foundling divinity shattered on the pavement. I run at her as hard and fast as my body is capable of pushing. But she runs just as quickly.

We sprint, hard. There is nothing save for our footsteps, my breath, my heart pounding through my skull. Arms pumping, legs burning, lungs screaming. I will catch her, and I will kill her.

To think she can infiltrate my territory and mark it with such horrors, to think she can exist here when I do. The wolf licks its chops. Its hunger only grows.

We come upon an intersection, and cars are flowing. She's going to have to stop or turn. I can feel her hair in my hands already, the crack of her skull on the sidewalk, her body pinned beneath mine. She sees the cars and slows just enough. I am nearly on her, I am seconds away.

And in a move so fast I have to blink to believe I see it, she darts into the traffic.

Seconds. Mere seconds only. Two cars passing, three. And then they slow. The light changes. But there is no girl. I run across the street and search every corner, look down every path. A homeless man is slumped against a waxing salon.

"Where did that girl go?" I say.

"What girl?" he says.

"There was a girl. My size, my age. She just ran this way. Where did she go?"

"I didn't see any girl."

"She was right here. Right in front of you," I say. "She was dressed like me."

"Are you sure?" he says.

XXXVIII

Rage does not do it justice.

Fury. Frenzy. Savagery. Madness. Spleen. Bile. Wrath.

There is no word for what fills me.

A screaming monkey, a howling wolf.

She got away.

I touched the doll. I desecrated it.

The girl got away.

I stalk back on the Strip, prowl the street just to move. If I stop moving, I do not know what will happen. I do not believe I am capable of it. I pace until another hour has passed and music pushes out from the clubs and bars, until the people come.

I pass by the Viper Room, and I am a person enough now that words catch my eye. I have to breathe, slowly, to convince my brain to do something as simple and still as reading, but there the words are. And I realize why I have stopped. The band playing tonight, the very same advertised on the poster with my grandmother. The very same.

Inside, the band is onstage. Feedback squeals from their amplifiers while a black-and-white image of my grandmother flashes behind and over them from a projector, a different image of her.

A younger Tallulah wearing a jean jacket and leaning against the hood of a Cadillac. She looks directly at the camera, her sunglasses reflecting daggers of light. An iconic moment in time from a film that won two Academy Awards, and yet this band uses her image as a prop. As cheap nostalgia.

I stand motionless in the audience, waiting. Dancers swarm around me. Lights streaking, sweat, liquor, vape smoke, eyes closed, teeth flashing in laughter, mouths singing along to words. All these bodies moving. The band swaying them all.

Tallulah over everyone.

I stand very still.

XXXIX

Tour buses, it turns out, have fabulous sound systems. And it really is impressive that a Viper Room act should have a tour bus at all, but I am certainly not complaining.

An unlikely pick for best among Halloween songs, but one that has really resonated with me time after time, is Tami Sagher, Robert Carlock, Jeff Richmond, Donald Glover, and Tracy Morgan's "Werewolf Bar Mitzvah," created for a TV sitcom as a cheesy bit outlining the unlikely scenario of, as the lyrics repeat, *Boys becoming men, men becoming wolves!* Frankly, their use of the classic Halloween song musical themes and the playfulness requisite of so many of the best songs lands it firmly in the canon, and high among the other songs, if I am one to judge. It pokes fun at itself, which is so much the beauty of the holiday. To expose the darkness, and to find the pleasure in it. So we listen to it, the band and me, and we have a lot of fun. Just jammin'! I read somewhere that Donald Glover had to sub in on some of the verses in the full-length recorded version and imitate Tracy Morgan's voice, which is a tidbit I share with the band before me now, though they don't seem all that interested in learning.

I began by incapacitating two of them so I could focus on each one by one. I did this with a samurai sword my grandmother used in an extremely racist and outdated film Hollywood has conveniently forgotten. I had a moment to slip back to the house and let them settle into their bus before I came to pay them a visit. I suppose it's just that three guys in a tour bus really don't expect a girl to slice at them full of extreme violence, so it really wasn't all that difficult to let myself in. Element of surprise and all that. I stabbed through the singer's chest, quickly, upon entry to the bus, then took the sword and sliced through part of the bassist's abdomen. I knocked the drummer unconscious with the hilt. The drummer was down fully, but had nearly placed a call to their manager, and I got to the phones of the other two before they were able to reach anyone. I tied them each up with various articles of clothing and odds and ends I found around the bus, and here we are now. The drummer still lies unconscious; the bassist, tied to a chair, and singer in the driver's seat, are bleeding heavily. Just so he doesn't cause any trouble, I knock out the bassist as well.

Once the singer and I are effectively alone, I make a small incision in his forehead along his scalp line and then tick mark cuts about an inch apart from each other perpendicular to the incision down one side of his face. I use them as a guide to peel his skin down, bit by bit, in strips, until the whole of his face is exposed. He screams, and I turn the music up louder. The second band plays inside, and the Strip is always alive at night. All the sounds feeding the gods of Hollywood, the spirit of the place. Perhaps we are the gods. Perhaps Tallulah is. I watch his face move as he screams, without the skin to conceal what lies below it. Muscle and tendon and ligament and bone and blood. It is so beautiful, deconstructed like this. How can anyone look at anything without craving to know what lies beneath?

He howls questions to me: *Who are you? Why are you doing this? I didn't do anything to anyone. I don't deserve this. Why me?*

This is a failing of men. This same violence, applied to a woman, she does not ask *why* it is being inflicted upon her, she only struggles unsuccessfully to free herself and grieves the fact she has grieved her entire life, one that she understands fundamentally and innately. That violence simply occurs.

His screaming continues and even with the beauty of his movements, the sound hinders my ability to appreciate the song I've selected for us, so I stand and use the sword to cut through the tissue just in front of his ear on the other side of his face and slice down, carving through tendon and muscle and ligament on each side until I am finally able to disconnect the jawbone. His cries persist throughout the process. It is difficult work and takes a long time. I press repeat so that the song won't end.

The drummer wakes in his chair. Once the singer's jawbone is free, some meat still hanging down from it, I toss it hard at him. I miss. Drummers are always sort of a lot. I'm not in the mood for it. Still, he's the one who's awake, so he's the next one to play with. I turn back to glance at the singer, jawless, slumped and unconscious. His face hemorrhaging blood. The loose skin of his lower mouth dangling along with a tongue that has nothing to keep it in. Well, he's certainly quiet now.

With the drummer, it's tape over the mouth (found in the bus emergency tool kit) and sticks through the ears. I hum along with the song as blood sprays out from the burst eardrums and his muffled yelling intensifies. I shove them in farther and twist. The circumcision joke of the song comes, and it sparks a perhaps tired but still worthy idea. I think it will be lots of fun.

I leave the drumsticks where they are, decide to shove them in just a bit farther, and push him back so I can unzip his too-tight pants. He's already circumcised, it turns out. I click my tongue. What can I say, I guess I'm a little disappointed. But I've got him here, so I decide to take a little more off. Just the tip. Just to see how it feels.

Perhaps one would expect the chopping of a penis to feel a bit like the chopping of a hot dog, and it does. It is more fun than I anticipated, so I chop a bit more. Chop, chop, chop. Crying tears. Bleeding from the ears. Howling through the tape.

Once his crotch is a bit of a mincemeat situation, I give him a firm little stab through the throat, just so I don't have to hear any more from him, though he will likely lose consciousness in a minute anyway. People pass out so easily, it's really disappointing. In my experience, the women seem to hold to consciousness longer with extreme pain. But perhaps my data sample set is not large enough to really make an accurate statement. Perhaps I need to collect more.

The bassist I've saved for last. Bassists are generally the quiet ones, in my experience, and they are always the most intelligent of the band, or the least. This one seems smart to me, I'm not sure why exactly, but I just feel it. He's still passed out, and I consider him and decide to go for the hands. Break anyone's fingers, and they'll be sure to wake up. We do all ten, and he's up by number three. I taped his mouth too, and he's sufficiently tied, so there's really not much for him to do. I give his fingers each a little chop and shower them around the bus, place a couple of the pieces in fun hiding spots for someone to find later. Like a scavenger hunt. Finger confetti for everyone! I pull off the tape, kiss him, and suck his tongue into my mouth. I bite, hard. It takes a couple tries, but finally I bite through. I open my mouth and let his tongue dribble out, falling with a little slap into his lap. His eyes crazed with terror until they roll back in his head. He slumps forward again.

I take a moment and stretch. Spit out the rest of his blood

over him. My own hands are tight and tired from all the week's ministrations, and I really have to focus in on the music to finish my work. The silly back-and-forth, the playful banter between the actors, and the ridiculousness of the premise.

Werewolf bar mitzvah, spooky scary!

The rocking little melody. The backup vocals that come in toward the end. It's just magic.

I peel a lot more skin and shove a lot of body parts into a lot of orifices, and finally I step back and take in a deep breath. I wipe my forehead with the back of my hand, and there's a piece of skin and ligament or something else drippy and sinewy hanging from my pinky finger. I consider it for a moment then open my mouth and drop it on my tongue. I chew thoughtfully.

The tour bus is covered in blood and cracked bones, and I confiscate a Ziploc freezer bag holding a fair amount of cocaine and add in bits of brain from each of the band members. Just enough to be a proper souvenir. The ancient Egyptian art of excerebration takes very little time if one only makes good use of available tools and knows what one is doing. They had enough lying around that I was able to make it work. I take my new pliers out of my back pocket and snag some teeth too, for the jar at the Tata Tiki Lounge. For the piña coladas. For The Bartender. I take one of the phones with me, since mine is now in pieces in my grandmother's cellar.

I head back inside the bar and drop some more brain bits into unclaimed drinks around the space, for a little extra Halloween flavor. There's more cannibalism in this town than most people realize. I might only be adding to cocktails that already are full of brains. I might only be just now joining the party.

Behind the bar, a familiar face chats with customers, pours a line of shots. Tattooed skin and all-black clothing, showing enough cleavage to make rent money tonight. She looks good.

I picture her naked there at her post, picture her with Gideon shoving that dildo in and out of her. Feelings, at the reminder of Gideon. Feelings I cannot and will not identify. I blink hard. I cling to the rage. I feed it.

I slip through the crowd, my eyes on Claire's. I linger near her end of the bar. When she looks up and sees me, I give her a little wave and smile.

She jumps back. There is pure distilled fear in her eyes. Trauma, I realize. This is what I have done to this woman. I consider staying and asking for a drink, giving her a good long night of it, but I have a better idea. She watches me warily, that terror unwavering, as I hold her eyes and walk along the bar. Once I've hit the other side, I blow her a long, slow kiss and turn away.

At the bouncer's stand, before leaving, I ask if I can borrow a permanent marker. I write Claire's name on the bag of cocaine and brains and ask the bouncer if he wouldn't mind giving it to her. I tell him she will know who it's from. I give his cock a nice little squeeze in thanks.

Because I can.

XL

I do not return to the house. I am wired and alive and adorned in the blood of men who I know nothing about and who are no longer men at all. I dip into every bar on the Strip, my own little pub crawl, and receive many compliments on my bloody Halloween look, one night early. I end up at the brothel bar because it is the only one that stays open all night long. The women's room, generally one of the least shitty (no pun intended) bathrooms in town, is fully occupied by tittering females adjusting their makeup and cleavage and hair, so I stumble into the men's instead.

I pause as the door slams shut behind me. I am astounded. There is a couch and a television inside this bathroom. The TV is set to local news, and it's built into the mirror over the sink. The women's room has soft lighting and wide mirrors and smells of perfume and Febreze, and the men's room has a couch with a flickering side lamp and a TV. It's disgusting, and the couch is a sort of Frankenstein abomination of perhaps three couches sewn or pushed together into one, in dark browns and greens, though it is difficult to tell in the low light. The room is not small. You could come and read in here. You could do anything, really. Facial or pubic hairs mar the sink. There is a dark stain on the couch that looks like blood. The couch smells of cigarette smoke and bad decisions. The whole room reeks, really. But it's so big, so . . . expansive.

A guy comes in, and I turn to him. "Have you seen this?" I say, pointing to the couch and the TV and the room at large.

"Uh . . . what are you doing in here?" he asks me.

"You don't think this is insane? This room, this couch, all this space. I mean, what the fuck? It's . . . *magnificent.*"

"Um," he says, "this is the men's room."

I pull my eyes from the beauty of the couch to stare at him. He wears a designer V-neck tee and a newly polished diamond-encrusted dog tag on a chain, bares meticulously groomed eyebrows, and his Tom Ford cologne competes with the shit and semen essence of the space. He stares at me incredulously, his nonsense tribal tattoos leading to manicured hands covered in a curated collection of rings.

"God. Never mind," I say. I roll my eyes and slam myself into a stall.

The guy and I pee next to each other, and the local news-woman on the bathroom TV discusses the *Talk of the Town* Halloween parties, says that everyone who is anyone either has an invite already or is trying to secure one. I stand without flushing and head out to wash my hands. Images flash on the screen of various celebrities as the woman drones on about which studios are throwing which parties at which hotels and venues. I reach for a paper towel, and I stop. My jaw drops open. There, just for a second on the TV, inlaid into the mirror in which my bloody body is currently reflected, is an image of Gideon and Kate. There, and then gone. Other images replace them, of celebrities and well-known athletes and producers. I think maybe I have imagined it. I must have imagined it.

"Uh, are you gonna stand there all night, or . . ."

The guy behind me is waiting for the sink. I am standing

frozen with the water running and the paper towel in my hand. He raises his threaded eyebrows at me. I turn around and shove the wet paper towel into his mouth.

Outside the bathroom, I stumble to an empty barstool and pull out my phone. Formerly the singer's phone but now wiped and reset. I search their names, and the same image of Gideon and Kate shows up on TikTok. *Double Trouble: The Hottest New King and Up and Coming Derek Popova Film Star Are the Brother Sister Duo Everyone is Talking About!*

I feel a presence at my elbow and look up. A man in a suit with the tie undone hovers over me and opens his mouth to ask what I am drinking. I speak first.

"Not one word unless you want to be skull-fucked by a bottle of Svedka."

He pales and scatters. I return to the video.

And there they are. Gideon and Kate. I grip the bar top for support. According to this, they have both made the "exclusive and coveted" guest list of a studio's Chateau Marmont Halloween party. The post also speculates that Kate will be going as the date of Derek Popova and splices in footage of them caught together around town. She looks happy. Thin and tired, but happy. A photo pops up of Gideon beside a photo of the actress from the Chateau pool. The one who was *born dead*. Then those are replaced with one of them together that must have been taken that day I was there, both of them wearing what I saw them in. His arm around her shoulders, knocking back a drink, her smiling for the camera she clearly knew was there. It says she has been gone on an ashram retreat and no one has seen her for weeks, and the article speculates as to whom Gideon might take instead, showing a photo of him similarly cozied up at a restaurant with a dark-haired model named Svetlana. His eyes are on the model's, their hands inches apart on the table between them.

The theme for the party is HALLOWEEN ICONS OF FANTASY AND NIGHTMARE.

I throw the phone over the bar, and it smashes open a bottle of Fireball.

I shove the door open to the Tata Tiki Lounge. I do not know what to expect as I have never been in at any time of day except during my afternoon bi-weekly appointments. The sun has just risen over the Strip, and I am not sure I will even be able to get inside. But the door is open, and inside, I find Johnny, and I find The Bartender. Just like always.

The latter eyes me once, flips the station to Halloween music, and blends me a piña colada. I step in slowly and take in the room. It's just Johnny and The Bartender. Nothing different. I am wary as I take another step into this space that I know so well. But I was certain that at this hour *something* would be different. The fact that it's open at all . . .

"What?" The Bartender says. He is in a worse mood than usual.

"You two are just . . . here?" I say.

The Bartender stares at me flatly. Johnny sits with his head down, examining his palms.

"No one else," I say.

The Bartender holds my stare and without a word sets my drink down on the bar.

Alright then. I scan for the doll which is mercifully gone. I do not let myself think about the fact that it means the girl has returned to claim it. After another long moment, I accept that the Tata Tiki Lounge is, somehow, as it always is. Stranger things have happened. I reach gratefully for my glass. The Bartender makes me another.

At the end of the bar in his habitual spot, Johnny sits up tall now and bears an expression of utter bewilderment. I think it might be simply that it is dawn, and here he is just as I am. He turns and looks at me, surprisingly clear-eyed, and as if he expects me to solve some great riddle of life for him. There is something profoundly different about him.

Neither man says anything of my bloody appearance, which I find mildly insulting.

"What's your problem?" I say to Johnny, wiping my mouth with the back of my hand and slamming the empty glass on the counter. Gideon and the actress. Gideon and Svetlana. Kate and fucking Derek.

Johnny, imposter Johnny, shakes his head, and I know the feeling so intimately. It is the doll on the ground and the girl getting away and Gideon and Kate and my grandmother and my job and my whole fucking life.

"He's out of my wine," Johnny says. Incredulous. Bereft. *Sober.*

Holy shit. This makes me forget my troubles, momentarily. Johnny is standing before me sober. I can't believe it.

"It's . . . there isn't any," he says. He holds his hands out as though he has never seen them without the wine, without the glass and bottle. As though he does not know who he himself is in this moment or how he ever came to be here. He looks at me as though I can solve the mystery for him. As though I must have the answer to this, the question of all questions.

Talking Heads' "Psycho Killer" comes on the speakers. The Bartender heads to the back to get something, or more likely, to avoid us. There is a new piña colada on the counter waiting for me. I open the teeth jar and drop a few new ones in. I reach into my pocket and then drop in more. I replace the lid.

"Hey, Johnny," I say, taking my drink and knocking it back.

"Yeah?" he finally manages, that same look of complete incomprehension on his face.

"You wanna fuck?"

As Johnny, who I am now more convinced than ever is the real Johnny, is for the first time in the whole of my knowing him sober, he is surprisingly adept at said fucking.

He came back to himself upon my asking the question, I guess triggering one of the few words that he knew to be concretely tied to his identity. Now, we take up the whole of the small graffitied and tiki-ed bathroom, my ass to him and my tits over the sink. In the mirror, he watches himself, his still good body, his hand running through his hair, posing himself in a manner he has clearly posed himself a thousand times, every time he shoves into me, tilting his head slightly further this way or that. If he has noticed the blood coating my skin, it seems it does not matter.

My eyes find themselves in the mirror. These eyes the last thing the band saw, the last thing Liz and Andre saw, the last thing the girl with the dolls will ever see. Blood on my face like war paint. I look more like myself than I ever have. To think I have ever fought this. To think I would ever want to hide it.

The eyes of Tallulah Fly.

The eyes of Maeve.

Today is Halloween.

I walk home with new purpose. I will find the girl, and I will end this.

I step inside and prepare for the night ahead. I will do my grandmother's makeup. I will restore her face, paint her nails back to their classic red, perhaps even uncover some of her jewelry. She deserves to experience the holy day as herself.

I walk through the house and down her hall. Her bedroom door is slightly open, so I suppose I will find Lester the Cat inside. I do, and I nearly trip over him. He sits in the middle of the floor, staring up at me and loudly meowing. It is an accusatory sound, pointed and harsh.

I try to push past him, but he claws at my leg. I swear and shake him off. Maybe he needs more attention. I can get him another mouse. Perhaps a cat tree.

My grandmother looks peaceful when I get to her bedside. I press my fingers to her throat and plan out which jewels I will pull out. She's got them all in a safe downstairs, and I know the combination. There are probably more in the bank, but whichever she has here will have to do.

It takes perhaps seconds, perhaps longer, for the realization to come.

It pushes its way into my mind slowly and painfully.

There is no pulse.
   Beneath my fingers,
   there is no pulse.

There is—

XLI

ilence.

XLII

The inner workings of the mind sifting and sorting and liquid trickling down through permeable rock and soil and ash and tar and dust of the self, searching for a place to settle. Only ever farther to fall, more to filter through. Only ever sinking deeper into the bottomless dark.

Death happens so fast. Just like my firing. Just like Kate's part. One is alive, and then not. Just like that.

What is the self when one half of it disappears? What if it was the stronger half? What is a self at all?

There are no spoilers in life. There is only just the one ending.

But something miraculous happens. Something that I did not anticipate.

I feel her.

Tallulah, I feel her inside me.

She is not gone. Why did I ever think she was gone?

She is not dead.

Nothing can kill Tallulah.

Why did I ever think anything could?

We take the stairs down one at a time, my grandmother and me. She looks beautiful with her makeup on. With her jewels. She is light in my arms, as though she never weighed anything. As though her weight and my weight are one in the same and it is no more to carry us both than it always has been.

"We'll just get a nice dinner," I say. "We'll just have a nice night in our town."

"Careful, Maeve," she says. "This is my favorite blouse. It shall not be wrinkled."

"No," I say. "It shall not."

At Jones I sit at a table with two plates of spaghetti and two Old-Fashioneds. The maître d' has been paid to play Billie Holiday. I clink my glass against hers, and we discuss the night ahead. Outside, the moon hangs fat and full overhead.

My wolf howls. My grandmother howls back. They know what's coming.

They howl together.

XLIII

Back at the house, I change my grandmother's bedsheets and smooth the edges down, tuck them in tight. All adults make their beds. Any person who does not is frankly playing an extremely unconvincing game of personhood. And my grandmother will no longer need this bed because she is no longer sick.

Hilda was wrong. I knew she was wrong.

I turn on my Halloween playlist, and Oingo Boingo's 1986 hit "Dead Man's Party" comes on. It is an absolute smash. I dance through my grandmother's room as Lester the Cat bites at my heels, weaves in and out of my feet. I open her closet and search through the Chanel and Gaultier and Laurent until I find a little box at the back of the room that is the very one I am searching for. I blow the dust off the top and take the box over to her bed where I carefully pry it open. Inside, the costume is still as beautiful as it was when it was made for her. I lift it up and admire the boned corset, silken and tight and just my size.

I apply my grandmother's makeup carefully and with precision, consulting the photograph as I go. Beautiful and bloody. I fasten the wrist and neck cuffs, spray myself with my grandmother's perfume. I select heels from her closet, and finally,

I don the bunny ears.
I stand and admire myself. We both admire me.
"You're beautiful," she says.
"I look just like you."

XLIV

Holy shit, you look just like her! That photo, that's crazy!" the valet says.

I toss him the Mustang keys and then stop and turn. I grab the back of his head and slide my tongue in his mouth. When I pull back, he is stunned, and sporting a semi.

"Young men are just so delicious," I say.

I begin the walk up the carpet, the lights and music from inside spilling out into the night, calling me in. Welcoming me home.

The Chateau looks as though Halloween has exploded on every surface, in every corner. The outdoor pool area has been enclosed and transformed with hanging ghosts and witches, the bar and lobby completely overhauled with cobwebs, lights, and smoke, packed in with costumed partygoers, dark and full of movement. Props from famous Halloween and horror movies hang everywhere, and emerging from the pool are the animatronic great white from *Jaws,* the Creature from the Black Lagoon, and Swamp Thing, fog drifting over its surface between them.

Inside, movie prop weapons hang down from the ceiling: axes, chainsaws, swords. And the costumes. The costumes are exquisite. There is Chucky, Ghostface, Pinhead, Pumpkinhead,

the Stay-Puft Marshmallow Man, Norman Bates, Frankenstein's monster, Tyler Durden, David Kessler, Two-Face, Darth
Vader, Dracula.

And there is me.

We are what we are what we are, after all. And I am a dead
Playboy bunny and I am a fly and I am a wolf, and I am any
wise man's worst nightmare.

The DJ spins a non-Halloween song, the bass pounding
through the floor, and Miley Cyrus and Billy Idol dressed as two
characters from *Rocky Horror Picture Show* sing into mics along
with the song in a spur-of-the-moment reveal, judging by the
elated reaction of the rest of the partygoers. I do not see Kate or
Gideon among the cheering and dancing costumed Hollywood
royalty. I head over to the bar and take three in a row of pre-
poured shots on a tray. I have one more and let my fingers graze
Freddy Krueger's crotch as I pass.

I make it to the middle of the dance floor, and I begin to
sway. I am a dead girl at a dead girl's party, and I am going to
act like it. Maeve may not crave the spotlight, but Tallulah lives
for it. And we are both here. My grandmother deserves a good
time.

I close my eyes and swing my arms, roll my hips, arch my
back, kick my legs, drop to the floor and stretch up to the ceiling. I move and I thrash and I spin and writhe like the true
queen of Halloween town, like I am going to summon forth all
the spirits of the dead, awaken the wolves and incorporeals, the
demons, and every monster. I dance and dance until I feel that
I have done it. I have given them life. Inside, and all around.

When I open my eyes, the floor has been cleared, and it is
only me. Pennywise and Hannibal and Bateman and Leath-
erface all watching. I smile. I pull them in. Sweat, Halloween
store plastic, couture, liquor, spit. I grind into Jack Torrance,

slide my hands down the Joker's chest and stomach and hips, I press myself between Michael and Jason, shimmy with Jigsaw, and I throw my head back and howl.

Through the lights and the sweat and the fog I catch sight of her. Kate dressed as a sort of sexy-version Linda Blair from *The Exorcist,* in a smaller and tighter nightgown, the lacerations accentuating the delicate lines of her face. She's hired a professional makeup artist to do it, and it is spectacular. Hollywood has traditionally given us so few iconic female horror villains, and nearly all of them became what they were after being brutalized by men or possessed by male demons. Still, who doesn't love a good exorcism? Beside Kate is Derek, of course, dressed in a priest's or, I suppose, Exorcist's uniform. The symbolism would be more on point if Derek were the minor demon possessing her, but the feeling is there all the same. But perhaps that is giving him too much credit as well. It is something larger than Derek that possesses Kate. And it possesses nearly every person in this room. It is this town and all we are promised here. It is already in us.

I work my way through the crowd to talk to Kate, but she turns and heads outside with an actress I've seen in things but whose name I can't remember. Kate didn't see me. At least I don't think. Derek grabs two new drinks and sets them on a high table to the side of the room. He produces something from his pocket and drops it in one of the glasses. It fizzes and settles. He prepares to follow after Kate outside.

I sidle up next to him. "Hey, you," I say.

He startles and then turns to me, his eyes trailing up and down my body. The drugged glass is on my side, the other on his. His pupils dilate, and he licks his lips. I do look amazing.

He tries to place where he's met me before, his eyes catching on my chest. I lean in close to his ear and whisper, "You don't know me, Derek, but I am a mega fan. I have seen every one of your movies. And I just wanted to come over here and tell you how much I appreciate your . . ." I let my hand trail down his stomach and graze just below his belt. ". . . visionary work. I'd really love to spend a little time with you, get to tell you how much of an inspiration you are to me."

I pull back, and he blinks a few times. He comes to, and my hand is on the glass nearest me. "A toast?" I say. "To new friends and inspirations?"

His feeble mind calculates the willing and barely dressed girl holding the glass full of Rohypnol before him, flashes to the girl he came here with, weighs whether he will be able to manage both, what he might be able to pull off. But no man who roofies drinks ever brings just one pill, and every man loves a challenge.

He clinks his glass against mine.

"To new friends, and inspiring each other," he says.

I smile and drain my glass. He does the same.

"Listen," I say, "can you meet me in the bathroom in a few minutes?" I lean in again and whisper just what kind of inspiration he will receive.

The song shifts, and the pop stars still sing with the DJ, but this time it is something I know. I sing along as I weave through the room once more, making my slow way toward the bathroom.

Dead, I am the one exterminating son.

Derek is early. I pull him inside.

We fumble in the dark of the bathroom as Rob Zombie's lyrics fill the room. Derek smells of expensive noxious cologne and new wallet leather. I undo his belt buckle with one hand and reach into his pocket with the other.

"I brought something fun," I say. Stroking his cock, unimpressive in its half attention, I slip his roofie bag open, grab two of the tablets with my free hand. I drop the bag to the floor and stick both pills on his tongue.

"What are these?" he asks around them.

"A good time," I whisper. I slide my tongue in his ear, stroke his now mostly hard cock, and close his mouth. He swallows and groans in response. I tease him and kiss him and make it all feel worthwhile enough for him to stay while the time counts down. I check my grandmother's Cartier watch. It should be just about . . .

Derek sways on his feet.

I put the toilet seat down and sit him on it. I straddle him and take the cable ties from between my breasts. I grind on him and shove my tits in his face as I hook his hands behind his back and bind them together. A third cable tie binds them to the pipe in the wall.

He smiles and licks his lips in appreciation. These limp-dick *artist* men all such predictable bottoms.

"Hey, Derek," I say, and he groans.

"I just want to know," I say, licking and sucking his ear, his jaw, his throat. "How you thought you could come to a party full of people and drop something as basic as a roofie in your starring actress's drink? Like, could you be any more 2007?"

He moans and then pauses. Tries to stiffen and pull away from me, but his muscles won't quite let him.

"We've met before, but it's okay that you don't remember. What you probably should have remembered though is that Kate is not a fucking idiot, and she has friends. Friends who would kill for her."

"What . . . How are you . . . ?"

"Oh, how am I not drugged? I switched our glasses. I mean, honestly, Derek, it is actual child's play. You got duped by a *switched glass* because a girl in a bunny suit touched your penis. I can only imagine it was about the power, because we both know Kate would have slept with you anyway. But you liked drugging her and being a little rough, and you liked the fact that she didn't always remember. You had complete control over someone else. But you don't have the power now, do you, Derek? No . . . you don't." I smile compassionately.

Derek begins the usual attempted struggle, blah blah, but the drug has kicked in, and the subsequent two will overcome him soon. I run my hands over the crucifix hanging around his neck, considering fun ways of using it. He has a second chain on beneath his costume, and I fish it out. I hold it between us, rolling my eyes so hard they might get stuck.

He says something I don't listen to, and I take the silver cocaine spoon from around his neck and shove his head back with my other hand. I shove his head back as far as it will go and take his dumb fucking waste of metal cocaine spoon, and I dig out his eyeball.

He screams. Like they all do. I twist the spoon.

He makes a gurgling sound, and I can't get the eyeball disconnected, so I just let it hang from the socket, dangling down his face.

He mumbles something, tries to speak, but all I hear is *Dragula.*

I want to do so much more to this man. But I can't kill him if Kate is going to get what she wants, and I can't take his other eye if he's going to continue directing, again, because it affects Kate. It's a shame, but I believe I've made my point.

I caress his face and lick his lips. He is nodding off, his

eyeball lolling and smacking against the skin of his face on that little tendril of shiny red tissue.

"The thing is," I say, "you're going to leave here and, if you do remember what happened through the drugs, which seems unlikely to me, you'll tell someone what I did. But, Derek, here's the secret."

I lean in close and whisper in his ear. "They're not going to believe you." I smooth his hair down. "No one will believe you. Ever."

I shove the cocaine spoon up his nose until I feel it hit cartilage or bone and his head knocks back and blood sprays out over my hand. He cries out again and then slumps forward.

I bend down and tongue the socket of his eyeball.

I extricate myself from him and give him one hard kick in the throat.

"Can't wait to see the movie, Derek. I'm sure it'll be a total fucking hit."

XLV

Back on the dance floor, Derek's blood and ocular fluid have really completed my costume in the most fabulous way. I stretch my arms out to my sides and breathe in the decorations and the costumes and the music and lights and alcohol and party. This, the single best night of every year, the night when the veils are lowered, and the spirits can walk freely between worlds. All Hallows' Eve, Samhain, night of the witching. Magic fills the air, and I am a part of it.

"What. The actual FUCK, Maeve!"

I open my eyes, and Kate is before me. Between her fury and her makeup, she is momentarily terrifying.

"Wow, Kate. You look amazing."

"Fuck you, Maeve! I have friends over here saying the girl dressed like Tallulah Fly is making out with Derek by the bar?"

"Oh. No, it's not—"

"What is it not? My brother wasn't enough, you had to go for my boyfriend too? And my fucking career? If you cost me this part, Maeve, I swear to god, I do not know what I'll do." Tears of fury fill her eyes. Tears of fear. She thinks that I would do this to her, that I would ever jeopardize what she cares about. I am stunned.

"Kate, it's not like that."

"What is it like then," she says.

"I . . . He's not a good guy," I say. "You shouldn't be spending time with a guy like that."

"Oh that's real fuckin' rich."

"What is?"

Kate throws her hands up. "I shouldn't spend time with him, the man who is making my career and giving me what I have always wanted because he isn't *good*? What, and you're good, Maeve? You're some paragon of virtue?"

"I just mean that—"

"You spend all your time wallowing, watching these weird fucking videos and obsessing over music that no one will listen to ever, subjecting us all to it again and again, and you do it all like it's going to make any difference. None of that shit makes you any more of a person, Maeve, and it doesn't make you any less alone. Which frankly, you're gonna be. Like, what do you even want anyway? You have no goals and no future, so you just tear apart any hopes and wants of people who do."

She is openly crying now. Because of me. Kate is crying, and all of this has poured out of her as though it has been roiling inside her, waiting for some time to make its way out and into my receiving ears, and her terrifying glorious makeup is smearing because of me. "This is my whole life, Maeve. I *do* have dreams, I *do* have a future with people who *love* me, and you can't handle that."

"I want you to get everything you want," I say. I mean it. I take a step toward her, hold her eyes and try to convey that I really truly mean it. I reach out for her hand, and she pulls it away, disgusted, offended that I would make the attempt.

She takes a step toward me, looking more lethal and wild than I have ever seen her, and I am so full of love for this person and so full of terror that this is the moment, understanding that it has come, is coming even as she speaks. "Do you? Do you really? Your grandmother is Old Hollywood royalty, and you never thought of pulling some strings to get me meetings? You live in this big house on the hill and in this fantasy life, and you have no idea what it's like for the rest of us. But you want to trap me there with you, and guess what, Maeve. You failed. I am going to be something huge and glorious, and you are going to wither and die on that hill just like your grandmother."

The ground trembles beneath us, just a little. Just enough.

Kate stops there, strains at the words that she did not mean to come but did. They hang between us, and she does not know, cannot know what has happened, but even if she regrets her words, they are hers, and she meant them.

She meant them.

She opens her mouth and then closes it and shakes her head. She turns and kicks the wall and yells, "Fuck!" Then she turns back to me and says, "Just *please*. Stay out of my life, Maeve. Forever."

Forever.

I stand there for many songs. People walk by, compliment my costume. Some try the door on the bathroom which is, of course, locked. "Thriller" comes on, and I force myself to accept what has come, what I knew would inevitably come. There are no spoilers. Everything comes to an end.

Tallulah is not sad, Tallulah says that girls like Kate come and go.

Tallulah says to dance.

So I move. I do not stop moving. I do not allow myself to stop

for a long time. Song after song. I let the wolf take over. I let
Tallulah take over. I lose myself. Until—

There is a pull, on Maeve. A tug on a tether that she did not
know was there. I open my eyes, and take in the room. There is
a commotion by the bathrooms, and a swarm of people pushing
in closer and running away. I hear screams, just a few. Derek
must have awoken, or someone found a way to get inside. A girl
yells that someone needs to call 911. Bouncers moving purposefully, speaking into radios, caterers trying to get a better view
and whispering to each other. But none of this is what called to
Maeve. None of this is what pulled me back to the night.

Through the bodies and the lights and the fog, through all that
is dancing inside me, a man makes no moves toward or away
from the commotion. He stands across the dance floor from
me, stock still. Purposeful. Eyes that I think are two different
colors but I still do not know. Eyes that see me, in darkened rooms
and in the light. As much as I can be seen. Gideon is there, and
I am here.

He makes his way through the crowd in a red riding hood,
a beautiful woman I do not know wearing a sexy huntsman's
costume watching him walk away.

Gideon's eyes on mine.

And there is no one else. There is no party. No commotion.
No bleeding director or heartbroken friend.

Why have I ever thought there was anything else?

Everything I have devoted my time to, the dolls and the mystery girl, the hours wasted trying to emulate the lives of writers
and characters from books and films, trying on lives other than
my own. What has any of that meant? Perhaps I am nothing if
not other people. Perhaps I am nothing if not Tallulah. But
Tallulah is not here now, and I wonder if she really was. There is

grief and self-loathing and fear and rage and anguish, but now they are quiet. With his eyes on mine.

They are quiet.

The ground shakes again, stronger this time. I don't know. I don't care.

His eyes on mine.

There is only Gideon and Maeve.

Only us.

XLVI

We leave the car at the hotel and exit just as the red and blue lights come flashing. For the whole of the walk, I am tingling. I am thrumming with a restlessness and a want and terror, with a satisfaction, and the certainty that is the man beside me. We don't speak. There aren't words for this. If it has been written or sung about or put on film, I have never witnessed it.

We approach the house, and I pause on the doorstep. I turn to him, fingering the key, Hilda's bones strung up above us, the Halloween decorations lit up and moving. The children have long since run up and down the street for candy. I've set bowls of it out, in front of Frankenstein and the possessed girl, in front of the mummy and the ghost, and it has been successfully ravaged.

I've never had a man in my grandmother's house before. In our house. My house.

I wait for Tallulah to speak, but she says nothing.

"Do you," I breathe, and I find I too can barely speak with this man here before me. With these feelings that I do not allow myself to name. My chest is tight, and I am too full, too full of wants, too full of life. The poisonous cacti on either side of me.

"Do you want to come inside?"

A red riding hood falls to the floor of the foyer.

Bunny ears.

A shirt. A corset. Pants.

He shoves me up against the wall, and a prop vase shatters to the floor. I groan as his tongue finds my neck, as his hands find parts of me that are screaming out for him. I push him into the living room, up against the couch, ripping his briefs, and we topple over it. On the couch, on the floor, on the coffee table and the chairs. His hands on me, my fingers on him, tongues, lips, teeth, sweat, fingers in hair, hot breath on throats and nipples and hips and thighs. We devour each other. We take, and we give, and it is too much, and it will never be enough. I can't get close enough to him, I can't get enough of his skin on my skin. I can't—

Neon and party noise from the Strip and the city bathe us through the glass.

That thing that has been growing inside me that is not rage and is not spite and is not fear or pain. It expands and pushes and pulls at my insides and lights me up from within and out. It is exquisite and painful in its own way, and it is all-consuming, all-exciting. This man inspires it in me. Because of him, I am so alive.

We don't play any songs. We don't use any toys. The monkey and the wolf and my grandmother are silent.

There is Gideon, and there is me.

His eyes and my eyes.

Nothing else.

I had no idea.

I didn't know.

I didn't know.

He thrusts into me again, and we erupt, together.

XLVII

I wake to wrinkled sheets and the impression of a large body beside me on the bed. I pad into the living room and find Gideon sitting and reading with Lester the Cat. They share a chair that was put to better use last night than it ever has been before. My body responds to the memory, and that hunger wakes again. For more, more of him.

First things first. I head into the kitchen for coffee. He's already made a pot. I eat four almonds and a small square of dark chocolate before walking out to sit in the chair by his.

"Which book?" I say.

"Goethe's *Faust*," he says, finishing the page and then setting the book down. That particular copy is in German.

"You can read it?"

He raises his eyebrow. "You still think I'm only an athlete, with no other interests or talents."

"You possess *some* other talents," I say, and then I take a long slow sip of my coffee, hoping he doesn't see my face.

"Maeve Fly. Are you blushing?"

"I don't blush."

Gideon sets Lester the Cat down on the floor and turns to me. "You know," he says, standing and bending down over my chair. "Your face turns just about that color when you come."

He leans in and kisses me, long and slow, then says, "To completion."

I pull back and make a face. "Did you really just say *completion?*"

"Yeah, Maeve," he says, "I did."

We make use of much of the furniture in the house. Early morning light streaks in, and the space is full of movement, heartbeats, breath. Of two humans, and a cat. Of life. I had thought that Gideon would feel like an outsider here. By all rights he should. But somehow, he suits the space, and it him. Perhaps I have imprinted enough of myself on him to make his existence here work. The walls have not rejected him. And I have not.

Hours pass, but I do not feel them. Time, for the first time in so long, feels not to be something that must be filled, that stretches on interminably and cruelly. Time operates differently here, now. We are suspended and outside it. We are exempt from its rules.

I allow the thought to form, the ember of a hope that has been growing and burning since he came here. I could see him here, in this house. I could see myself, with him. Maybe, over time. Putting up the Halloween decorations together.

The sun is sinking below the horizon when his stomach growls. We order food, and I retrieve the cellar keys from my bedside drawer to head downstairs and get us some champagne. Gideon strokes my hair, my forehead to his chest, the two of us standing in my room. "I didn't expect this," he says. "Moving to LA. I had no idea."

"I'm happy you did," I say. I mean it. I hardly know who I am anymore, but I don't mind it. Not right now.

"I knew you would be there last night," he says.

"How?"

"A Halloween party at the Chateau. Where else would you be? It's why I went."

I bite at his nipple so he doesn't see that I am smiling. His skin is hot where mine meets it. He is here, with me.

He pulls back so we see each other. He looks . . . nervous. "Maeve," he says, and Lester the Cat enters the room, mewing loudly. Gideon clears his throat again. "Maeve, I brought something, something I want to show you."

Lester the Cat screeches at me, and three loud knocks sound from the metal front door knocker. Gideon runs his hand over his face.

"Okay," I say. "I will get the food, feed him, grab us some champagne, and then I want to see." I drop the keys and reach for a sweater to pull on over my naked skin.

Gideon nods and exhales. He bends down and kisses me again. I lean into him. I lean all the way in.

I open the front door not to food, but to two police officers, the very same two who stopped by to ask about Hilda. Senior and Rookie.

I pull my sweater in tighter around myself, and Cop Senior attempts with impressive control not to glance down at my bare legs. Hilda's bones are strung up above us. Most of them.

"Oh, hello, officers. What can I do for you?" I say. My voice cracks just a little, and I put on a sweet girl smile.

"Hello, Miss Fly. We're sorry to disturb you. We're here to follow up about the Hilda Swanson case."

I wasn't expecting this, for them to come here.

"Oh, yes," I say, keeping my voice steady. "Of course. Has she come back yet?" I slow my heart rate. I breathe.

The older one clears his throat, and then the babyface cop behind him makes a big show of examining all the Halloween decorations closely. He looks at the bones. "No, ma'am, we're just making a quick stop. This might be hard for you, but as a friend of Hilda's, we wanted you to hear it from us." He pauses to take his hat off, a sympathetic gesture. "Miss Fly, we believe at this point that Miss Swanson has gone missing."

I don't speak for a moment.

"Oh god," I finally say. "Gone . . . missing? Hilda? Like, disappeared? How is that possible?" I sway a little on my feet.

"Do you need to sit down, Miss?"

I brace my hand on the doorframe. "No, no, I'm fine. Thank you. I just can't believe . . ." I look up at them. "Do you have any leads?"

The officers observe me for what seems a long time, and then the young one leans forward to look inside the house, his hand on the gun on his belt.

"Sorry," I say. "Where are my manners? Um, you're welcome to come in. I do have, uh, company at the moment, but . . ."

Cop Senior flushes red, and his eyes sweep behind me and catch on the clothing still strewn on the floor before carefully coming back to my face.

"No no, that won't be necessary," he says, "but thank you. Sorry to disturb you, and for the bad news. Just thought you'd want to know, and please give us a buzz if you hear anything, or if anything comes to mind?"

I exhale and nod. And just as I think they're about to leave, Lester the Cat weaves between my legs, then brushes up against the officer's leg, purring. He chuckles and bends down to pet him. "What a cute little guy," he says, and strokes his back, which I can now see is matted with a sticky red substance. I don't know how Lester the Cat could have blood on him, what he could have gotten into now, but that is clearly what it is. We stand for what seems to be minutes or is maybe only a second, Lester the Cat purring, the bones in the branches swaying with the breeze, the officer's fingers on someone's dried blood.

The officer grimaces, stands, and wipes his hand against his pants. "Well, we'll leave you to your evening. Again, please don't hesitate to call us if you think of something or need anything at all. This city is full of danger, even this neighborhood. It always pays to be safe."

"Thank you, officers," I say, and Cop Senior heads back to the car. The trainee lingers a moment longer and then steps up to me. He pulls his notepad out, fumbles with a pen from his breast pocket. "Um, ma'am?" he says.

"Yes?"

"These decorations . . ." He leans forward to inspect Hilda's femur, just inches away. "They're pretty impressive. Lifelike. You buy these or make 'em?"

"Oh," I say. "Thank you. It's a mix."

He stares at the bones a while longer, then at the possessed girl hanging from the tree, around the yard. His eyes come back to me.

"Are you by chance a professional decorator? My wife and I just love Halloween, and this is like really, really good. We would totally hire you next year."

The food is delivered shortly after. I quickly feed Lester the Cat and head into my bedroom, ready to pounce on Gideon again, but he is not there.

I head back to the kitchen and open up the containers, pull out plates. He still has not emerged from the bathroom. I walk back toward my bedroom and see that the bathroom door is open. He is not in it. I retrace my steps, step back into my room, run my eyes over everything. The unmade bed, the clothes strewn about on the floor and the furniture. The books now replaced on my shelf.

The cellar keys are gone.

I do not feel my body as I move toward the stairs. As I go down them one by one. I do not allow myself breath or thought or sensation. One step and another. Movement, methodical. I do not allow myself anything.

I see the open cellar door.

The cellar door is open, and Gideon is inside.

XLVIII

"Come. I'd like to show you something," my grandmother said to me that morning in the kitchen. "I'd like to tell you a little story."

I followed her downstairs, and she held a set of keys in her hands. She turned to me beside the cellar door. I was not allowed in the cellar. My grandmother had said she was extremely possessive of her wines and that she did not want me, or anyone, accidentally touching something they should not. I had never been inside.

"Maeve, people will steal anything and everything from you that they feel they are permitted to." She wore a silk robe with fur around the collar and hem. She wore slippers that made her steps silent.

"I became pregnant with your father at the Chateau by a married man. He was quite famous, and so was his wife, and he wanted me to terminate the pregnancy. Naturally I wanted to terminate it anyway, and mind you this was not the norm back then, but it was possible. But when that man told me to do it, I swore that I would not. It was a simple decision, perhaps the swiftest I have ever made.

"He was angry. He threatened to ruin my reputation, my career, to accuse me of misdeeds that were not mine. It would have been fine. It was only that he thought he could get away with it. This man that I had let into myself. He thought I would let him destroy me. He thought he would survive me at all."

She looked hard at me. "If there is one truth you need to know above all others, it is that to let someone inside here, to let them inside you, is to end them. Because no one will ever see you, not really. And when they do, it will be too late for them. You are what you are, and no matter what you think, you cannot change it. A wolf is only ever a wolf. So if you're smart, Maeve, you'll never open this door for anyone who you would wish to step back out."

She turned and placed the key in the lock, swung the large wooden door open.

She stepped inside the dark.

"Come in, Maeve," she said, "and meet your grandfather."

XLIX

Gideon stands in the cellar of my grandmother's house, of my house, in complete stillness.

It is as though the room is breathing, as though the walls are pounding, pulsating with a life that was not intended to be shared with a living breathing mortal. None other than me.

Gideon takes it all in.

My grandfather in a chair, his bones arranged in the manner my grandmother arranged them all those years ago. Various other bones and body parts she collected in a large wicker basket beside him. I've never known who they belonged to, but it has never mattered. Then there are the bones of the others from me, here and there, over the years. The ones my grandmother taught me to kill because she said one day I would need to know how to do it and how to dispose of them after. As always, she was right. I should have known, even then.

There are Andre's bones, Hilda's finger, the souvenir Lester the Cat saved for me while the rest of her cooked and uncooked remains went to my decorations. There is Liz, still a corpse, one that is now beginning to rot, in the corner of the room, her intestines and other organs spilling out from her stomach. The pipe and the dead mouse still there, sticking out from between her splayed legs, the mouse ears still on her head. She is more pulp than body, crusted and rank.

My grandmother is propped up on a daybed I dragged in, among her fine pillows, dressed and made up and surveying it all.

There, behind her, the bottles of champagne. The one I would have grabbed for us to drink tonight.

I see it all, the way Gideon must now for the first time, and I understand my grandmother's words. If he had known before, he would never have stayed. How could he? And now he does. Now he knows.

Gideon turns slowly, a look of complete incomprehension on his face.

Finally, he speaks. "I thought . . . I mean, maybe I suspected . . . *something*, but . . ."

There are tears in his eyes. There are tears in this enormous man's eyes, and there are tears in my own.

"Gideon," I say.

And it is so clear. I was such a fool. To let myself believe that he is like me, to let him convince us both of it. This man who lost his childhood best friend and thought it made him something dark, thought it made him some kind of monster. I was so stupid. I have been so, so stupid. To let myself believe I could ever be anything but alone.

"Maeve," Gideon says, and I take a step inside, and then another.

"Why did you come in here?" I ask. Now that he knows . . .

"For the champagne, but—"

"You shouldn't have come in. I didn't invite you in." I swipe another tear with the sleeve of my sweater.

"I need to show you what I brought," he says.

"What?" I say.

"Please, Maeve. I need to show you."

You did this, Maeve, Tallulah says. I glance at her, and she is watching us, witnessing all of this. I turn back to him.

"Maeve, I'm not upset," Gideon says.

You let him inside you, inside our home, and now he will take it all. He will take everything. Because no one is like you, Maeve. No one will ever understand you.

"Maeve, listen to me," he says. He raises his hands. "I'm not going to do anything. Let's go upstairs, and I will show you—"

You let him into our house. You brought this upon yourself. He has seen, and he will expose you because he can't understand.

"Maeve, please—"

My fingers find the jar, open it slowly, and reach inside. I am crying, truly crying now. Tears streaming so that I can barely see.

I walk toward Gideon, and he stiffens but does not back away.

"You don't understand," he says, tears in his own eyes, a look of wonder or terror on his face. Of complete disbelief. He reaches out for me. "Maeve, me too."

Never open this door for anyone who you would wish to step back out. You are what you are.

"I do understand," I say. "I really do." And I smear the cactus poison in his eyes.

"Fuck! What the fuck!"

"I'm sorry," I say. "I'm so sorry." I back away from him. I am shaking. The whole of me is shaking.

"I can't see," he says. "I can't see anything. What the fuck was that."

"You weren't supposed to find any of this, Gideon. I'm so sorry."

"Maeve, just stop talking for a second and listen to me. You don't understand—"

You know what you have to do, Tallulah says.

"Maeve, goddamnit, I can't see you!"

He yells things to me, but I do not hear them. I hear screeching monkeys and two howling wolves and my grandmother's voice again and again.

There is no one like you, Maeve. No one but me. What a foolish stupid girl you were to forget it. And now look what you've done. You've brought him down with you. You brought a lamb into a wolves' den. You did this.

My fingers find what I am reaching for, and I choke on a sob. She is right. I am so stupid. I let him in. I let myself believe.

I am saying something, again and again, asking a question, but I don't even understand my own words.

Gideon can never love me, not what I truly am. Not now that he knows. He can never.

I am still speaking to him, still asking the question, but now I choke on the words. I have no choice. I have no—

I swing the mace, and it collides with the man I love.

He tries to fight me, but he is blind, and he does not know this space. Because it is mine, and it was never meant for him to see. He stumbles forward, trips over my grandmother's collected bones. I swing the mace again and again.

Until he is still. Until he is silent.

And then I collapse beside him.

The words still pouring from my mouth, but now I understand them. Now they are the only sound in the room.

How did you get in?

How did you get in?

L

I close and lock the cellar door. I shower in hot water and cold water. I cannot stop shaking. I clean the house. I return my grandmother's costume to her closet.

I have done everything that is to be done and have left Gideon's clothes for last. I stand in my bedroom and stare down at them. I do not want to touch them, cannot stand to feel them. But I must do it.

I fold his shirt, carefully, and set it on my bed. I do the same with his red riding hood. With his socks. I lift his pants and find there is something in the pocket. I imagine it is his wallet, but when I take it out, I realize it is not.

It is an envelope, folded. I unfold it, slowly, and open the flap.

Inside are photographs printed on paper. I drop them, my eyes unfocused. I force my hands to spread them out over my comforter. I blink.

I wait for my eyes to take in the images and for my brain to synthesize them.

Bodies.

Each photo a different one. Some of the images old and pixelated. Some newer. Each of them freshly dead. Still. And one of them, a young man floating in a river, alongside a newspaper clipping. Jared Rao, accidental or self-inflicted death, fall from bridge, 2009. An image in the newspaper of a young Gideon, Jared, and Kate. Another image, the most recent, of an actress I saw not so long ago by the pool at the Chateau, with Gideon. He said he didn't like how things ended with Jared, that it was ugly in the end. He meant the very end. He meant the final moment.

I drop to my knees.

There are eight of them. Eight bodies. Gideon's tattoo.

I thought that maybe Jared's jersey number had been eight, on the hockey team. I thought—

That thing he said in the cellar. He told me. He told me, and I didn't listen.

I couldn't hear him.

Maeve, me too.

 # LI

I get in the Mustang.

As I pull onto Santa Monica Boulevard, the air stirs around me, picks up through the whole of the city. My hands shake on the wheel.

Gideon's skin on my skin. Gideon sitting beside me. Gideon beside me in the dark.

Gideon telling me I didn't understand.

Gideon's voice drowned out by Tallulah's.

Maeve, me too.

The wind rustling through the palm trees, their trunks swaying slightly, dry fronds scraping against each other.

Louder and louder as I approach.

I pull up in front of his house, the great Tudor with the too-green yard. There is a sudden crack above me as I close the Mustang door. A brutal sound of impact as a large mass lands before me on the ground.

A palm frond has fallen. I stand there, and I stare at it, on the grass.

Like great bird carcasses, he said. *Like trash.*

I look around and see that all the trees are swaying, that the whole of the atmosphere is upset.

The air stirs faster around me, and a breeze pushes me forward toward the house. As another frond falls, to my side. And another.

I use his keys to let myself in with shaky hands. He has no alarm. It is quiet inside without him here, the only sounds my own breath and the wind outside. This house scooped out and hollow. Empty.

I have never seen any of the rooms on the main or second floor besides the kitchen and living room. I step into each of them, most empty or just partially furnished. With each new room, I hear more of the wind, more movement outside. I hear my own breaths coming faster.

Upstairs, I find the master. I find two guest bedrooms. And a final room, at the end of the hall. It is locked, but the smallest key on his keychain opens it.

I swing the door open and step inside.

There is a body here. The actress. Her corpse has been preserved with something, partially preserved. Maybe sawdust. Formaldehyde. She is splayed out on the floor just as she was in the photograph. Rope wrapped around her throat. Almost lovingly. Almost.

Paints lie around the space, worktables and work benches. Art supplies. Body-dismantling supplies. Some kind of hockey trophy shoved in a corner.

And on the main worktable . . .

My hand over my mouth. I am nearly sick. I am so much. Too much. Because this is not possible.

The wind pushes against the side of the house, the trees rustling, more sounds of impact outside, and I shake with it. The whole of the city is shaking. The whole of the world.

And this before me . . .

On Gideon's worktable are doll parts and plastic toy parts. Vials of blood and jars of human hair.

And right in the middle, a newly completed doll. The last one he would ever make.

A wolf's body with a fly's wings. A smiling face, blood dripping from the mouth. A hollowed-out turnip beside it on the table, carved into a tiny jack-o'-lantern.

Three words written in blood on the doll's side.

Three words.

The wind driving in great gusts against the walls, rattling the foundation. Shaking the city as it always has, and always will.

Words in the mind, words that mean nothing.

My name is Maeve Fly.

This is my story.

Maeve, me too.

I didn't hear him.

He told me, and I didn't hear him.

I didn't—

The doll with the little carved lantern beside it.

You are what you are what you are.

Tears stream down my face, and I do not brush them away. I let them fall. I think they will never not fall.

It was always going to end this way.

There are no spoilers in life. This is my story.

It wasn't Tallulah's voice that drowned out Gideon's words.

It wasn't Tallulah's voice because Tallulah is dead.

It was mine.

We are what we are what we are.

Every man shares the same fantasy, and it is this.

Three words on the doll that Gideon made, and me standing here, alone.

I See You.

ACKNOWLEDGMENTS

There are so many people without whom this book would never have seen the light of day. To start, it is with humbling gratitude that I thank the world's best editor, agent, and manager, Kelly Lonesome, Chad Luibl, and Adam Goldworm. Thank you all for taking a chance on *Maeve Fly* and on me and for your continued belief in this project. You are, in every way, the absolute dream team. Here's to many future drinks and many future novels. To Adam especially for taking that initial chance on a writer who was convinced she just might never find representation by the time you entered the picture. I am so glad we are here, now. An enormous thank-you to Grady Hendrix, Jean Kyoung Frazier, Kyle Kouri, and Anya Lewis-Meeks, my early readers. I am such a fan of all your work and am humbled by your words. Thank you so much to copy editor extraordinaire, Angus Johnston, and to the most magical cover artist, Carly Janine Mazur. And to Jordan Hanley, Ashley Spruill, Saraciea J. Fennell, Christine Foltzer, Jessica Katz, Kristin Temple, Devi Pillai, Roma Panganiban, and everyone else on the Tor Nightfire, Janklow, and Aperture teams who has read or given feedback on this book, or contributed to its publication, you hold my gratitude eternally.
She clawed her sudden and violent way

out of me, but ultimately, she took a village to bring fully into the world. And what a glorious village it is.

To my most wonderful professors at Columbia and NYU: Sam Lipsyte, Rivka Galchen, Victor LaValle, Nicholas Christopher, David Burr Gerrard, Laura Slatkin, Andrew Romig, Hallie Franks, Kristin Horton, Matthew Stanley, Susanne Wofford, and Chris Spain, who first got the ball rolling on this writing journey for me when I was certain I was on another path. To my earlier teachers, Dalila Hannouche, Mark Savage, and Steve Durning. All of you have shaped me, and my writing, in innumerable ways. Thank you for pushing me, believing in and challenging me. And to Mike Harvkey, no one deserves a teacher, and now friend, as supportive and wonderful as you have been every step of the way. There is nothing to say but thank you, a hundred times over.

Thank you to all my favorite writers, especially Stephen King. Just for existing. For showing what is possible and providing a light at the end of a sometimes excruciating tunnel.

To my family, who may or may not want to be attached to this book once they read it (!), but who have been throughout my life so supportive I will never be able to fully convey. My cousins, aunts, uncles, stepfamilies, and all the Kouris, thank you for loving me unconditionally. I am the luckiest girl in the world. Special shout-out to the current Doctor Leede, for always responding to my texts after ER shifts to answer questions regarding what could be done to a human body, questions that I'm sure would put me on a hundred watch lists.

To my friends (my friends!), how anyone gets through this life alone, I will never know. Anya, Evan, Jean, Mina, SJ, Brady, Natalie, Christina, Nifath, Nadya, Santo, Sydney, Matt and Lexi, you have all been there for me in the last six years, when I needed friends most. You mean more to me than you will ever know. I love you all so deeply, even as I owe many of my worst hangovers to you. Thank you for being you. To my littles, Ivy, Arthur, Delainy, and Franki, thank you for keeping me young always! To the Los Angeles community who welcomed our human-canine family with open arms, you have been a vital part of this book's conception. Especially the WONDERFUL couple who inspired the HORRIBLE couple in a certain Beverly Hills engagement party scene! To Chris Molnar— without you ever handing me that copy of *Story of the Eye* late one night at a party, this book would never have come to be. Thank you for thinking I was the kind of girl who would enjoy it. To the Anarchists, thank you for always giving me a running soundtrack for when I need a break from writing. And to Kelsey and Mia. You are my family, now and always. I could not be the person I am now without you both. I love you with my whole heart.

My parents. There just aren't words, and will never be, for what you have given me. Thank you for accepting and celebrating the person I am, for always pushing me to strive for the greatest possible happiness, and for never allowing me to settle for anything less. You have gifted me a truly incredible life, getting to do every day what I love most. You are my favorite people. To my grandfathers, other family members, and loved ones who have passed on too soon, I will carry you in my heart always. To my grandmothers, who I continue to model much of my life after, thank you for being the most fabulous women to ever walk this planet. The world truly was not ready for you!

And to the greatest partner in this life I ever could have imagined. You have taught me it is okay to feel deeply and messily, to be uncertain and chaotic, and to make big mistakes. You have stood by me in the darkest moments, survived a pandemic shut inside with me, and without you, your insight, and your encouragement, Maeve could never exist. Without you, I would not be who I am now. You are the best hockey date, dog father, travel partner, and live-in editor, and there is no one in the world with whom I would rather sit and discuss writing at any dark tiki bar. You are my person, and it is an unimaginably beautiful thing, to see and be seen.

Finally, to my most-prized reader. Thank you for lending Maeve, and me, your most precious headspace for a time. You are as vital as every neon sign, as all the fallen palm fronds. May your drinks stay frozen, your jack-o'-lanterns burn bright, and your fangs glint always in the moonlight. And may this be only the beginning of our journey together.

Happy haunting.

Turn the page for a sneak peek at
CJ Leede's next novel

AMERICAN RAPTURE

Available October 2024 from Tor Nightfire

EMERGENCY BROADCAST.

My entire life I have been told what happens to those who sin. The wicked ones who turn from God's light. The ones who question, who seek forbidden knowledge, who bend to temptation, disobey.

I have always known the consequences for being a girl like me.

EMERGENCY BROADCAST.

But this?

EMERGENCY BROADCAST.

Clothing torn, tears streaming down my face. I drive away from the only life I've ever known.

Covered—dripping—in so much blood.

I tighten my grip on the wheel. Just for a moment, I close my eyes and pray.

HOW TO RECOUNT THE END OF THE WORLD:

1. Don't spare any details, no matter what the cost.
2. Back up and start from the beginning.

CHAPTER 1

Silent Symphonies

B irdsong outside my window.
Bright midwestern morning. Fresh sun, clear air. Bird-
song outside, and silence inside. Dust mites floating, settling,
gathering on stuffed animals, crucifixes, Bibles, in the corners
of the wooden built-ins my father designed. Paintings of Jesus,
of Mary, in their wooden frames. Beige curtains, beige carpet.
Silence in my room.

The window before me is sealed shut. Sealed because I
opened it, the night my brother was taken from our home. The
night my world went silent. Five years ago today.

I can feel the season's change is almost here, but I do not yet
know it holds the beginning of the end. I do not yet know anything except the inside of this room and the screams of my brother
that live in me forever. Echoing, dancing with the dust mites.

Downstairs, bacon sizzles in a pan. My mother calls my name.
I pull on my plaid pleated skirt, collared shirt, and sweater. The
birds outside have flown away.

In the hall, I press my palm to Noah's closed door, the framed
painting of Jesus beside it, one of so many in the house.

I picture my brother, sitting on his bed in the low lamplight.
The last good moments, ones that replay all the time. Our birthday was coming, we were almost twelve, and I had snuck into his

room, afraid, like I always was. I never could have known what
my being there would do. That these precious moments would
become our last together.

We were both homeschooled and took classes at church, but
Noah was smart, years ahead in math and science, and our
mother was perpetually embarrassed by it. She said it wasn't
Godly to indulge in such vanity, said it was dangerous. But when
we were much younger, a man in our congregation had seen Noah
scribbling and asked him about it. A math teacher, he ran a
summer camp at his farm where kids went to tend animals.
Because he was in our church, our parents agreed. Noah went
every summer, and they had no idea that while the other boys
were baling hay and milking, he sat in the kitchen scribbling
numbers and learning about the world. I was envious, so envious of it. While I was left at home.

Noah knew things that I didn't, had experiences I didn't
have. But in every other way we were equals. We were everything to each other, always. And he always came back and
shared with me all the things he'd learned.

Noah across the bed from me, a worksheet in front of him.

"What are you working on?"

*"This science project. There's a contest, and the winner gets to
go to the Dells."* He shrugged. *"Maybe this could be our way in."*

What we wanted for our birthday, more than anything. We
read about the Dells in a magazine that someone left at church
and Noah stole for us, hid under his bed. The Wisconsin Dells
were a place where everything was designed to be spectacular.
Fun and colorful. A water park, a science museum, a bookstore.
So many shops, so many adventures. We'd never been anywhere like it.

"Think Mom and Dad will ever take us?" I asked.

"Sophie! Breakfast!"

I stand in the hall, alone. I will turn seventeen in a few weeks, quietly and unassumingly beneath this roof as I have every birthday up to now. Noah will do the same in a loveless facility, away from me. Each of us a half person, a half self. There will certainly be no trip to the Dells.

Downstairs, my parents eat breakfast.

My father—thin, sweatered, in his signature round glasses— eyes me over the top of his newspaper and says, "You're going to school like that?" The gentle architect, the meek father. He wasn't gentle that night. His hands on Noah's arms. On mine.

I look down at my clothes, the uniform I wear every day. "What else would I wear?"

He turns to my mother, and they share a look. My father says nothing more. His newspaper reads: PHILADELPHIA, NEW YORK CITY CLOSING ALL INNER-CITY SCHOOLS TO COPE WITH FLU OUT-BREAK.

My mother withholds the cereal and milk until I've prayed, and when I'm finished she releases the food to me.

The flu, from what I have gleaned reading the back of my father's newspaper and overheard conversations, won't affect us, even though it's bad this year. It's isolated in the Northeast, and they've quarantined that whole part of the country. The priests remind us that we don't have to worry, we are protected by Christ's blood. We invite and accept Him inside ourselves, again and again.

Our home, wood, stone, glass. Careful lines, beige carpet. My father, like every other Taliesin School–inspired architect in the region, designed it in Frank Lloyd Wright's classic prairie style, organic materials, clean lines to blend into the surround-ing nature, except he added an upper story. Design couldn't trump the need for space. The need to make a show of having space, of tucking children away. The upper story that only I now inhabit. My father designed our church in the same way. An even larger, more spacious version of our home. Functional, harmonious. Built-ins, shadows across beige walls and beige carpet created by clever window casings and walkways, so many windows, natural light. Architecture that asks for silence, that muffles the world, that encourages standing still. Dust mites, floating. My waking hours spent inside these rooms designed by my father, imitating the work of another. My mother likes to say that God is an architect too, that we should all imitate Christ, every day. I never say anything to this.

We eat in silence as we have each morning since that night. I don't want to exist inside this house. I barely want to exist at all. That in itself is a sin. God gifted us this life, these parents, and we are meant to be grateful. We are meant to repent on our knees and receive salvation ecstatically and somberly on our tongues.

One thousand, eight hundred and twenty-six days.

So begins, through the taut film of unspeaking, the daily silent symphony that has lived in Noah's place, ever since.

My father sips his coffee, sets it down. My mother sips her coffee, checks her watch. My father flips the page, sips the coffee. I chew.

Sip, place, sip, click, crinkle, sip, crunch, crunch.

The rage and ache in a curated spotless house. Long shadows across the carpet.

Sip, place, sip, click, crinkle, sip, crunch, crunch.

The rhythm of it follows me out the door.

Sip, place, sip, click, crinkle, sip—

My mother shuts the driver's-side door behind her, and we are in the car.

Foreston's population is in the single thousands. There are two schools, one for girls and one for boys, both Catholic, and kids come from all different farm towns nearby. My school, St. Mary's, is five minutes from my house. I would walk if I were allowed. As it is, however, I am not allowed much of anything. Including any kind of device to alert my parents to my safety if I *were* to go anywhere without them. No phone, no unsupervised time with the computer. But the town of Foreston is basically the congregation of our church, so there's not much danger anyway. Before this year, I was still homeschooled, but we got a new Monsignor who was blessed by the Pope, and he told my parents that I needed social interaction. So now I attend St. Mary's. I felt a thrill at the idea at first, of a new freedom, any kind of freedom. Until I got to school two months ago and realized it was all the same girls from church I had been with my entire life. Beige home, beige church, beige school, beige life.

Still, it gets me away from my mother.

She pulls the car to a stop. I sit up, and she holds out her arm to prevent my exit.

"Your father had a point today," she says. Her sweater is the color of Sunday wine, and she smiles at me briefly, almost sadly.

"What point?" I ask.

"I've ordered you new uniforms," she says.

"What's wrong with the ones I have? We just got them."

"We'll go for a shopping trip, get you some new church clothes too. This weekend."

I can't spend a day with her alone, can't imagine she would ever want to spend a day with me. We don't do this. The other girls are making their way into the building, the bell sounding, their overlapping voices, the school chapel's incense wafting to us on the breeze. "Can we talk about this later?"

She turns that smile back on me. From here she will just return to the house, maybe go to the store, to the church events rooms, then home again. I can't fathom what she does with her time, her thoughts. Her hair is like mine, dark and thick, but she wears hers pulled back tight, so that it must hurt, stretching at the skin of her scalp. This austere woman, that pure unflinching smile.

"Don't worry," she says, "We'll get you sorted this weekend."

With this, I am released.

ABOUT THE

CJ LEEDE is a horror writer, hike
an MFA in creative writing from
and a BA from NYU's Gallatin Sc
mythology and the Middle Ages.
ing around the country, she can b
boyfriend and rescue dogs. She is
winner of the Octavia E. Butler C

Sydney Angel

r, and Trekkie. She has
n Columbia University,
hool, where she studied
When she is not driv-
e found in LA with her
he author of *Maeve Fly*,
olden Poppy Award.